Also by Robi

Bloody S

Vacuum-Packed

Praise for previous novels

'Writes about the dark side of desire with a horrible clarity.'
QX magazine

'An emotionally gripping thriller.' *Attitude magazine*

'Follows in the tradition of Bret Easton Ellis and Michel
Houellebecq. You'll be dazed, appalled, intrigued.' *Metro*

'Describes the emptiness of pop culture and the wreckage
of lost young lives with a world-weary cynicism that
can sting with its bite.' *Daniel Gawthrop, The Nation*

'While this is essentially a book about gay men,
it is so much more. The themes here are universal,
especially the search for love.' *Amos Lassen*

'Raw and deeply moving.' *Author Ian Casocot*

'*Vacuum-Packed* is one hell of a disturbing read.
The descriptive details are remarkable and the
situations uncomfortably riveting. This is gritty,
thought-provoking stuff.' *The Independent Gay Writer*

Bangkok Burning

Bangkok Burning

Published by The Conrad Press in the United Kingdom 2021

Tel: +44(0)1227 472 874
www.theconradpress.com
info@theconradpress.com

ISBN 978-1-913567-53-8

Typesetting and Cover Design by: Charlotte Mouncey, www.bookstyle.co.uk

The Conrad Press logo was designed by Maria Priestley.

Printed and bound in Great Britain by Clays Ltd, Elcograf S.p.A.

Bangkok Burning

Robin Newbold

For Gil

Ship me somewheres east of Suez,
where the best is like the worst,
where there aren't no Ten Commandments
an' a man can raise a thirst.

From Mandalay by Rudyard Kipling.

Chapter one

On the run

Graham knew he only had seven days, just a week to get what he craved – a new life.

A cacophony of voices in pidgin English broke him out of his trance, the grabbing, everywhere hands accosting him as he neared the entrance. He was back, the tawdry plywood exterior looking even poorer than he remembered illuminated by the tacky red neon sign announcing Christie Cabaret Show. Greeted by the same throbbing Thai pop music, beating in time to his heart, the gutter stink of cheap perfume, the place looked much smaller and far more decadent than it had in his mind's eye over the last few weeks. In his dreams he'd expected to walk in and find her, poised, as if she'd been waiting for him, but Graham felt cheated as he looked around frantically at the other ladyboys. Though how he hated that word, the fact he could possibly be desperate for one of their ilk. Staring out at the braying red-faced punters, Thai girls curled serpent-like around bovine white men, their eyes calculating every move, brains computing every sentence uttered he saw a kind of hell and of Natasha there was no sign.

'God,' he said to himself, feeling his muscles tense, mouth desert dry, palms leaking sweat, chewing at nails so destroyed blood was oozing out of them.

'Can I help you, Sir?' said not a divine being but a heavily made-up boy.

'Where's Natasha?' he said, wheeling around, scanning the bar again.

'Natasha?' said the boy with a shrug.

He flopped down at a bar stool overlooking the ramshackle stage, sighing as the first strains of Whitney Houston's 'I Will Always Love You' – one of wife Sheila's favourites – struck up and a ridiculously elaborately dressed ladyboy appeared, lip-synching in all the wrong places.

'Beer, please,' said Graham to the boy who'd continued to hover and he was gone with a practised and unnecessary shake of his arse.

'All right, babe. As one alcoholic would say to another, you look like you need a drink,' said a man to his right, fruity voice cutting through the din, a gnarled hand seemingly weighed down by a worrying amount of gold jewellery enveloping his arm. 'Great this, ain't it.'

'Graham, what's yours? Though everyone calls me Gray as in Mr Gray. Like my life,' he said, turning to look at his new best friend, taking in the yellowing skin which was the hue of old newspapers, the gin-coloured hair.

'Nigel... Nigel Monroe.'

'Good to meet you, Nigel Monroe.'

'You can live like a king 'ere, dear,' he said, voice a shouty amalgam of Cockney and camp, raising a glass unsteadily with one hand, patting the boy's arse with the other. 'These girls, you see, know what they want and how to get it.'

'Do you know Natasha?'

'Let's see, I've been here since 1990, so that's twenty years now. Twenty bloody years man and boy...'

'Where were you before?'

'Before? Was there a before?' he said, looking out into the middle distance. 'All over. And you?'

'South London.'

'Don't sound like it.'

'I don't have a strong accent. Guess you could say I'm well read. Like my crosswords and that. But, come on, what have you been doing here?'

'Ah, the first rule of being an expat, never ask that question 'ere,' he said, shakily raising a hand. 'People get offended. But, you know, this and that...'

As he tailed off, Graham sensed regret, his companion staring off beyond the nonsense on stage and into the darkness beyond, as though wondering how he'd 'lost touch', so the phrase went, with friends and family, with his roots, with who he actually was, traded it all in for a seat in a dive bar in a city halfway around the world. He didn't want to bloody end up like that.

'Listen,' he said, his turn to put a reassuring hand on his neighbour's arm. 'I need to find someone... a girl.'

'A girl, eh?' said Nigel, stroking his stubbly chin. 'And who might she be?'

'Natasha.'

'Ha, bullseye,' he shouted above the din of the warbled bars of Whitney. 'But she ain't no girl. Very pretty mind.'

'So?'

'And I, eeee-I, will alwayssss love you...' came the racket

13

from the stage as if to mock Graham, the ladyboy's eyes boring directly into his, while Nigel had gone back to concentrating on his real interest, the drink in front of him.

'Very popular that one,' the old man replied finally, as the seemingly infernal noise from the stage ceased, a mischievous smile lighting up his face. 'I'd talk to Mark if I was you.'

'Who the hell is Mark?' he said, familiar knot of pain across his shoulders, arms trembling.

'Mark, babe, is the owner of this fine establishment… I told her to engage with the fucking audience, why is she looking at the floor?' he said, pointing at the ladyboy nominally on stage, for she clearly wasn't interested, Nigel slamming another empty glass down on the counter.

'What's it gotta do with you exactly?'

'You're speaking to Nigel Monroe of the Nigel Monroe Dancers fame, West End impresario and choreographer,' he said, the boy refilling his glass, ushering away another empty bottle of whisky from the scene like an embarrassment.

'The Nigel Monroe Dancers?'

'Those big telly shows in the seventies and early eighties. The glitz was personified by the Nigel Monroe Dancers. Even made it on *Top of the Pops* once,' he said, spreading his hands as if to reveal a name up in lights but there was only a dark emptiness.

'I see,' he said with a tight smile.

'I'm creative director here.'

'How about Mark? When can I speak to him?' he said, wanting to get back to the topic but wondering how someone barely able to raise a glass to their lips through the fog of alcohol could possibly direct anything.

'He's around. Probably out back getting hammered again.

But he'll be back. Where else would 'e be?' said his companion, patting Graham's knee.

'I don't even know what I'm doing here. What the hell am I thinking?' he said, though he thought back to when he'd first seen Natasha – her ample, perfectly symmetrical breasts spilling out of a skimpy basque top, crimson lipstick accentuating the lure of her mouth, unruly shock of blonde hair hinting at sexual abandon. Before 'seduction' was just a word from the crossword puzzles he obsessed over to distract him from the paucity of his life.

'Go on then, what's your story?'

'Story? There's no bloody story,' Graham said above the thumping disco beat, mimicking the palpitations of his heart he'd been suffering the last awful three years, since that day, that bloody day, the bastard day of the accident that changed everything. 'I made the mistake of coming over here earlier this year with the missus on my fortieth birthday, didn't I. Natasha, she was giving me the eyes… I couldn't help myself. We kissed. I can't stop thinking about it. My life back home in England, it's so empty.'

'What about the wife? Kids?'

'Kids? I don't even wanna go there, Nige. Another time. But my wife, Sheila, she hates me. We haven't touched each other in years, bloody years. I sit driving my cab through the night, those cold London nights, rather than go home. It's freezing on those winter nights with the pissheads getting in, throwing up, running off but I prefer it to her cold, hard back. So bloody cold.'

'And where you meant to be now?'

'Told 'er I was going to Canada to see my brother for a week.

He emigrated there years ago but he's got terminal cancer. All the nonsense about life being too short but it really is.'

'I know, babe. I know.'

'Every chance the wife gets she tells me how crap I am, how I don't amount to anything. She blames me for everything. Is it any wonder I'm having a breakdown? Doctor gave me these pills but I haven't taken 'em yet. I feel enough of a bloody failure,' Graham said, waving the packet of happy pills in the air, defeatedly chucking the box down on the bar, shoulders slumping, blinking back tears, again.

'Dear, it's the way it works I'm afraid. Life I mean,' Nigel said, holding up a placatory hand as he did so. 'Not being funny but look at yourself in the mirror, look at me... no, go on, I mean take a fucking good look. What could you or I have that could possibly be of interest to these twenty-year-old visions of beauty? It's not our looks, it's not our sense of humour, it's not even our great personalities.'

'I know but...' he said, looking out at the lithe bodies on stage, then catching a glimpse of himself in the mirror behind the bar, the image Nigel had warned him about – and he took in the thinning blond hair only partially disguising the pathetic balding pate, the craggy forehead lined with twenty-plus years of worry, the length of his marriage, the darting, desperate eyes.

'Graham, ain't it. You need to hear this and we're only going to have this chat once. After this, like all of us, you're on your own,' said Nigel. 'It's a so-called playground for white men, a paradise if you like, but we've created a monster. Look around you. I know for a fact most of these boys have several different foreign *boyfriends* all unaware the other exists, all under the illusion they are paying for little Johnny to go through university or save his dad's buffalo herd from foot and mouth.'

'How about the girls then?'

'Girls? They're not girls. Don't kid yourself. You're down here in the gutter with the rest of us. If that's what you like, though, do yourself a favour and be honest. Sounds like you done living a lie.'

'I'm not gay,' he said, feeling like he was going to vomit out his insides, head swimming, hating having to even utter the word, *that* bloody word.

'Love, no one's judging you. Try to let it go,' said Nigel, placing a hand on his shoulder. 'Be careful though, the lady-boys are the worst of the lot, they have the accoutrements of women, yet they think like men, they're dogs when it comes to sex, like us. But just enjoy it, if that's what you really want.'

'So what you saying?'

'Sorry for the lecture but in a roundabout way, I'm saying it's even worse being alone, if you crave the touch of another, tenderness, any kind of contact, what we all need. If you're alone, you're just swimming with sharks,' he said, watery eyes looking older than time.

'You had someone?'

'I had someone and I was the one that ruined it. I ate up all the ridiculous temptations like sickly sweets, I kept fucking around and he couldn't take it anymore. Now all I 'ave is this,' he said, wrenching the glass from the table, whisky slopping down the sides. 'I can't get involved in the game now. It's too late for me.'

'What about me?'

'I don't profess to have the answers. You want to give up everything to set yourself up here but what are you really giving up?'

'A life,' he said but Graham didn't really believe it. What life? he thought savagely, looking at the box of Xanax on the bar, hinting at a kind of existence that made him so anxious he was prescribed pills just to get through each day.

'These girls, boys a lot of them are interchangeable but they can give you what you want. For a price. This is the East.'

Graham noticed a serene look come over the old man's haggard features as though he'd just spoken a sacred truth. 'Okay but…'

'Shush,' said Nigel, finger to his lips, pointing him to a figure behind the bar as he went back to his drink.

Graham took it to be Mark, lending an even seedier edge to proceedings, something of the Dickensian rogue with his ragged clothes, rat-like features, hair plastered down with sweat, brow glistening as he frantically counted money – what looked like the night's paltry takings. He put the slender sheaf of notes down, silently shaking his head at the dark, almost empty auditorium.

'Hi, I'm…'

'Can't you see I'm busy, mate,' he said in a grating Liverpudlian accent, brandishing a cigarette he was puffing manically on.

Undeterred, Graham grabbed a stool opposite as the man went back to his counting.

'So what can I do you for?' he said finally, looking up from his small mound of notes and receipts, making eye contact for the first time, though it seemed a worryingly dead-eyed stare.

'You're Mark, right?'

'Who wants to know? Listen, mate, if you're looking to buy me out, the whole gaff is up for sale lock, stock and two

18

smoking fucking barrels,' he said with a smile.

'Nigel…'

'What does that fucking divvy know? He keeps telling me how to run the show and look,' he said, waving at the emptiness of the place, indicating the lack of talent on show, the amateurishness.

'I'm not that innocent,' lip-synched one of the ladyboys, completely out of time as she mimicked fellatio in what was meant to be the gap between the words as if to illustrate Mark's point and Graham let out a nervous laugh.

'You think it's funny?' Mark said, stubbing out another cigarette in an overflowing ashtray.

'No, course not,' he said, beginning to feel he didn't know what he was dealing with, like he'd swapped south London for the Wild West, where he didn't know any of the rules, if there actually were any.

'I've got Nigel in one ear, Christie in the other,' Mark said, slamming a palm against his sweaty brow.

'I'm actually here about Natasha.'

'Natasha,' spat Mark. 'You really don't want to go there.'

'Well, I need to find her,' Graham said, fiddling in his pocket, meeting Mark's gaze but there was nothing in the blank stare to provide reassurance or even to register an interest, though he hoped the two 1,000 baht notes he'd just placed on the bar would change that.

'Okay, if you really, really want to know,' he said, spiriting the notes away as he did so. 'She's in Soi Cowboy at Casino Royale. She's *the star*. Well she bloody would be, wouldn't she. That's what I heard anyway.'

'Soi Cowboy? And why'd she leave here?'

'Soi Cowboy is another part of the jungle. Not too far in a taxi. Get your guidebook out. She has to be number one, *numero* bloody *uno*. That's why the silly cow left. Felt she was being upstaged. I think we're done here old son,' said Mark, turning from the bar, disappearing into the blackness behind it.

It was the same trait he'd noticed in Nigel, that Bangkok expats were only interested in someone that could do something for them, otherwise you ceased to exist.

'Soi Cowboy… Casino Royale,' Graham repeated, relieved to have a whereabouts, even if he didn't know where that was, he had a name and what a name, he chuckled, Natasha channelling peak Bond girl, though he guessed there wouldn't be any flashy casino.

But as he prepared to leave, thoughts drifted back to the image of Mark frantically counting money, calculating whether it was enough to live on, and he feared he'd caught a glimpse of his grubby, threadbare future. Walking out past Nigel Monroe of the Nigel Monroe Dancers at closing time, he saw his eyes were glazed over at what was unfolding on stage, a performer stifling a yawn as the old man watched, waited, finally bringing another half-empty glass to his lips.

***

Arriving back at the crumbling concrete block of a building that was his hotel, vowing to continue his search the next day as the city's bars were now closed, at least the legal ones, Graham caught a glimpse of himself in the cab's rear-view mirror, a white ghost in a lurid world. The irony of the hotel's name spelt out garishly on its grisly edifice making him laugh for he felt a long way from the Paradise it promised.

He grabbed for the phone vibrating in his pocket, knowing

instinctively who it would be, forty years old and only one person was ever interested enough to call, yet it was also the one person he least wanted to hear from. Still, out of a sense of what – Duty? Habit? – he picked up.

'Where the 'ell are ya,' said Sheila.

'Whaddya mean, where the hell am I?' he said, knot tightening across his shoulders.

'Graham, I've spoken to your sister in law, you're not in Canada. I wasn't able to contact you earlier and I was worried. Where are you?'

He breathed into the phone, short, sharp breaths but the words wouldn't come out.

'Well?'

'Thailand.'

'Thailand? I might have bloody known. You and those bloody ladyboys.'

'Just for a few days. I need to find myself.'

'Find yourself. Find your bloomin' self. You say you're anxious and you're taking those stupid pills. What abaht me? Graham, you're not some teenager on a gap year. You're a forty-year-old man with *re-spon-si-bil-i-ties*. The last three years 'ave been hell and you're running away. What would Emma say, eh?'

'Emma? How dare you bring her into this, my daughter, my lovely Emmy.'

'Your daughter? I hold you completely responsible, you bastard. And this… this Thailand, it's all about sex.'

'Sheil, I'm not looking for sex, I'm looking for love. Love you dopey cow. How many times have you rejected me over the years? Even Em said, before she… that I should get a life. I want the touch of another human bein' for God's sake. I'm

21

not a monk. I can't go on like this!'

'You think I want anything to do with you? To even touch you? Look at yourself in the mirror. Kissing you is like kissing a toilet. You're bloody disgustin'.'

'Love, you ought to know there's someone else,' he said, cutting her off, punching the wall, jagged pain raking up his arm.

Chapter two

Finding Natasha

'*Rot tit* [traffic], *rot tit*. Red shirts no good,' said the taxi driver sighing, waving a hand in the air.

'Red shirts?' he said, transfixed by the gleaming, glinting molten sea of cars stretching ahead as far as Graham could see in the blanched landscape.

'Red shirts, crazy. Support Thaksin, old prime minister. Yellow shirts support king,' said the driver, turning around shaking his head.

'Oh,' replied Graham, balling up his hands, having seen from the morning's *Bangkok Post* that protesters – guessing it was the red shirts the cabbie had referred to – had set about one of the city's most chichi shopping districts burning and looting, barricading themselves in.

'Yellow shirts no good either.'

Crossing his legs to stop them shaking, fixated by a pall of smoke billowing on the horizon, screaming sirens in his ears, he thought if the unrest couldn't be explained by them, rationalised, then what hope did he ever have of understanding, making sense of this place.

'Soi Cowboy,' said the driver, announcing his destination.

He turned around giving Graham that wonky smile, which he'd seen numerous times since he'd landed and which he knew normally not only spelt trouble but involved money – nothing to do with the sickly tourist slogan invoking inanely grinning locals. 'Land of the smile, my arse,' he said under his breath as he shoved a couple of notes at the driver and got out.

He passed innumerable shops and restaurants where there seemed more staff than customers, striking him as the classic goldrush development and by the looks of things the gold was running out. It was in the desperate eyes of the shopkeepers and stallholders, their vaguely threatening exhortations to 'come look', followed by an arm around the shoulder – harassment was another name for it. The gaudily painted signs an attempt to disguise the brutalist concrete boxes but the profusion of low-hanging electrical cabling and dusty, potholed pavements unmistakably spelled Third World bloody hellhole. It was like the little money that was made had never been put back, the whole place thrown together, with the constant whiff of shit in the air a sign of an infrastructure about to literally burst at the seams. Sun, which was beating down unrelentingly, and sex were obviously the only attractions, Graham thought, as he walked past a bar to the catcalls of its scantily clad female occupants, looking washed out in the unforgiving light.

And there among a profusion of fast food outlets and convenience stores was the grandly named but dilapidated Casino Royale. Graham felt his throat tighten as he approached, cheap perfume and hairspray rancid in the air, crowd of ladyboys inside as though found out in the glare of daylight. In the middle of it all, as though the very centre of attention, there she was, Natasha. But it was far from the Hollywood reunion he'd imagined in his dreams, no eyes across a crowded room, instead she squinted at him either from vague recognition or that he could be trouble.

'Natasha,' he said as she towered above him in heels, proffering a hand for her to shake, mottled skin so at odds with her youthful radiance.

'Yes,' she said, switching on the dazzling smile but it was only as brief as her handshake.

'We met... er, my wife was there,' he said. 'Graham.'

'Oh, yes, darling,' she said, eyes twinkling, full actress mode.

'Would you like to go for a coffee?' he said reddening, like of course she bloody remembered, the bawling of the other ladyboys indicating they had an audience.

She was sporting plumes two-foot tall for Christ's sake and he wanted to go for a quiet drink – he felt infantile and she looked ridiculous. He had gambled everything for this, *this*? Graham was looking at the ground, writhing his hands, having given into temptation, finally following his instincts yet his whole body was in pain, the damn guilt. He shook, feeling totally exposed, as everyone would know his business now, what he was, given he was planning to be seen out with her.

'Are you serious, dear?' she said, eyes drilling into him.

'I've never been more serious in my life, Natasha.'

'You need to make it worth my while and I not cheap, honey,' she said, rolling her eyes.

Graham felt winded, unable to get the words out, swaying from one foot to the other, her long nails appearing like talons as she reached out to grab him, hand noticeably larger than his, deep manly laugh only adding an air of menace, so at odds with the ravishing picture of femininity.

'It's rehearsals now. Meet me tonight, after show,' she cooed, answering for him and grazing his cheek with a kiss.

Natasha's grating pidgin English made her sound uneducated, naïve even, but all Graham saw was the energy, the confidence, like she wanted it all and knew how to get. No, she was far from bloody stupid.

***

He got back to Casino Royale early, so early the show hadn't even started. She was among a gaggle of girls outside trying desperately to hook tourists inside with the promise of 'the greatest show on Earth'.

'Oh, so pleased to see you,' she said, pecking him on the cheek, taking him by the hand as she led him into the bar.

But bar seemed a bit of a misnomer with the ramshackle, near empty venue open on three sides, with a covered stage at the far end, the trademark Bangkok go-go joint just a couple of short steps from the gutter. As if to emphasise the point, Natasha kicked out a long leg, accentuated by ridiculously high heels, to shoo away a stray dog that had taken up residence. Despite his shakiness, he enjoyed the cat-calling, the attention from the other ladyboys as he sat down – it was like he'd gone from invisible fortysomething to having some kind of cachet. But having looked around he realised sadly how anyone could have cachet in a place like Casino Royale, it was otherwise known as having a wallet.

Even the *Castaway* impersonator at the bar with his wild hair, long beard and raggedy clothes was being fawned over by not one girl but two. Provided you put your hand in your pocket you were popular, thought Graham, but as the place slowly filled up with a profusion of single men and a few others with visibly bored wives, a pairing like he'd once been a part, it attested to a strange kind of allure – a sleight of hand, an optical illusion the Far East presented in the most easily digestible and readily accessible format. He knew at its crudest it meant being able to get a sensual kind of relief in the toilets, while the wife sipped her G&T, all for under a tenner. Everything seemed to glitter, at least on the outside.

'You want drink?' said Natasha, like the perfect hostess but mimicking holding the neck of a bottle, or something else, and then swallowing hard.

'Beer, please and whatever you're having, darlin',' he said, biting the inside of his cheek to stop twitching, metallic taste of blood in his mouth, hoping the Xanax he'd just popped would kick in, take the edge off his deafening thoughts.

'Okay,' she said, doing her bottle stroking impression again. 'But I have to get ready for show… later.'

Then in a whirl of plumage and a blur of those long legs she was gone but she left behind the scent he'd smelled that first night. The very one, which despite all the worrying signs and reservations, meant adventure to him – a vital piece of the jigsaw of his life he felt he'd mislaid at the end of his teenage years, half a lifetime ago. His hag of a wife refused to touch him, said he 'didn't turn her on' but forbade him from going outside the marriage. What kind of a prison cell was that? Till death do us part, Graham thought. More bullshit.

'All right, mate,' said a young Englishman, sitting down beside him.

'All right,' he said, staring straight ahead.

'These girls are amazing,' he said, though none had approached him, while several were draped over some of the older patrons.

'What would your mates say?' said Graham, shouting over the now thumping disco music, desperate to gauge the reaction of his peers to what he regarded as a perversion, a perversion he could no longer run from.

'Mate, one of mine's been shacked up with one of 'em for a week. Gone native,' he said, nudging Graham, eyes sparkling with a kind of wonder, though there was something uncertain about his laugh.

'What's wrong with him?' he whispered in Natasha's ear, as she plonked another beer in front of him.

'He never pays,' she hissed, making a cut-throat gesture with her claw-like hands, bending down to say something into the young man's ear and almost instantaneously he got up, leaving a half-full bottle of beer on the counter.

Quite relieved to be alone again, with the prospect of meeting Natasha later, he sat through the show getting quietly drunk. It was the same out of synch lip-synching to the familiar canon of camp songs in the all too garish costumes he'd seen before. Even Graham, brought up on a diet of seventies variety shows, knew it could be done so much better because the one thing that was lacking was variety. The ridiculous germ of an idea had been growing in his mind and looking around as the audience lapped up the amateur rubbish, blinded by the faintest dusting of glitter, he licked his lips and smiled. It didn't have to be the furrowed brows and frantically counted receipts of Christie's, it could work. But as the closing strains of Abba's 'Thank You for the Music' boomed out and the curtains closed on the waving 'performers' he wondered if he could sell any of it, his plan to open a bar, to her.

Amid the grimness of the alleyway outside, with the backdrop of rubbish strewn gutters, rickety food carts and prowling stray dogs stood the cast, ball gowns skimming the dirt despite the deliciously stacked heels, waving goodbye to their admirers or offering more, much more, later. It appeared pukka from a distance, thought Graham, though as he got closer some looked grotesque, the street lights giving the over made-up features the harshest of tints but still Natasha radiated an odd kind of feminine beauty mixed with a worryingly male cockiness.

'This is my friend, Daeng,' she said, introducing Graham. 'He is choreographer. We go together now.'

'All of us? I see,' he said, looking at Daeng, the sprite of a Thai boy with the breathtakingly prettiest of features at odds with the most unforgiving of stares.

'Let's go to Sheraton,' said Natasha, indicating her and Daeng with a discreet hand gesture and unblinking eyes.

And even though she'd changed out of her plumes into a little sequinned number, he wasn't quite sure what they'd look like in the bar of a five-star hotel but that was it, wasn't it? It was like a test, he was either in this 100 per cent or he wasn't. How gay would he look? There'd be no going back. Yes, she had the accoutrements of a woman but as Nigel said, she was in fact a he.

'Okay, we go,' he said, kissing her lightly on the cheek, Daeng's eyes still blazing into him.

They clambered onto her motorbike, which looked new and expensive, setting Graham's mind whirring all over again – How could she afford it? Which foreigner bought it for her?

– questions that couldn't be silenced but he tried to ignore the doubts as he sat on the back, Daeng sandwiched in the middle like a chaperone. He watched as she caressed, rather than drove, the motorbike with one hand, while she tended her blonde locks with the other but he couldn't help thinking how bloody ridiculous he looked, sitting on the back of a bike with two queers up front. What did that make him, eh? All he could hear was Sheila's voice in his head, imagining that mocking sneer.

'May I help you, Sir?' said a grinning concierge as they arrived at the hotel reception.

'We're going to the bar,' Graham said, biting the inside of his cheek again, blushing under the withering stare of the squat hotel employee, feeling judged, pigeonholed, in the blink of the man's unforgiving eyes.

'You need to relax. Don't look so embarrassed. Do I embarrass you?' said Natasha, roughly grabbing his arm, shoving her face into his.

'No, no course not,' he said but his whole body trembled down to his fingertips, attempt at a reassuring smile coming out as a grimace as they were led into a grand lounge done out in the clichéd colonial pastiche of rattan chairs and whirring ceiling fans.

The concierge sat them behind a strategically placed potted palm, which was more to save the embarrassment of other guests, thought Graham, than to afford them any kind of privacy. He continually shifted in his seat, fiddled with his hands at the fussing of the waiter, the looks from those on adjoining tables. What were they thinking? he thought as he tried to hide behind one of the over-sized drinks menus, eventually daring to come out and order himself a beer.

'Hey, you need one of these. Take it easy. I don't bite,' she said, shoving a pack of cigarettes at him.

'I kind of gave up but thanks. I do need one,' he said, whipping one out, which she lit, taking down a massive lungful.

'Anything else, Sir?' said the waiter, dispatching the drinks, something garish with umbrellas in for the Thai twosome.

'No thank you,' he said, almost done the cigarette, relieved to get a drink in his hand.

'What do you want?' said Natasha, looking him over, putting her palms together like she was praying.

'You,' he said, feeling Daeng's stare, gripping onto the sides of his chair, knuckles white with the effort.

'You can hardly look at me. And you look around the room like you frightened of everyone else, scared of what they thinking.'

'Natasha, that's why I'm here. I want to live, be myself. I've hated myself for so long, my life. When I saw you, that first time, I knew I wanted to change. Had to change,' he said, finally looking her in the eye, feeling his body still at last.

'How? How can you have me?' Natasha said but touching his hand.

'Opening a cabaret bar in Bangkok – Natasha's – your name up in lights,' he said, spreading his arms as if to indicate that glittering sign.

'What about you?' he said, looking away, down at the floor, words almost dying in his throat. 'What do you want?'

'Look at me, be brave. Look me in the eye. Graham, I don't care about looks, even money. I want man with a good heart. Someone that not going to hurt me,' she said, breaking eye

31

contact, looking shy, bashful, for the first time.

'Someone hurt you before?'

'I not talk about that now. I can trust you,' she said, grabbing his hand under the table, holding it. 'But how you know anything about show? About running bar? About ladyboys?'

'I will get Nigel Monroe on board,' he said, bullshitting, yet to even having mentioned it to Monroe, some pisshead he'd only recently met.

'You have money, darling?' she said, eyes gleaming, smile on her lips, her hand caressing, cajoling.

'Yes, I have money,' he said, hands shaking violently, forehead sprouting sweat, frenziedly calculating his recent inheritance would cover it on a vague ballpark figure from Monroe that £200,000 bought a decent-sized bar, aware Daeng was looking on dismissively as her smile only widened.

'We want fifty-fifty. A fifty per cent share of the business between us,' she said, patting her friend on the shoulder, his grin revealing a mouthful of rotten, jumbled teeth at odds with his delicate, doll-like features.

'Him as well?' he said, thinking so much for her professing not to be all about the bloody money.

'As choreographer, yes, to work with Nigel,' she said, grabbing Graham's shaky hand again, stilling it, stroking his fingers.

'Okay, whatever you want, baby,' he said, clinking her glass, memories of Sheila sitting in front of her beloved telly, which even had to stay on when they had guests, already beginning to fade. That lifeless world when he'd sat there and felt the grey walls closing in had been replaced by an expansive Technicolor vista – no more cold nights in his cab picking up pissheads

32

or even colder nights in the marital bed – those nights when he'd stayed out rather than go home to the ice queen and her cruel taunts or even crueller silence, breath frosting on the windscreen.

'Try to look happy,' she said, putting her fingers to his lips, manoeuvring his mouth into a rough approximation of a smile. 'If you're with me, you forget what other people think. It's about what you think.'

'I know,' said Graham but it's what he was thinking that terrified him.

'Sir, the bill,' said the waiter.

'Lovely. Thank you so much,' he said, the substantial total bringing him back to the here and now, throwing down his credit card, Natasha and Daeng looking on silently.

'You come with me,' she said as they stood.

He leapt on the back of her bike, wrapped his hands around that slender waist, smiling, though as he watched Daeng recede in the mirror, he realised the boy was staring right back.

They drew up outside a crumbling multi-storey block, bars on the windows making it look like some kind of prison. Graham wondered with a shiver whether the cages were to keep the thieves out or the tenants in, dreary washed-out laundry hanging limply from most of the windows like flags of surrender. The sweat was pouring off him, heart beating frighteningly fast but instead of running, he followed her through a shadowy entrance, which was so uneven it seemed like it had been hewn out of the concrete by hand, more like the opening to a cave than a building. He squealed as something batted against his head in the dimly lit interior, then another and another and he looked down as he crunched something under foot only to realise they'd disturbed a swarm of cockroaches. Natasha looked back at him, holding his hand even tighter, unleashing a smile through the gloom.

They got in a tiny lift, the awful metal box coffin-like in dimension. Graham frantically wiped at his leaking forehead, noticed how someone had scrawled 'HELL' next to the 'B' for basement button Natasha had just pressed, feeling hotter and hotter as they descended down and down. Lurching lower he heard laughter rumble through the lift shaft from somewhere in the building, paranoid that even though they couldn't see him someone found amusement in his predicament. All Natasha could do as they finally juddered to a halt was smile that devilish smile again.

'Shush' she said opening the door to her room, clicking on a light. 'My sisters.'

He looked at the small space bathed in a red glow, displeasure audibly rising from at least three of the four bodies on a bed in the corner, each sporting the telltale tangle of ladyboy big hair. 'Where are the windows?'

'Come on,' she said, pulling him onto an empty bed in the opposite corner, drawing across a rudimentary curtain with all the finality of slamming a door, like it offered the complete privacy they needed.

As she brought her lipstick smudged mouth to his he drank in the opportunity at escape from her lips, pawing at her clothes, ripping at them, suddenly overtaken by lust. Her plastically perfect breasts finally bounced free in front of his face and he nuzzled into their perfection. Natasha cradled his head, moving his mouth to her nipples, then turning over, pulled her panties down.

'Fuck me,' she growled, wriggling free of her thong.

'Condom?' he said but she simply shrugged.

'Oh, Daddy,' she sighed as he grabbed clumsily at her.

'I love this,' he said, thrusting away but rapt by a yellowing, unblinking eye staring back at him from a gap in the curtain, imagining he was close as he'd ever come to being in hell, unable to escape the doubts, the self-hate screaming in his mind in the suffocating underground tomb.

Chapter three

Entanglement

He looked at the view, fifty floors up, peering down at the rest of Bangkok, insulated from the grime. Viewing the drinks menu, five-star prices to match the five-star venue – the appropriately named Vertigo bar at the Banyan Tree – Graham had no idea what he was doing there. Was it some Thai con trick? He was planning to buy a spit 'n' sawdust bar yet here he was in a wicker chair like some colonial bloody master in one of the city's classiest watering holes, drumming slimy fingers on the pristine table as a besuited waiter delivered the obligatory nuts and olives.

'What you thinking, honey?' said Natasha.

'Thinking?' he said, looking across at her in the little black dress, loving how she filled it amply in all the right places but aware they were getting looks from other patrons that were far from admiring and he felt the sweat prickle under his arms, a throbbing behind his eyes. 'Everyone's looking at us.'

'Gray, are you ashamed of me? You know, that means you ashamed of yourself and what you are.'

He reddened, words stuck in his deathly dry throat, unable

to answer, speak up for himself.

'He's tourist, just a tourist,' said Daeng laughing, nudging Natasha as if they were inseparable.

'Bloody tourist. Yeah, I'm just a foreigner, *farang* you call it like it's an insult. I heard you sayin' it all the bloody time. But without me you wouldn't be getting the bar,' he said, pointing a finger in his face.

Daeng merely smiled an unreadable smile, another one to be filed away with the rest, raising his expensively bought for drink that of course was on Graham's tab, Graham who felt every muscle in his body tense as he fantasised throwing the boy over the side of the building, watching as his body became just a black speck before exploding red on the pavement way below. What was he thinking, indeed, signing his life away, or at least his life savings, to these two. But he'd chosen life and looking across at Natasha, her sparkling eyes, the way she looked at him, like she could no longer do without him, that feeling of being wanted, if this is what it meant – he was all in. He would try to ignore the guilt, balling his hands into fists under the immaculately appointed table, grinding his teeth, attempting to write off what he took to be looks of disgust from others that only reflected his own self-hate, paranoia.

A man approached the table, a table littered with expensive refills, the tab forever growing. He was a squat, rotund man with slicked back hair, eyes shielded by mirrored sunglasses reflecting the blinding afternoon, though the most striking detail was the brown police uniform that always seemed to be worn unflatteringly skintight in Bangkok, epaulettes glinting, ostentatiously attesting to his worth. The officer eased himself down and began babbling away in Thai as though Graham wasn't even there, Natasha and Daeng in his thrall.

'So, Mr Graham, pleased to meet you. I'm Police-General Peeklong,' he said finally, as if the title was a non-negotiable part of his name, holding out a hand to be shook, unreadable behind his sunglasses.

'Pleasure's all mine,' he said with a fixed smile that he knew would've done a Thai proud, though Graham imperceptibly shook his head – Natasha, Daeng and now this? Where did Peeklong fit?

'I hear you're interested in buying my bar.'

'Your bar?'

'Yes, yes… it's a little sideline, shall we say,' he said, removing his glasses, black eyes boring into Graham.

'I didn't even know the place was yours. Like I know anything,' he said, maintaining eye contact but shaking inside, thrusting his legs against the table to stop them trembling. 'Why you selling?'

'A glass of your best Scotch,' said the policeman as a waiter approached. 'Why am I selling? How about I want to help you out.'

'Help me out, eh? You normally help *farangs* out?'

'Mr Graham, it's how Bangkok works. I help you, then you help me,' he said, placing a service revolver carefully on the table along with his sunglasses, the firearm glinting in the sun.

'I see,' he said but transfixed by the gun, cold, hard steel looking up at him, Peeklong toasting him with his Scotch and a smile, taking advantage of Graham's largesse, a pig with his nose in the trough.

'We agreed fifty-fifty,' said Natasha, taking Graham gently by the hand but addressing Peeklong. 'So Gray own fifty per cent and me and Daeng fifty per cent.'

'Will we, Nat?' he said, taking one of the cigarettes she'd offered, dragging the smoke deeply into his lungs. 'Will we, indeed.'

'It's 10 million baht... 10 million. You have the money?' said Peeklong, voice deep, intimidating, as if rumbling up from below, at odds with his squat figure.

'I have it,' said Graham, grimacing as he frantically calculated the numbers in his head, though he'd known the ballpark figure this was becoming real, the cost in English pounds – £250,000 – familiar tension streaking across his shoulders.

'Well done, honey,' said Natasha, high-fiving him, eyes twinkling, though Daeng stared straight ahead.

'I want to inspect the goods first, though. I'm not prepared to buy sight un-bloody-seen,' he said, putting a hand to his aching head.

'I can see you're quite the businessman. You won't be disappointed,' said Peeklong, laughing as he held a set of keys tantalisingly under Graham's nose.

***

'So here we are,' said the police-general, chuckling as they piled out of the taxi in the heart of Bangkok's red-light district.

The laughter ringing in Graham's ears saying to him, 'Look at the pup I'm about to sell you, sucker. You can't do a thing about it. Try saying no in front of those two.'

He stepped gingerly onto the pavement outside, which was slippery with a slick of grease, filth, stained with the rotting remains of cheap street food and worse. At the very entrance was a big black lump that Peeklong kicked like he was taking a penalty. The smell got Graham first, the butcher's shop stench hitting his nostrils and looking down he noticed not a lump but a dead dog, innards spilling out where it had been booted, entrails all over the laughing policeman's patent leather boots, cloud of bluebottles in the air that had been feeding hungrily on the carcass.

'Don't worry, my driver will remove it. Too many things die young in this town,' said the police-general.

'Yeah,' said Graham, sidestepping the body blackened by decay, hoping it wasn't some kind of awful omen.

'Natasha's,' she said, taking him in her arms, giggling like the dead dog was nothing, indicating a blank space outside the bar where a sign should've been, would be.

Was she actually taking the piss though, thought Graham, remembering back to the time he'd promised her name up in lights, looking at the cheap chipboard facade, wringing his hands at how it could ever work, the throb behind his eyes again, pain twisting at his shoulders. Mark's place opposite appeared similarly, depressingly decrepit, with half the neon bulbs depicting Christie's having stopped working or simply missing, like the owner had given up too.

'Come. We go inside,' said Peeklong.

The policeman had his hand in the small of Graham's back, propelling him forward. They stepped over the threshold through a set of squeaky louvre doors that were on the piss, like a clichéd entrance to a saloon bar in some sad spaghetti western. Peeklong snapped on a couple of strip lights, which hummed below the creaky corrugated iron roofing, illuminating a bar at one end of the pitch, raised platform doubling as a stage at the other – the usual format for a Bangkok fleshpot.

The policeman wrenched open a rusting metal shutter with a clatter, unlocking a door to the side, appearing behind the bar with a crooked smile, switching on a set of fairy lights that flashed once and died to a collective shrug.

'Drink?'

'Whisky, please,' said Graham, Natasha leaning into him, Daeng marauding around like he was some kind of bloody surveyor, knocking on wood, running a hand along the dusty bar, while Peeklong poured Johnnie Walker Black into four glasses, dolloping in ice, topping it up with Coke that sloshed everywhere such was his haste.

'Cheers,' said the policeman.

'Up yours,' said Graham, knocking it back, hoping it would relieve the tension in his body, ease the nagging questions in his mind, sitting down on one of the rickety stools strewn about haphazardly, part of the ramshackle inventory, its lining ripped, innards spilling out like that of the dead dog. 'Can I have a look at the books?'

'That's what I said, quite the businessman, ah. But books? You think I keep books?' said Peeklong, unleashing another mocking laugh, Daeng and Natasha joining in.

In the ensuing silence, punctuated only by the humming of the strip lights, Peeklong laid a piece of paper on the bar, smoothing it down like it was of high import, taking a shiny pen out of his top pocket, a pocket adorned by a flash of insignia.

'I'm wondering what this place makes in a month,' Graham said, head swimming with the afternoon of drinking that had turned into an evening, though there was something else, the three pairs of eyes looking back at him as though what the fuck, just hand over the bloody dosh.

'Let's just say, Mr Graham, it's enough. And if the bar's a success, good for me, good for you,' he said, thrusting the piece of paper towards him, the pen. 'This is the title deed. Let me see the colour of your money.'

'Here's the ten per cent deposit. I'll wire you the rest of the money tonight, as you asked,' he said, swinging the holdall that he'd been gripping with all his might onto the bar top, the cash he'd just withdrawn from Bangkok Bank in bundles with Natasha and Daeng at his shoulder as though ready to step in if he'd had second thoughts.

Peeklong unzipped the bag without an invite, dove a hand in and snagged one of the bricks of money, sniffed at it with his pig-like snout, a light seeming to go on behind those typically dead eyes, lovingly bringing out one bundle after another as he counted under his breath.

Graham gulped back all the questions he'd been meaning to ask as the count continued, like some dodgy drug deal, focusing on preventing himself from shaking, giving away his sole experience of business was getting a mortgage twenty-odd years ago and then he'd had his hand held all the way by the old school bank manager and solicitor. Now it was all on him, he thought, listening to Peeklong finally zipping up the bag with a contented sigh.

'Sign here,' he said, pointing at a blank space on the paper otherwise filled with indecipherable Thai script.

Graham cleared his dry throat, about to say something but those three pairs of eyes again, and he looked at the paper, knew it could mean nada but instead of querying the only sound was the scrape of his pen, pressing so hard his signature was scored into the bar as Peeklong snatched it up, indicating for Natasha and Daeng to follow. Catching the bunch of keys the policeman threw at him nothing had felt heavier, more weighty, the four of them now inextricably linked. Graham was in lock, stock and two fucking smoking barrels as Mark had memorably offered up. He was also fully entwined with a ladyboy, the bile rising in his throat. What the bloody hell did that make him?

***

'What the fuck do you want, mate?' said Mark, glancing up from the litter of his desk, scattered envelopes everywhere that looked suspiciously like unopened bills, the seemingly forever burning cigarette in his hand explaining the filthy, overflowing ashtray.

'Look, I've come in peace. There's no reason why we can't all get along. I'm your new neighbour,' said Graham, noticing the jarring tic under his rival's right eye.

'For fuck sake, drop the hippy-dippy claptrap. Plus a little bird told me you've already nicked my master of ceremonies, my main man Nigel. You don't know what you've got involved in,' he said, waving a finger in Graham's face.

'I'm sorry about Nigel but he wanted the challenge. Just what have you got against her, Natasha?'

'Yeah, yeah, Nigel wanting to go to pastures new. Let's see how long it lasts, how long he can stay off the ale. And Natasha? Mate, you don't want to know.'

'No, Mark, I really, really do want to know. I feel up to my neck in this already.'

'Does she know you're here you bloody divvy?'

'Why?'

'Look, she's territorial like a dog, she demands loyalty. A gentle warning… if she finds out you've been to see me, handed out the olive branch, she'll get angry,' he said. 'And when I say angry, mate, I mean angry. She might look like a woman but it's just a mask. I've had a machete to my neck.'

'What?'

'Some little fucking disagreement and she went straight to the kitchen drawer. She would've used it as well. Lucky her mum came in, disturbed us.'

'So you were together, you two?'

'Mate, that's what I mean, you don't even know and you don't want to know. Course we were an item but she's literally like a big, filthy leech. She sticks to your major artery and sucks you dry until you've got nothing left. Nothing.'

'Go on.'

'It's little things at first. You'll go out for those first few dates and she makes any effort to pay for the odd thing here and there. Wait, I bet she even did your laundry,' he said, laughing as Graham nodded almost disbelieving in assent. 'By the time she's made you rely on her to navigate this fucking jungle of a city, not only are you funding her but her family, the even sicker buffalo and half her mates as well. Graham, don't think you're the first person to ever discover paradise because she'll exploit it until there's nothing left.'

'Bloody hell.'

'Look, it might be different with you, for all I know, if you're careful but she broke me and I'm not just talking financially. Okay I make a tiny profit from the bar but that's after years of losses when she was involved and you know the funniest thing,

44

she fucking owns it.'

'Owns it?'

'Don't look so shocked. She owns it but Christie came along and put her name to it when Natasha left, like saving face, my face. That piece of paper you sign means nowt because in Thai law a foreigner can only have a minority stake in a local business.'

'She said it was split fifty-fifty,' he said, throwing up his hands, wincing at the shooting pains in his stomach, thinking back to the time he'd signed the scrappy piece of paper under her and Daeng's unflinching gaze, how it had all felt so wrong.

'Well she would say fifty-fifty, wouldn't she? Technically she should still be getting a rake-off from my place but I'm not busting a gut behind this bar for her anymore. But what do I get for years of hard bloody work?' he said, sending a whole wedge of the unopened envelopes on his desk tumbling to the floor. 'This is how paradise ends.'

'Mark, I'm sorry... I... I don't know what to say.'

'It's okay, drink?' he said, pointing to the tellingly half-empty bottle of whisky on his desk, Graham nodding. 'Sounds like a cliché but when you have nothing left, there's nothing to lose. I don't even have any fucking friends. The only people that remember my name in this town are barmen.'

'What about the customers here?'

'Oh, yeah, you get all the old expat crowd but people come and go. Never get too close to anyone as they'll be off to pastures new in a year, year and a bit or end up dead.'

'Why did it end with you and Natasha?' he said, taking a big slug of whisky.

His question was met by a howl of laughter. 'I couldn't take it. The lies, the abuse, the sleeping around. She might be your girlfriend but if I'm honest, she's a complete slut. There's an American guy, was a regular at the bar and the bastard still comes in. Untouchable in Thailand as he's rich. Money buys you everything here. Mr Paul fucking von Eil the Second he bills himself as. Wanted back in the States for fraud. Typical expat, running away from a past life. Reinvented himself as some bloody big shot.'

'So she was with this Von Eil?'

'She was with him all right. Probably still is.'

'Still is? But she's with me. He better not bloody try anything,' he said, banging a hand down on the desk, shaking his head.

'Oh, I'm scared,' said Mark, head tilted back with laughter, tears in his eyes. 'Mate, mate, oh poor you. You've no idea what you're dealing with. It's the way he looks at people, he's like the Godfather.'

'The flamin' Godfather?' said Graham but his body was trembling again, shaking uncontrollably, sensing somewhere out there was this powerful man that wanted what he had, was going to spoil his dream.

'You look like you've seen a ghost. Don't worry, you'll meet him soon enough. Always comes sniffing around. Evil bastard too. Into real sleazy stuff, kids the lot, but he's rich so that's all right then. Never got that about this fucking country. Everyone's a Buddhist monk but I've never found somewhere that worships money more. You and me are walking ATMs but it runs out unfortunately. Then there's Christie, she and I hardly talk,' he said, stubbing his cigarette out and sending dog ends overflowing onto the table, lighting up yet another.

'What, ever?'

'That's the thing, Graham, I could've been the best husband in the world. I loved her but a silly little thing like love doesn't count in their world. How could I possibly compete with Von Eil? With these girls, or whatever you want to call them, there's always someone like that in the shadows with a wallet full of gold cards. She treated me like a kid, like I was soft, and that's what I've become. I've gone backwards since coming 'ere.'

'How about Daeng and Nigel?'

Another howl of laughter. 'Look, Nigel's pretty harmless. Would do anything for a drink mind and he speaks the lingo, so I often find he's on their side. As for Daeng, don't ask.'

'Come on, Mark, what's his game? I just can't make him out.'

'You'll see soon enough. I despise him even more than I do her. It just makes me laugh when they try to take the moral high ground and blame everything on crazy foreigners when their own set of values are the most fucked up I've ever come across. It makes me sick.'

'I can't believe what I'm hearing…' said Graham, shoving a hand in his pocket and caressing the box of Xanax.

'Mate, the normal rules don't apply here. As Nigel always says, nothing is as it appears. Don't be surprised by anything. Look at the paper. It's an uncivil war,' Mark said, pointing a shaky finger at the morning's *Bangkok Post*, headlines screaming *'Red shirts in bloody stand-off'*.

'That's another thing,' said Graham, thinking it was almost tragi-comic that he'd run away partly due to anxiety only to end up in the most anxiety-provoking place in the universe, the red and yellow shirts summing up the contradictions of the country, contradictions so ingrained they were prepared to kill one another.

'Amazing Thailand,' said Mark laughing, sarcastically invoking the country's latest tourist slogan, raising a glass.

'I don't know what to do.'

'You've come this far, try to enjoy your time with her. Don't ask too many questions. That was my mistake. The Thais will always be in the driving seat, they stick together. You either shut up and get on with it, or like me, you go under,' he said, looking down, unable to meet Graham's gaze.

'You know you said that thing about running away, we're all running away, were you?'

'I was in the army, mate, Northern Ireland, Falklands, the lot. This is where me army pension's gone. In the end there's just nowhere left to run. Burnt all my bridges at home for this.'

***

Graham stepped into the welcoming shade afforded by the roof. He heard loud voices but it took him a moment to locate exactly where they were coming from, blinking away the brightness from outside, luxuriating in the blast of cooler air from the bar's electric fans before he allowed himself to compute what was being said.

'You're fucking undercutting me. You're trying to put me out of business,' said Mark.

'What's going on here?' said Graham, barging into the little dressing room backstage, watching as Mark got in Natasha's face, finger an inch from her nose, though she looked impassive, uncaring, Nigel and Daeng silent partners off to the side.

'Don't tell me you don't fucking know,' said Mark, turning to Graham.

'Try me,' he said, looking at the Liverpudlian's flushed face

48

contorted in hate, almost unrecognisable from their matey chat just an hour or two ago.

'Well, if you look at your blackboard outside you'll see you're offering two-for-one drinks between seven and nine. I can't afford to do that and I call that undercutting.'

'My dear, that's business,' said Nigel, lopsidedly raising a glass.

'Hold on here. Since when have we been offering two for one? We haven't even opened yet,' Graham said.

'It's a business decision,' said Natasha, shaking out her long hair, shrugging.

'Yeah, a business decision that'll put me out of business, you bitch!' said Mark, slapping her across the face but before he could disengage Daeng was on him, bundling the Scouser to the floor, raining down hefty blows on his head with the sick metronomic thump, thump, thump echoing around the bar.

'Enough,' said Graham, running over to the pair, Daeng standing triumphantly above Mark about to hit him again. 'Daeng, I said that's enough.'

The Thai slowly backed away seeing the pathetic, bloodied mess he'd left but Natasha stepped forward, unable to leave it.

'If you come back here again, I kill you,' she said towering above her ex.

It was the slow, deliberate delivery that put a chill through Graham, his body trembling, because he knew she meant it, in that instant realising what she was capable of. He helped Mark to his feet as Natasha finally backed off, drawn to a face swollen like some outsized fruit rotting on a summer lawn but it was the hurt in his eyes that looked more painful. The Liverpudlian hobbled away but stopped at the exit, the two bar owners coming face to face again – old hand and novice.

'I will be sitting opposite to watch this whole fucking enterprise fail,' Mark said, spittle showering everyone in proximity as he nodded to indicate Daeng and then Natasha.

'Keep looking over your shoulder,' Daeng said, shoving Mark out the door, sending him stumbling again, falling to his arse on the blackened pavement, where he stayed as though totally defeated.

Graham was hugging himself, disbelieving at what he'd just witnessed, at what he'd got himself involved in.

'We need to get rid of him,' said Natasha, like she was talking about sacking an underperforming member of staff.

'What? Why?'

'Just 5,000 baht all it would take to get someone to finish him,' she said, clicking her fingers.

Nigel and Daeng's laughter sent that now familiar chill through him once more.

Chapter four

Love in a hopeless place

'That's where Mark got it wrong see. He reckons it's all tits and bums but it's showbusiness,' Nigel said, spreading his arms as if indicating a stage. 'We've got to entertain, dear.'

'That's the spirit,' said Graham, never having seen him more animated or more sober, looking around the claustrophobic, brightly lit backstage area filled with preening performers in garish costumes and awash with first-night tension, pleased the choreographer was fully aboard, the last piece of the crazy jigsaw.

With a swig of his drink for courage he peeked out of the curtain and once he'd finished blinking the brightness of the stage lights away he was looking into a near-empty bar, tawdry and faded under fairy lights with no presence out front to lure in the unsuspecting.

'For Christ's sake,' he said, every muscle in his body tensing, a pounding across his temples, envisioning that night when he saw Mark frantically counting receipts. 'Don't we have any girls outside the bar?'

'Relax, honey,' said Natasha, draping a hand over his shoulder.

'How can I relax? Thirty minutes until showtime and not one paying punter. Where the hell's Daeng?' he said, brushing her off, thinking the Thai style casualness about everything could undo him yet she looked a vision in plumage, very much the star of the show, if there was a bloody show.

'Gone for food.'

Graham threw his hands up and just stopped himself letting out a diatribe about the boy who was meant to have orchestrated the outdoor promotion, which was as sophisticated as grabbing people off the street. He looked from Natasha to Nigel, though his compatriot was busily preparing the performers, fixing a wig here, plumping a feather boa there but what good was a show without an audience, a bar without customers?

He glanced out of the curtain again, slightly placated by the fact a few punters had actually ventured in. Drink orders were being taken, bills written in the antiquated Thai way of triplicate, receipts he knew he would be poring over at the end of the evening – just like he'd seen Mark do – to calculate how much they'd *lost*. He'd resigned himself to operating at a loss for a while, which is why they lived in a virtual slum, that after the five-star luxury of his first trip was making him see the country in a totally different light, a light filtered through the shitty brown detritus of the Third World.

Graham exited backstage and onto the street, a large rat scuttling away into the gloom, unsettling him, as did the thought of Mark waiting for him in the shadows having already made an enemy. He walked round to the front of the bar, Natasha's Cabaret picked out in neon against the dark Bangkok night and a smile tickled the traces of his mouth – the first time he'd genuinely smiled since landing in the country. But he looked back down to street level and at the garishly dressed ladyboys standing somewhat forlornly, oblivious to everything except themselves.

'Girls,' he said, clapping his hands. 'You need to be ready to greet customers, not talking to each other. Or looking at your bloody phones.'

However, he felt vaguely ridiculous after saying it as they turned sombrely away from each other and back towards an almost empty street. The uncivil war that was raging having put off many tourists meaning it was not a good time to be opening a new establishment. Embarrassed he decided to go back in and take up what was soon to become his customary place behind the bar – all too close to the optics and fridgeful of beer, pouring himself another Thai whisky, fiddling awkwardly to light a cigarette, having gone back to smoking full time again after years of abstinence. He only just about resisted counting the number of customers in the sparsely populated bar but unlike most of the fickle clientele that anxious knot behind his shoulders refused to leave.

'Ladies and Gentlemen, tonight we welcome you to experience great dance, great music. Let us introduce to you the greatest show on Earth. Cabaret!' boomed Nigel's voice, making the tinniest of speakers reverberate and distort. 'Mama Mia…' heralded the beginning of the Abba medley the old man had been banging on about, reflecting how painfully out of touch he was in relying on the platforms and bouffants of the seventies, as though he was still wishing to regain his heyday but Graham knew all the crap music in the world wouldn't bring that back – it was lost to them both.

He looked on as the old melodies warbled from the speakers,

at the stilted, nervous dance routines, the too bright costumes of the ladyboys, made still cheaper by their fake smiles and the mistimed lip-synching and he wondered how it could ever work, though he felt hope in Natasha's sparkling eyes, long-legged strut. He was proud to be the man taking her home every night, though that pride was still shrouded in shame, he thought, as he took another swig of his drink. But this was everything he'd wanted, wasn't it?

A few other punters came and went as the evening progressed, even taking a girl or two along the way, but it had dwindled down to one by the time of the finale – the appropriately titled 'Last Dance'. It could have been entitled anything, for the remaining customer was splayed across the bar, totally drunk, a girl hovering over him waiting to lift the remaining contents of his wallet no doubt, along with the rest of his dignity.

Almost on cue, as the music ended, and the drunk stirred, Graham noticed Peeklong had entered with two colleagues, a visit he'd been expecting, though their brown well-filled uniforms and shiny boots looked incongruous in the surroundings. They certainly didn't seem about to order drinks as they approached the bar.

'Ah, the first night. How's it going?' said Peeklong, looking around the near-empty venue, dark glasses glued to his face despite the hour.

'It's going. What can I do you for?' said Graham, fixated by the gun holstered conspicuously on the policeman's hip, unsettled by it and the fact the other two officers were trampling through the premises, thinking where the hell was Natasha when he needed her, just the sound of her laughter bubbling up from behind the curtain.

'Just paying a friendly visit,' he said, swatting a mosquito that had landed on the counter, waking the drunk who stumbled off the stool and away, the other two policemen having sat down at a far table and lit cigarettes.

'Drink?'

'I thought you'd never ask,' said Peeklong, throwing his head back in laughter, which set off the other two goons.

'Whisky? And how about your friends?' asked Graham, stalling, hoping Natasha would return before they got to the crux of the matter because he knew there was going to be a punchline, this didn't feel like just a friendly visit from the local neighbourhood bobby or the former owner for that matter.

'Scotch, yes. Don't worry about the other two, not your problem.'

He turned from the bar and poured a more than generous measure of his best whisky with what he was dismayed to find was a trembling hand but he couldn't face another drink himself, he was trying desperately to sober up, to be ready for what was coming. Graham had not been in the country long but he'd already got used to its formal way of doing things beneath the facade of informality, as behind the politeness and smiles often lurked if not a killer blow, then something close to it. He handed Peeklong his drink.

'You will not have one with me?'

'I've had enough,' Graham said but wondering what exactly he'd had enough of.

'Turn the music down, please.'

'Yes, of course,' he said, reaching for the volume control, only just realising through the fug of alcohol they'd been shouting at each other above the Thai pop, a hub-bub now audible from behind the curtain where Natasha was obviously having a party with the rest of the cast.

'Mr Graham, how much did you make tonight?' he said, taking off his glasses, finishing his whisky with another gulp, banging it down on the bar.

'Pardon?'

'Mr Graham, it is simple question. How much money?' spat Peeklong, snatching his glasses from the counter and repositioning them on his greasy nose.

'Six thousand baht,' he said to a chorus of laughter, three pairs of eyes looking at him.

'We visit Patpong every night. We know everything. And we also know that new businesses are vulnerable, vulnerable to attack from rivals, jealous people,' he said in almost a whisper, running a hand smoothly across the counter like it was made of the costliest mahogany, taking a lighter from his pocket and lighting the flame just an inch or two from Graham's face.

'I... I see,' he said, feeling the heat, propping himself against the bar to prevent the trembling.

'No, *farang*, I don't think you do see,' said Peeklong, voice louder now, rhythm harsh, where it had been so soft and lilting before.

'Look, what the hell do you want? I'm legal and above board. We had an agreement,' he said, the other two officers moving menacingly around to his side of the bar, picking up bottles, roughly putting them down again like they were looking for something incriminating.

'Work permit? You have?' said Peeklong, like they'd never even met, let alone done a business transaction. 'We want a third of the takings. It's Thai way. Then you have no problem from police. No problem for me, no problem for you. See? That's what I meant when I said the bar's good for you, good for me.'

'A third!' Graham shouted but his shoulders slumped. 'How can I afford that?'

'You will afford it, or you close down,' said Peeklong, smashing his gun down on the counter with a crack, holding out an open palm for money with his free hand.

Graham was uncomprehending at what the hell things had come to, asking himself how he'd got into such a position, as he limply acquiesced and began counting out 2,000 baht, the ridiculousness of the comment 'you will afford it, or you close down' seeming to perfectly sum up the paradox of it all, the paradox of the whole country. Peeklong wordlessly folded up the money and shoved it into his top pocket, ambling off with his goons.

'I've just been robbed by the bloody police,' he said to no one in particular as he burst through the stage curtain, kicking the floor so hard he felt the pain throbbing up his leg as he frantically calculated the rest of the night's pitiful takings were going on the after-show party in front of him, robbed twice over.

'Don't worry, tonight's drinks are on me,' said Nigel, quick with a consoling arm around his shoulder, obligatory drink in the other hand.

'What the hell is this? I've just had to give most of tonight's takings to the police,' he said, indicating Daeng who was like the puppet master sitting in the centre of a circle of staff on the floor doling out drinks and snacks but the Thais continued to ignore him.

'Shush,' said Nigel, pouring Graham a drink, shoving it at him.

'You're telling me this is normal? This is how it's done?' he said, pointing at the crowd of them, their carefree chatter clashing horribly with the screaming worries in his mind.

'Graham, Graham… it's our first night, dear,' Nigel said, nodding towards the party going on in the other half of the room. 'Let's celebrate. It's about the here and now.'

'Bloody hell,' he said, no longer worried about hiding his anger from Natasha, not that he thought she'd care anyway as right on cue her insistent laughter cut through the air like a buzz saw.

Looking at them, eating and drinking with abandon, he knew he could never accede to the Thai way of 'living for today' because it simply indicated they didn't have a future – it was how people lived in a slum, where there were no opportunities. He could see how Nigel had lasted so long in Bangkok, the Nigel that didn't feel guilty any more about getting smashed every night because he was surrounded by similar people with no hope.

'Listen, it's a feudal system. You're always in debt to the most powerful Thai. However long you stay here, however much money you've made you're always a bloody *farang*. Don't forget that. I did…'

'Yeah, feudal system is right. I'm not just a *farang*, I'm a bloody serf. Nige, I'm also totally lost,' Graham said, putting an arm around his friend, looking for an answer but he ended up simply staggering back towards the bar.

He wrenched the box of pills from his pocket, only for emergencies Graham had thought when he cashed in the first prescription. Until what had become the all too familiar feelings – the heartbeat thumping in his ears, the sweat pouring from his brow, the desperate clinging onto the edge of the bar as if to retain his balance.

'You okay, Gray?' said Natasha.

'Love, I, er… don't know…' he said flinching, not having seen her coming, body wracked with an urge to run, just like what he'd suffered back in London only to be told at A&E it was no heart attack but panic, then the shame, the impotence that went with it almost worse than the attacks themselves.

'You sick?' she said, her eyes all over him.

'Look, it's just my heart sometimes. It gets a bit excited. If you know what I mean,' he said, as she plucked the packet out of his hands, scrutinising the brand name but seeming none the wiser or at least he hoped she wasn't.

'Excited. I like it when you excited,' she said laughing, grabbing Graham to her.

'Oh, Nat,' he said, her embrace better than any tranquiliser.

'We're going out tonight.'

'Tonight?' he said, looking at the clock, past twelve, thinking the night was long over.

'Yes, Daddy.'

They hailed a cab from outside the bar, Graham sliding across the backseat but Natasha sidling up close, the cabbie giving him an odd look in the mirror, that sick feeling in his stomach again, like he was being judged by his mates, his dad, for sitting alongside what? A bender, a poof, a freak, that's what. And what did that make him? He closed his eyes wanting to blink it all away but her presence was comforting – Nat wanting him, for all his doubts Graham wanting her.

'Love you,' she said breathily into his ear, lips brushing his lobe.

'Natasha,' he said, turning to her, drinking in those eyes, so long since he'd heard those words, if ever, feeling desire despite himself, a tide he could no longer hold back, hating the way he felt but loving it at the same time, tension easing but head swimming.

'Don't think too much,' she said, hand caressing his thigh.

'I know,' he said, giving the cabbie the imaginary finger, looking out the window, late-night Bangkok, or early morning, and the place was buzzing, smiling as he took in the Silom night market, hawkers still trying to sell their knock-off sex DVDs, fake Rolexes, dodgy Armanis, alongside the profusion of eateries with roadside grills fizzing away, the cut and thrust of this never-ending place.

'Tonight we go to DJ,' she said.

'DJ?'

'DJ Station. It's gay club, you know.'

'Gay?' he said, finding it hard to even enunciate, moving away from her, grabbing the seat with both hands, knuckles white.

'Gray, take it easy. We just drink. Have fun. You don't have to *do* anything.'

'Yeah,' he said but in his mind's eye all he could see were the blokes in The Sydney, his local pub, could imagine their pointing fingers, red faces, tongues loosened by beer spewing hate, hatred directed towards him, a fucking queer and that's what he deserved, a queer who'd deserted his wife and shacked up with a Bangkok ladyboy.

'Come on,' she said, having to drag him out of the taxi.

It's like he hadn't even realised they'd stopped but Graham followed her lead, those flashing eyes, jostling through what seemed an endless throng of people, finally sitting on little plastic stools by the blackened roadside, pleasant food smells in the air. A woman almost unbidden, big, bustling mum type all business, plonked down two cups of iced water in brightly coloured plastic beakers. Natasha addressed her, presumably ordering food.

'It's chicken rice. Give you energy for tonight,' she said with a smile.

'And what do I need energy for?'

'Oh, baby,' she said, waving her trigger finger under his nose and they both laughed, Natasha rooting around in her handbag as she did so.

'What's this?' said Graham, as she placed an envelope on the table, a pink envelope, his name on the front in curly script. 'Didn't realise it was my birthday.'

'Open it,' she said, nudging him gently in the ribs.

He ripped it open like a kid on Christmas Day, Natasha looking on like a proud parent. Graham may have been sceptical about it all, was on the precipice of hating himself for what he'd done, but he could see the love in those eyes as his own clouded and he couldn't deny as each individual word seeped into his soul that somehow it was the right thing.

'*I'm so glad you came along and changed my life. You need to be patient with impatient but just know I'll always be there for you, that I love you. We're a team now,*' he read, unaware of the tears until he felt them streaming hot down his face, throwing up a hand trying to stem them, hide his emotions, like he always did.

'No one's ever sent me a card before. Not like this,' he said, pulling the hands away from his face now, letting the tears

61

come, reaching across to Natasha.

'Nigel helped. My English not so good. But I mean it,' she said, pointing at the food that aunty had just laid down. 'We eat now and then we have fun.'

'Yeah,' he said, carefully putting the card back into the envelope, handing it to her for safekeeping – a team, he thought, ladling down his food like he hadn't eaten for a week.

'You know my parents hated me for being like this,' she said through mouthfuls.

'Like what?'

'This.'

'You look amazing,' he said, entranced as she sat erect, flashing that perfect smile, like she was some kind of supermodel.

'No, Gray, I didn't feel like that. Not then. It's in your head. I felt ashamed when I was younger. When I stopped being ashamed, I'm like this. It's like turning into a butterfly. But you've got to forget what's in your head now.'

'What about other people?'

'Don't care. I don't care what they think. My mum and dad… they threw me out when they found I was ladyboy. My dad, he beat me…'

'Beat you?' he said, looking at the tears in those normally smiling eyes, balling his hands into fists, feeling protective as he grabbed her arm.

'I don't want to talk about that. Long time ago. It's okay now, it take time. I was patient with my parents because they are my blood. But who are other people? Who cares what they think. You just be yourself.'

'But what happened after your parents threw you out…'

'I was young, so young. Just fifteen and I'm not proud of

62

what happened then, my past. But I'm not talking about that. I'll tell you some time. Come, let's go.'

'Nat, I wanna know…'

'We're talking about you now. We talk about me another time. Let's go.'

'Okay,' he said, like her eyes forbade him to say another word, following her as she stood, Natasha pressing a couple of notes into the stallholder's hand, smile affixed back to her face like the recollection of bad times had simply been a passing storm, Graham admiring how she could just brush things off as he felt the shooting pains in his stomach, twisting at his guts.

The irritable bowel syndrome that seemed to be constantly with him was a reminder of all his worries but yeah, he needed to be himself, hopefully that would help. Graham was desperate for something to work having been unhappy for so long, like anxiety and depression were a default setting, instinctively feeling in his pocket, the Xanax still sadly there.

'You don't walk behind me anymore, you next to me,' she said, wrapping an arm round his back, propelling him forward. 'Don't be ashamed of me as that mean you're ashamed of yourself. If you're going to be embarrassed by me, we can just go back and you pay me.'

There was a queue outside the club, Graham looking at the mostly young lads laughing and joking wondering where his time had gone, having already been hitched to Sheil at that age, his so-called childhood bloody sweetheart but he had no idea what'd been sweet about it, more like a twenty-year prison sentence than something to be celebrated, eulogised with meaningless phrases. But instead of standing in line, Natasha who was chatting away to various faces in the crowd, ushered

63

him to the front like some kind of film star on a red carpet, all that was missing the popping bulbs of the paparazzi, though the feeling of celebrity was contagious and he was a somebody for the first time as he glided into the club with her.

His forehead immediately slicked with sweat and the beat of the music pounded in his ears as they inched through a swarm of people, part of a seething mass rather than individuals but Graham had a smile on his face as what the hell had he been worried about? Downing the whisky soda she'd just got from the bar, again skipping the queue, VIP status, he felt good, though it was like a man with vertigo on the edge of a cliff. He was already craving another drink because he didn't want to think, to look down.

'Have this,' she said, discreetly indicating a pill between thumb and forefinger, as they pressed back into the swarm towards the dancefloor.

'What's that?'

'It's better than the drug I see you take before. Ecstasy,' she said, pressing her mouth into his ear again.

'Yes,' he said, Natasha placing one half of the pill she'd just split onto his tongue, Graham swallowing it back, bopping away on the edge of the dancefloor, the last time he'd danced at his daughter Emmy's birthday where she'd taken the piss out of his dad dancing and he didn't want to think again.

'What you think this place?' she said above the boom of the music.

'Amazing,' he said, the crush of bodies feeling sensual, erotic, rather than intimidating, not something to run from as he'd first feared, tension magically disappearing from his shoulders, his entire being, first time in a gay club and it was liberating.

'Why didn't you bring me here before?'

'Oh, Gray,' she said with a smile as they clinked glasses.

'I think we can do this, we really can,' said Graham and it was the first time since he'd arrived back in Bangkok that he believed it, was starting to see all the things he'd denied himself over the years because what? He'd been so bloody frightened that's what, terrified of being himself, though he also knew it could be the drink and drugs talking and tomorrow he'd be in another black hole.

'Come on,' she said, dragging him onto the dancefloor.

'I can't.'

'Don't speak for once,' she said, enveloping her arms around him.

He folded himself into her embrace, the music reverberating through his being, feeling the rhythm in his fingertips go right down to his toes and he really was moving in time to the beat. Graham looked out at the sea of other faces, most with wide grins, arms aloft, all bouncing in time to the metronomic sound and it was almost as if they were one.

He swiped at the sweat coursing from his forehead, gratefully accepting a swig from a bottle of water waggled under his nose from a boy to his left, as if everyone was speaking the same language. Though he noticed his and Natasha's cosy little twosome had been infiltrated by a young white man, backpacker attire of shorts and singlet, beaded dreadlocks *on a white guy*, like he was desperately trying to find himself. What he had found by the looks of it, seethed Graham, was Natasha. He was now right in her face, his muscled back a wall between them, the lad bending down whispering something in her ear.

He tapped the backpacker on the shoulder but it was as

though he was glued to Natasha's ear, her twinkling eyes, that smile for someone else only riling him further. He wrenched the lad round to face him, he wasn't little old Graham anymore, hadn't given up his old life just to let this one slip through his bloody fingers.

'Can't you see I'm busy, mate,' said the guy glaring at him, harsh Aussie accent cutting through the music, face flaring a radioactive kind of orange, Natasha impassive in the background, all innocence.

'Yeah, busy with my girlfriend,' he said, manoeuvring himself right into the boy's face, feeling the adrenalin rip through his body, ready to fight, ready for anything, the warm fuzziness of the Ecstasy gone.

'Ah look, c'mon, this is Bangkok. What's mine is yours. No?' said the backpacker, taking a step back.

'No, what's mine is mine. That's my new motto,' he said, sending the boy stumbling backwards with a hefty shove, wiping the supercilious grin off his smooth features, a face so pristine like he hadn't even started shaving yet.

'Girlfriend, you say,' said the backpacker, lurching back into Graham's face, eyes burning. 'Mate, that ain't no girlfriend. Sometimes it's difficult to tell in this city but I've just twigged. I'll leave you to it, good for nothing queer.'

'Fuck you,' he said, slamming the Aussie full in the chest before the boy wriggled off into the crowd.

'Thanks, Gray. He just came to me. I don't even know what he saying but men here, they think they can just have me. They think they can just buy me,' said Natasha, placatory hand on his arm, tears in her eyes.

'I saw you smiling,' he said, brushing her hand away.

'Babe, I'm happy, so happy. Me and you together, the E, everything. He just push in. I not listen to what he's saying. I might look tough but I'm not. I smile so I don't get hurt. Men always hurt me. Always,' she said, looking at the floor.

'I'm gonna make sure they don't hurt you anymore. As you said, we're together now, we're a team. Team Natasha,' he said, high-fiving her as they slipped back into the rhythm, bouncing up and down to the music again.

'People say I'm whore but I'm good person, I try to be. I did some things in the past to get here. To survive. I knew when you came along you good person too, have good heart. I don't want a rich man, I want love.'

'Nat, I know. I saw you once, just that once. I pinned all my dreams on you. People think I'm crazy. Sheil, my mum and dad but my daughter… my Emmy once said to me find a better life. I knew it was possible,' he said, back in Natasha's arms, head lolling on her chest, never having felt more at home, that he belonged.

'Don't worry about other man, it's just you and me now.'

'I know,' he said, though Graham was looking beyond Natasha's eyes, those bright eyes, out into the blackness, nagging pain in his gut again, old fears piercing through the drug haze, the Aussie's accusation resounding in his ears. Maybe he was right?

Chapter five

Pact with the devil(s)

'That was a long night,' he said, glancing at his watch that showed it was afternoon and they'd only just surfaced, momentarily resting his sore head in his hands as they waited for the hotel lift.

'But a good one, Daddy,' said Natasha, pecking Graham on the cheek.

Also waiting for the lift was another microcosm of Bangkok life, an obese white man with a boy who was so pretty and petite he almost resembled a girl but he had a not so innocent mouth that offered up the requisite smile and gave the necessary platitudes to his 'daddy', leaving Graham wondering how much his acquiescence was costing, along with his arse. The man was dressed in what he'd come to already regard as the Bangkok uniform for aspiring sex tourists, obviously kitted out by his teenage companion – the clingy T-shirt and too fashionable jeans making the baseball-cap wearing fiftysomething comical if it all hadn't been so sleazy. They entered the lift and the boy pushed the man into the far corner, so Graham and Natasha had room. As they creaked downwards, he looked at the bloke as if to apologise – that was him always apologising for his bloody existence – though the tourist hid sheepishly behind his cap as the boy assailed Graham with the most smouldering of stares.

Just a bloody transaction, he thought, assuming that's what everyone would make of him and Nat too. Of course it was all good, the night out at a gay club and the altercation with the Aussie showed he was finally being himself, ready to fight for what was his, for what he was. But the comedown was staring at him opposite in the lift, the two queers. Was that what *they* looked like? Was that what people thought? And as he surveyed the scene in the lobby he clutched his head again, wishing he'd stayed in bed, could stay there forever.

'What, baby?'

But he was left peeking out from behind his hands like a kid confronted by a scary movie.

'What the fuck do you think you're doin'? Bastard!' shouted Sheila from her vantage point opposite the lifts.

When Graham dared to look up again, drag his eyes from the floor, no longer pretending it wasn't happening, Natasha was at Sheila's throat, sharp nails poised over withered skin, like she was going to rip it right out.

'Natasha, no,' he said, rushing to the grappling couple, breathlessly pulling them apart, a hand in both of their gurning faces. 'I can handle this. Please go.'

Natasha, eyes burning, skulked out of the lobby leaving husband facing wife – Sheila a mess of trembles and tears, aggression having melted away into emotion.

'Why? Why did you do this to me?' she said through sobs.

'Sheil, what were the last twenty years all about? I tried, really

69

tried to make it work. You wouldn't even touch me. Your own bloody husband.'

'That's your answer. We're married. Till deaf do us part and all that. And who the hell was that? What was it?' she said, slapping him hard across the face, the 'thwack' echoing through the lobby causing guests who'd discreetly observed before to become spectators.

'Look, please… we can't do this here. There's a restaurant next door,' he said, her crocodile tears spent, face looking harder, more cruel than Graham had ever remembered.

'Don't you bloody touch me,' she said, disentangling herself from his attempts at conciliation.

But to his relief she followed him outside and they walked the short distance to the garden restaurant in silence.

'Can I get you a drink, Sir, Madam?' said a waiter.

'Beer,' he said.

'Gin and tonic for me,' said Sheila.

'Why?' she repeated, as soon as they'd sat down.

In the ensuing silence Graham sadly recognised the fellow casualties from the Paradise sat at adjoining tables, feeling further humiliated by them, people he would have once looked down upon in his holier-than-thou, 'I am completely normal, happily married man' guise. He just hoped Sheila wouldn't notice the old sweating white men opposite their perfectly composed young paramours, though it would only take her to look around to find the answer to her question.

'Look, I can't live like a monk. We haven't even kissed in years, not properly, with feeling. I need the touch of another living being.'

'I don't understand you. We've been married twenty years

and all of a sudden I don't understand you. Look at the state of ya for a start. You look like one of those backpackers,' she said, wringing red raw hands. 'We are still married, by the way.'

'Sheil, you're just not listening. It's not a marriage, it's a prison sentence.'

'What about your vows? For richer, for poorer. Remember?' she said, repeatedly stabbing a finger into his chest. 'You're pathetic with your anxiety pills, your shaking. What kind of a man are ya? You're not getting any younger neither.'

'Love... I don't feel old anymore though, that's the point. I... I... it's a different way of life... it's... it's...'

'Don't 'love' me. Graham it's all about sex... and that... that thing you're with, how old is it? You're telling me you're a shirt lifter, a bloody queer. We've been togevver twenty years,' she said, loud enough other people in the garden were turning around to look.

'For God's sake. I feel different. No, I actually feel. And I haven't felt a bloody thing for years. I don't know what else to say,' he said, cringing into his drink.

'How about me? What am I supposed to feel? What about Emma, poor Emmy?' she said, slamming the glass of gin and tonic into the side of his face.

He recoiled as shards of glass minced the side of his cheek, face burning red hot but the icy liquid coating his shirt making him shiver with the shock of it all, her purple face in his, those grimy yellow teeth bared like a rabid dog.

'Don't bring Em into this,' he croaked, picking at the glass embedded in his skin, though it was like he was unable to move, fight or flight mode short-circuited, wondering what was coming next as he fixated on those awful teeth, remembering all those times in the past and why he'd run.

'You will bloomin' regret this for the rest of your life Mr Graham Floyd,' she said and wrenching his face to hers, she spat at him, lobbed a big load of gob.

He watched incapacitated by the shakes as Sheila walked to the exit, wiping a stringy bit of phlegm from his eyebrow, looking at the blood beginning to spot his shirt, unsteadily chugging down his beer.

'Bloody hell,' said Graham to himself, at last certain she wasn't coming back, that she couldn't hurt him anymore, staring down the looks from the rest of the diners, the last twenty minutes justifying his decision to do what he was doing all on their own, like he needed an excuse.

'Gray, what's happened? I was watching from over the street. Just in case,' said Natasha breathlessly, stumbling up to him in her stilettos, pawing at his bleeding face with a napkin.

'Lot of good you did,' he said, managing a laugh, patting her hand. 'Don't worry, she's gone now. The bitch has gone.'

'What the hell she do?' she said, stemming the flow of blood, cradling his head.

'Forget it, love. We need to move on now.'

'Yeah we need to move on. You need divorce.'

'You need to be patient. Rome wasn't built in a day,' he said, mouth so caked dry it was difficult to get any more words out, head in hands, heart thumping to a scarily fast beat he was so awfully familiar with.

'Rome?'

'It's just a saying. Be patient, impatient.'

'I can't be patient if we're living in that dump Paradise. We need apartment. You need that divorce paper in your hand.'

***

The taxi pulled up outside the bar, Graham popping a Xanax, thumping pain behind his eyes a reminder of the faceache Sheila had been just hours before. Getting out of the back of the cab he felt his grazed cheek, the stubbly chin, ran a hand through lank hair, what was left of it. Maybe Sheil was right, the state of 'im. Even when he used to go out to drive his cab he'd always made an effort, been smart, clean-shaven, attired in shirt and slacks. But in Bangkok he'd resorted to the slovenly expat bar owner wear of shorts, T-shirt and flip-flops, while he was stubbornly unshaven, as if since his carefully ordered life had disintegrated there were no standards left to be maintained.

They were huddled in the backstage area, which was the place Natasha held court from afternoon onwards, the telltale bottle of Thai whisky on the table, bucket of ice and assorted mixers, cost coming straight out of the evening's takings. Unusually though Graham noticed Daeng, Nigel and the lady herself were not in fits of giggles but looking incredibly serious.

'What's all this about then?' he said, half expecting to hear Nigel had come up with some new-fangled dance routines to wow the bar's dwindling numbers to justify taking a salary for virtually drinking the place dry.

'Private,' said Daeng, tapping his nose.

'Look, this is my bar as well. Nothing involving that is private. Got it?' Graham said, letting out a sigh as he pulled up a chair, having stood up for himself in front of Sheila there was no way he was letting the little Thai runt push him around, ready to stay and fight for what was his.

He looked Daeng in the eye, the boy shifting aggressively in his seat, almost willing him to kick-off but Graham was delighted when he kept schtum, another small victory.

'Graham, what we were discussing earlier, about Mark. You know…'

'I know what?' he said, hating the ambiguity Nat always dressed everything up in, the indirectness, unless it was about money and then she just fixed her prey with that glint in her eye and got exactly what she wanted.

'Graham, dear, they're going to finish him off,' said Nigel.

'Have you all gone bloody mad?' he said, Daeng immediately putting a finger to his lips but Graham stood up from the table, glaring round at each in turn. 'What the hell are you thinking, Nigel?'

'Nothing to do with me,' he said, holding up his hands. 'I'm just the messenger.'

'I didn't think things could go this wrong,' Graham said, voice barely a whisper, cracking with the effort of getting the words out. 'I'll… I'll go to the police.'

Daeng erupted in laughter, closely followed by Natasha, a horrible, mocking laughter and all Graham could see were Police-General Peeklong's black eyes boring into him when he'd signed the title deed, ensuring he was fully entangled in their grotesque plan.

'So I'll tell Mark then.'

With that Natasha grabbed his arm and twisted so hard he felt she was going to break it.

'You don't do anything okay. We take care of this. Understood?' she said.

He struggled to free himself from her grip but her hand

remained clamped on his arm, as though to stop him running off immediately and letting their neighbour know the murderous plan.

'Do. You. Fucking. Understand?'

'Yes,' he blurted out breathless from the pain, the pain zig-zagging up his arm, through his body, shoulders sagging, thinking if it was that easy to get rid of Mark then everyone's life was pretty much dangling by a thread, uncomprehending how Nat could go from kind and loving to murderous in one sentence. What the hell had happened to her? What had Mark bloody done?

'Don't think too much, Gray,' said Natasha, shoving a drink in front of him, pawing at the arm she'd just wrenched.

'Don't think too much. Don't think too bloody much. That's your answer for everything. No, I wanna know when and how. I know you're not gonna tell me why. Just some bullshit about how he's some kind of threat. But look at him, he's a joke,' he said, slumping onto the table, head in hands, unable to blink Mark's pathetic face away.

'You saw how he acted. Crazy *farang*,' said Natasha, slicing a hand across her throat.

'Doesn't mean he deserves to die. When and how?' he said, downing his shot of whisky with a shudder.

'Soon. In a fire,' she said, brushing absently at some blemish on her blouse. 'No bar, no Mark.'

'In a fire…' Graham repeated, a horrific vision of Mark's slight body charred and blackened among the ashes of his tawdry bar coming to mind.

'That's one show that'll bring the punters in,' said Nigel.

'You think it's funny?' he said, staring at his compatriot,

palms upturned.

'Dear, I told you this is Thailand, the East. The usual rules don't apply. Drink up, love. What else can one do?'

'So what's the plan?' said Graham

'You're the plan,' said Natasha, eyes sparkling, unleashing her most dazzling of smiles.

'What do you mean?' he said, lump in his throat, feeling the sweat trickling from his armpits, running down his back.

'He trusts you,' said Nigel. 'You call a meeting in his office like he's been asking for, bring drinks round, promise to get rid of the two-for-one offer, accede to his demands. Kill him with kindness.'

'Then?' he said to a horrible roar of laughter.

'Then excuse yourself to the toilet after ten minutes or so, deadlock the door from the outside as you go,' said Nigel with a clap of his hands, Natasha holding up a key, presumably *the key*, as he did so.

'What the bloody hell you doing with his key? Maybe he's changed the lock. Maybe…'

'Take it easy. You'll have heart attack. You know we were together once. This is just my insurance,' she said, waving it under his nose.

'Why me? And why can't you just bloody lock him in instead of all this… this charade?' said Graham, face burning red.

'He trusts you,' said Natasha, shaking him as she drilled deeply into his eyes. 'He hates Daeng and me. You need to meet him in office eye to eye, make sure he burns. We don't want any silly mistake.'

'Oh, God,' he said, banging a fist against his head as she let go. 'What about Nigel?'

76

'My dear, this needs someone with a clear head. I'm pissed as a fart by that time of day.'

'Look, this isn't some episode of the bloody *Soprano's*,' said Graham.

'Keep your voice down,' Daeng said, prodding him in the chest.

'Gray, you're not even here legally. You don't have work permit,' said Natasha.

'This has got Peeklong's fingerprints all bloody over it.'

'The good police-general likes order, simplicity and Mark has become a complicated pain in the arse, along with being lairy and they hate lairy here. But the main thing is his contribution to Peeklong's pension fund is almost nil,' said Nigel.

'I don't have a choice, do I?'

'No, dear, I'm afraid you don't,' said Nigel.

'And who else will be involved?'

'We take care of the rest,' she Natasha with a smile as she raised a glass, Daeng and Nigel following suit.

Graham just stared straight ahead, trying to still his shaking limbs, roughly pushing his glass away.

'You okay?' said Natasha, playfully punching his arm, the arm she'd nearly snapped.

'What's this I hear about foreigners not being able to own a business in Thailand?' he said, looking right into her eyes and with the way she'd refused to meet his gaze, turned away, Graham knew the answer.

'Thais always own majority stake. That's what I mean about you being just a tourist,' said Daeng.

'I was told it was fifty-fifty,' he said, hurling his glass at the wall, it exploding into pieces as he sprang across the table, grabbed Daeng around the neck, wrestling him to his feet.

'Gray, stop. Gray, please stop…' said Natasha.

'No, you listen to me for a change,' he said, tuning her out, hands clamped to the Thai boy's neck as he thrashed hopelessly around. 'I'm not sure what you're up to, Daeng, but I don't take orders from you, you got that. Natasha's mine. All this fifty-fifty bloody crap but the bar's mine too. I'll tolerate you because you're her friend, that's all.'

Chapter six

The unquiet American

He was stood out the front of the bar underneath the garish neon hoping the pathetic trickle of customers would turn into a deluge but sensed he really had no bearing on it – this white ghost, balding and going to fat, was no kind of draw. Graham realised he looked pale and washed out against the backdrop of another cheaply colourful Bangkok night. Even the sour-faced Daeng, who hadn't spoken to him since last night's little contretemps, was more accomplished at charming unsuspecting tourists, offering a dose of Eastern promise, a classic Thai sleight of hand, all glittery on the outside, rotten within. A lot of the dance routines, for instance, were culled from the country's ancient culture, though that presumably didn't include another practised Natasha's Cabaret move that could only be experienced in the toilets out back.

A car drew up and Graham immediately tensed, hypersensitive to any perceived threat, part of his bloody condition the doctor had told him back in England after Emmy… The super shiny, low-slung Mercedes convertible with blacked out windows looked textbook gangster, its radiant newness, its opulence so at odds with the poverty of its surroundings. His attention was drawn to the number plate that spelled EVIL and it made him shiver as though it was some kind of awful omen. He knew the whole area was a 'no parking' zone but for the driver of that kind of car, in Bangkok, the normal rules didn't apply and that wasn't just petty laws related to parking – 'the untouchables', Nigel had called them.

A white man with a healthy thatch of blond hair got out, clothed in a sober dark suit that would've looked ridiculous in the city's tropical climate had it not added to the aura the rich and powerful wore all too easily in the city, the way they splashed on good cologne, thought Graham. As the man hovered at the threshold of the bar it was if he was waiting to be greeted, fawned over, confidently lighting a cigar because who would possibly dare object?

'Hi, Paul von Eil,' he said to Graham with a grating American twang, name casually tossed into the ether, puffing out smoke as he did so.

'I might've heard all about you but I'm Graham, the owner here,' he said, jolted back to Mark's warning about the American, daunted by the firm politician's handshake, the judgmental gaze from those steely blue eyes, wondering how he could possibly compete, fill the shoes of the, no doubt, pricy Italian loafers the Yank wore.

'You actually smell new here, fresh meat,' he said, wrinkling up his nose, removing an unwanted hair from his suit jacket as though appalled by any blemish. 'But actually I've come to see my gal, Natasha.'

'Your girl? Your bloody girl? We're together. An item,' he said, stamping a foot on the ground, like he was marking it out as his territory, feeling the hairs on the back of his neck stand up as if in readiness, sensing danger as he had when the car first pulled up, when Mark had first mentioned his name.

'You Brits, don't take it all so seriously. This is Bangkok, man,' he said, patting Graham's shoulder.

'She's my girlfriend, that's all.'

'Sure she is. Sure she is. Lucky guy,' he said, tasting the dying embers of his cigar, throwing it to the ground where it landed just by Graham's feet.

'So what do you do, Mr Von Eil?' he said, kicking the dog end into the gutter, delaying the inevitable reunion with Natasha, adding the 'mister' only as a little joke to himself, taking the piss though he knew Von Eil had a big enough ego that he'd be flattered by the honorific, fine upstanding member of the Bangkok community he no doubt was.

'Sorry, I didn't catch your name first time round, bud,' said the American. 'You know it's rude to ask anyone in Bangkok what they do here, you might not like the answer. But if you really must know, I'm a banker.'

'Oh.'

'Yes, oh. I help finance property deals and when I say property I mean huge chunks of the fricking country. That street over there is owned by the Americans, that one by the Japanese, that huge tower so-called Communist China,' he said, arms flailing around to indicate vast swathes of the city, emanating a self-contented laugh as he did so. 'All part financed by an American bank. It's another form of colonialism but we are better at it than the Brits. This time it's permanent. I was right, wasn't I, you are a Brit?'

'Well, I'm English, yes. God save the Queen and all that.'

'Bingo. Not much gets past this,' he said, tapping his large nose. 'How's business, by the way?'

'Hmm, not so great now but we've only just opened,' said Graham, feeling the man had enquired just to be polite, half of his sentence swallowed up as he trotted along behind Von Eil into the noisy bar like an obedient dog, the American failing to look back, scanning the dark, deserted interior.

'What you need is tits and arse,' Von Eil said suddenly, shouting above the music as he turned around to face him, wicked glint in his eye. 'Tits and arse wall to wall, floor to ceiling. Sex sells. Virgins!'

'I think Mark tried that...'

'Fuck the loser,' he said, eyes blazing. 'Get the youngest, most beautiful girls. Then get some coverage in the papers. I know a night-time hack at the *Bangkok Post*...'

'Ah, Mr Paul,' said Natasha, appearing from backstage, like she'd been expecting him, already totally in his thrall as she gleefully wrapped herself around him.

'Natasha, darlin'.'

'How you like my bar?' she said, holding him at arm's length.

Her flamin' bar was it now, he thought, balling hands into fists behind his back as Paul von Eil the bloody Second twirled his girlfriend around, just as Mark had forewarned but he was nowhere near forearmed.

'As I was saying to your friend, sex sells. Sex up the place, baby,' said Von Eil, arm around the small of Natasha's back, gazing into her eyes.

'I'm her boyfriend remember,' he said, as if to no one, statement drowned out by a flurry of Natasha's giggles as Von Eil whispered into her ear, Graham wishing some horrible accident on the six-foot tall problem with the 'what the fuck you gonna do?' stance cluttering up *his* bar, stomach twisted in pain at the sight of the two of them.

'Daddy, could you make us both a drink,' she said, finally uncoiling herself from the American and putting what felt like a conciliatory hand on Graham's arm. 'Two whisky sodas.'

'Coming right up,' he said, banging and crashing about behind the bar, siphoning off more profit to keep Natasha and her friends in booze, hating Von Eil, hating both of them, hating the fact she knew exactly what he drank.

He snatched up a bottle of the cheapest whisky he could find and poured out the meanest measures, clearing his throat before unleashing a large dollop of gob in the American's glass, dispatching the drinks. The airy laughter that bubbled up from the bundle his so-called girlfriend and Von Eil had become in the corner sent an electric jolt through him, so powerful he was scared of what he could do with it, where it would lead.

***

'Where you been?' she said, accusatory eyes on him.

'I went for a drink with Nige, that's all. Sure you and your mate *Mr Paul* could handle it,' he said, Natasha looking cheap and mean amid the threadbare fittings and furnishings of the Paradise.

'Oh, Gray we just friends. I know Mr Paul for long time. What did you talk with Nigel?'

'This and that, not much really,' said Graham, desperate to probe about the bloody Yank but seeing how cleverly she'd turned it around and made it all about him and his recreational drinks with Nige – what a schemer.

'Long time to talk about nothing.'

'Nat, seriously, it was nothing,' said Graham, amazed he'd been able to keep the anger out of his voice having felt so strongly in the bar, moving towards the bed, to her.

'Okay,' she said, dragging him onto the bed, their lips locking.

'Hmm, this is nice,' he said through tongues.

But as he desperately breathed her in Graham tasted the unpalatable decadence of her lifestyle, the far from womanly whisky and cigarettes. Moving a hand to her once taut stomach, the little excess of fat there now seemed an unwelcome intrusion – one that hadn't been there when they'd first met, before he'd provided her with the means to get drunk every night. Still, he was thankful for the touch of another, like Nigel had said, the contact that everyone craved, needed. Where had he been just months ago with Sheil? Siberia that's where. A bedroom with ice on the inside of the windows.

'Babe?'

'What?' he said, tensing despite the joy of the breath in his ear, her hands all over him, never losing the knack of being sensual when she was about to ask for something, part of her well-practised ability to ensnare.

'You know hotel room, I was thinking…'

'And what were you thinking, Natasha?' he said, shrugging her off as he did so.

'It seems small for the both of us and...'

'Yes, so you've mentioned before but I was meaning to talk to you about that,' he said, preparing to utter words not in her vocabulary. 'It's too expensive.'

'Too expensive?' she said, screwing up her face, bottom lip

as if unfurling.

'We might own a bar but look at the figures, we're not making any money,' he said. 'I'm paying for this bloody hovel out of my savings.'

'But it will be successful,' she said, edging away from him.

'Will be? No, might be… we don't know for sure. I want to move to a cheaper place.'

'Sort your life out. You need that divorce, honey,' she said but beckoning him back towards her.

'I know,' he said, looking at the come-on in her eyes, like there was no way she was giving him up when he was worth something, grinding into her now, the eau de cheap perfume and hairspray coupled with the aroma of even cheaper whisky having some allure, along with her curves, but the Xanax had even managed to blunt his libido, Graham punching the bed as he disengaged, turning away from her in the tiny room.

'What you thinking?' she said, turning him around, waggling her little finger.

'Nothing's the matter,' he said, backing up onto the bed, though she followed on all fours, hot breath all over him.

'You can't even have sex now,' she said, pulling at his lifeless crotch. 'You have sex earlier?'

'Nat, no. Don't be bloody ridiculous,' he said, swiping her hand away. 'Actually something is the matter.'

'What?'

'Mark.'

'He won't matter soon,' she said, tone dropping an octave, sounding like a man.

'That's what matters,' Graham said, disbelieving at how unconcerned she was by it, murder.

'So it's still on?'

'*Chai* [yes].'

'But why? I just don't bloody get it. He's just some saddo. Look at the state of the guy. He needs help,' he said, face flushing, tears springing to his eyes, holding his hands together as if in prayer to stop them shaking.

'You don't know what men do to me. These men. They want own me. Mark was the same, he's bastard,' she said, looking past Graham out far beyond the tiny hotel room, face an ashen grey, eyes glassy, dulled, a tremble in her right hand.

'He what? What did he bloody do?' he said, shaking her, needing to know.

'When we together, I said 'no' one night but he rape me. Beat me up. Broke my arm. I stronger now but not then. I just young. So young. Is that what you want to know? Is it?'

Chapter seven

Bangkok grotesques

'Cor, look at your face. Cheer up, might never 'appen. You could always move back to London,' said Nigel, already settled in at the bar, drink in one hand, fingering a little black book in the other.

'London's fine where it is, thank you very much,' said Graham laughing, channelling hard-bitten expat Thomas Fowler in *The Quiet American*, one his favourite books despite the resident unquiet American in their midst, though Sheila had hated him reading of course. 'What's that in your hand, by the way? And I don't mean the drink.'

'This is literally my little black book. I've invited all my associates to our official opening. I also hear Chubby Bird's coming courtesy of Von Eil.'

'Chubby bloody who?'

'You know, 'the night's all a twitter'.'

'Nige, what the hell are you talking about?'

'"The night's all a twitter with Chubby Bird, the Bangkok bar scene's best friend". Don't you ever read his column in the *Bangkok Post*, dear?'

'Oh, that guy. What a name. And I thought you were the Bangkok bar scene's best friend,' Graham said, laughing again.

'I'm the Bangkok bar scene's lover and I don't know about 'all a twitter', he's just a bit of a twat but his column's well read, so it'll be good to get some coverage.'

'Is he actually chubby?'

'I wouldn't call him chubby, love, I'd call him grotesque. So big he has to be pushed around in a wheelchair by his young Thai boy assistant. Assistant in inverted commas.'

'Dearie me, this place really is something else. I thought he was into the ladeez of the night?' said Graham with a sigh.

'Hmm, he's from Texas, they're a bit funny about ginger beers there. I suspect he's still in the closet. I hear through the grapevine he likes young meat, probably explains why he counts paedo-in-chief Von Eil among his friends. I hope Little Miss Thing is on 'er best behaviour.'

'I meant to say, I haven't spoken to Nat since last night when I told her we need to move to a cheaper place. She was already out by the time I got up late morning.'

'For fuck sake, what did I tell you about frightening the horses? That's okay, I suspect she went to get some TLC from Daeng or someone.'

'Do you mind? She might be a joke to you but I'm bloody stuck with her, *this*,' he said, throwing his arms aloft.

'Sorry, dear, I didn't mean to say anything derogatory. Probably some retail therapy. You know how she likes a new outfit.'

'You're probably right. More outfits than days in the week. Either that or she was with Paul von bloody Eil the Second and it was more than just tea and sympathy…' he said, tailing off as the door swung open, seeing from the expression on Natasha's face that she'd been listening, another sodding headache.

'Hi, Daddy,' she said, leaning over the bar and kissing him but no word of an explanation as she blew Nigel a kiss too.

'What can I do?' he said, punching the counter as her back disappeared behind the curtain backstage, knowing she'd be back out in another moment to grab the obligatory bottle of Thai whisky, leaving him to mull over the death penalty she'd sentenced Mark to, biting the inside of his cheek, tasting blood.

'Have another drink, old man,' said Nigel.

Graham laughed, raising a near-empty glass as if in triumph, realising he was becoming a damn good actor.

'Hello, dear boy,' said the first customer of the evening, addressing Nigel, voice even resonating above the disco trash Natasha insisted upon – seemingly the emptier the establishment the louder the music. 'The sun's well past the yard arm, so make mine a G&T, please.'

'Graham, this is Mike Smale and vice versa,' said Nigel.

'Vice being the operative word. And it's Professor Mike Smale, I'll have you know. Hi there, pleased to meet the owner of this fine establishment,' he said, pushing a hand through what looked like a lovingly tended mane of grey hair. 'So what sexual predilection brings you to the tropics?'

'I... er... ha. You got me there,' said Graham, blushing, trying to concentrate on the red cravat and canary yellow shirt ensemble to distract himself, hide his discomfort, though it looked vaguely ridiculous and the face while ageing was tanned, soft as if indicating a gilded existence.

'It's all right, secret safe with me,' the professor said, accent plummy but with a hint of mischief, patting Graham's hand, still laughing at his own joke, revealing two rows of perfect teeth. 'I used to be into boys but ladyboys, wow, what a concept. I'm a tit man now.'

'You dirty old man,' said Nigel, doing his best Harold Steptoe impression, and they all laughed.

'Ladyboys, right,' said Graham to Smale, but reddening again under the professor's gaze.

'Oh, come, dear boy, don't be so bashful. You're among friends here. This is another country entirely. You can explore to your heart's content. Your sexuality I mean,' he said, laughing warmly, taking Graham gently by the arm. 'Don't be so squeamish.'

'It's not that...'

'You don't need to explain to Aunty Smale. I don't know what your set-up was in England. I'm guessing you were married. Don't worry, happens all the time.'

'You're bloody psychic. No wonder you're a professor. Professor of what exactly?'

'Awfully thirsty here, hint, hint,' he said, chuckling away.

'Oh, yeah that's the first rule of the Bangkok expat, never ask about past lives,' said Graham, busily preparing the G&T as he did so.

'Expat 101. You're learning fast but if you must know I do a bit of teaching at Thammasat, the university. Get to see all the bright young things. But I'm also a sub-editor at the local rag, the *Post*,' he said, receiving the proffered drink.

'That's on the house.'

'You're most kind. Here's my card. Why don't I return the favour and you get yourself over to mine for cocktails. Let's call it your induction,' he said with a wink, handing over the gold embossed card like they were at some professional networking event.

'But we've only just met and my mum warned me about strange men. Though I need all the bloody drinks I can get,' he said, carefully pocketing the card.

'Ah, but beware. There's the Thai saying 'keep a cool heart', too many foreigners lose their hearts and their heads here. This doesn't help,' said Smale, pointing at the booze before giving him a matey pat on the back.

'I'm here with Mr Chubby,' said a boy bounding up to the bar.

'Well, bring 'im in,' said Graham, unable to draw his gaze from the boy's beautiful face, strong angular features as if hewn from mahogany, the lad batting the lids of exceptionally pretty eyes, like an advanced guard smoothing the path for his master.

'Incredible, just incredible,' said Nigel, catching Graham's eye, Smale chortling monstrously along.

'But I actually need some help with Mr Chubby's chair,' said the boy.

'No problem,' said Graham, following the lad outside, sickened by the fact he couldn't help but stare at that curvaceous bum, his inability to turn away making him want to run all over again.

It took three of them to ease Chubby out of the back seat of the squeezed confines of the regulation Japanese-made cab, built for petite Asians not elephantine Americans. They managed finally to decant him into a wheelchair, though Graham wondered whether the old man's disability was really laziness on his part, a desire to be waited on for there seemed a real liveliness behind his eyes, no doubt a reflection of what he'd seen in the city's myriad barrooms, or 'gin mills' as he referred to them in antiquated prose seemingly stuck in the 19th century.

'Evenin' fellas,' he said, years living in Asia not having blunted his accent, face red and sweating from the exertion of *them* lifting him out of the cab, chins quivering as if in anticipation, thinning hair Brylcreemed back at the sides, though a baseball cap hid what was no doubt an expanding bald patch. 'What have you got for this good ol' boy tonight? Anything to get the juices flowing?'

What a sight thought Graham taking him in properly for the first time, momentarily speechless. He watched Chubby wobble as he laughed, his whole body seeming to shake, eyes and mouth tiny slits amid the fat, skinny arms resting absurdly on his huge tummy, copious Buddhist amulets around his neck like a vain attempt to ward off ill health. The 'Don't fuck with me, I fuck back!' T-shirt comical and pathetic all at once.

'Drink?' Graham said finally, watching as Chubby observed the bar, taking it in as if with an expert eye.

'I thought you'd never ask,' he shot back, now perched precariously on a bar stool, legs hanging lifelessly but hand placed firmly around the small of his boy's back for support. 'Great to be here. You must be Graham.'

'The very same,' he said, as Chubby lent a podgy hand to be shook.

Graham busied himself getting drinks, pleased to see three or four other punters had wandered in, ones not connected with Nigel's get-together, hoping for a favourable line or two in the notepad now open on the American's sizeable lap.

'Cheers,' said Chubby as Graham handed him a drink and

went to his pocket.

'No problem. It's on the house,' he replied, holding up an admonishing hand, playing along, wondering if the great American conman had ever paid for a drink in his life. 'One for the boy?'

'Much obliged but ma boy don't drink. I hear you've been paid a visit by the *gendarmerie*?' he said after greedily taking a big swig, comment uttered through the side of his mouth conspiratorially like they were in some speakeasy.

'Goes with the territory,' Graham said, trying to appear cool, knowledgeable but feeling cowed by Chubby's years of experience, the man who he noticed had made such a good job of demolishing a double whisky in near record time, even faster than Nigel. 'Another?'

'Oh, it would be rude not to. But where are the demi-mondaines? Don't I at least get to inspect the goods?' he boomed, assembled throng laughing along with him.

'They are preparing backstage but should be out soon,' Graham said, though he knew their preparation consisted of getting hammered, his stomach burbling discomfitingly, knot searing across his shoulders, feeling the desperate need to make it all work.

'There should be some presence. I was at least expecting a gaggle of gals out front. From the outside you look closed. Come to think of it, you could say the same about inside.'

This prompted more laughter but Graham, having moved away to fix drinks for the other punters, knew Chubby was right. He'd always insisted on a bunch, or whatever the word was for a grouping of ladyboys, out front and a few milling around in the bar but Natasha had taken over with her liquid 'pre-match preparations'.

He felt a firm hand on his shoulder as he poured another large whisky for himself, spinning around to find a suited Von Eil right in his face, accompanied by the bustiest of young ladyboys, possibly criminally young, breasts accentuated by a low-cut top, hot pants riding up her pert behind.

'One for me and, er, my friend. This is Paris.'

'Hi,' he said, stifling a laugh at the ridiculousness of the name, bringing to mind a certain hotel heiress but then he thought of Emmy, that they could've been similar ages, digging nails into the palms of his hand, biting his lip so hard it drew blood, knowing to Von Eil they were just fashion accessories, 'fuck toys', he called 'em.

'Before you ask, I christened her and I also paid for those, the deluxe version,' he said with a smirk, indicating her breasts with a gropey hand before patting her arse.

'Nice one, I thought you might be responsible,' said Graham, Von Eil's clear blue eyes staring into his, eyes that would've looked innocent if they hadn't been so blank, unreal, like something out of a picture that had been photoshopped and as he bent over pouring drinks, he added his own little flourish to what was becoming the American's favourite tipple, distributing the phlegm with a swizzle stick, a pathetic form of revenge.

'Cheers, my man,' said the American, taking a sip, fingering a large cigar he'd just slid out the silken inside of his suit. 'You and I need to discuss business. I have a little proposition for ya. But I'll be back to see you in a day or two. Where's the lovely Nat?'

'Up yours,' he said, clinking glasses, crossing his fingers under the bar. 'But why don't you mind your own business.

That goes for my lady and this bar.'

'You don't get it, do you? You just don't know who you're freaking dealing with. Laters,' said Von Eil, drilling his fingers into the side of Graham's head, mimicking the cocking of a gun, before turning on his expensive heel and going behind the curtain, Paris following in his wake.

'That bloody bloke,' he said, clenching his fists, sweat prickling under his armpits, stomach knotted in pain, heart thumping, wanting to run behind the curtain and pummel Von Eil's big face, wipe that smirk off once and for all, imagining the American undressing Natasha with those blank eyes, hands all over her.

'Come on, son. You got to pick your battles here. Just ignore the arsehole. You know what these Yanks are like. It's always faster, higher, stronger,' said Nigel, rolling his eyes.

'You make it sound like an Olympic event,' he said with a laugh.

'That's it, just keep smiling. Full house tonight, eh?' said his friend, nudging him, as if reading his mind.

'Better,' he said. 'It's getting better.'

'Couldn't be worse,' said Nigel, prompting laughter in both, bond strengthening another notch.

'Golly, I don't know about City of Angels, City of Degenerates would be more accurate looking at us lot,' said Chubby, red in the face, gently swaying as if in time to the music, though grip on his boy worryingly taut.

Amid the group's guffaws Graham looked at the fucked up tableaux of Bangkok life confronting him and thought the journalist had got to the crux – degenerate it was. But he sensed maybe degenerate wasn't a strong enough word for it, maybe degenerate bordering on evil for the fact he'd quit a twenty-year marriage, soulless life though it was, and shacked up with someone planning to murder their neighbour.

'Cambodia that's where it's at, Phnom Penh to be precise,' said Von Eil, returning to the bar, draped over Paris, licking his lips with a thick tongue as though starving hungry.

'I wonder what's so great about it? Bet it's not the sightseeing,' said Graham.

'Nonsense. Nonsense. I absolutely concur, dear boy,' said Smale, slapping the American on the back. 'Like Thailand twenty years ago.'

'Oi, Ronnie,' Nigel shouted above the increasingly loud disco thump to a tall, imposing figure who'd just entered the bar. 'I thought you'd never make it, love.'

'*Bonjour, bonjour*. Of course I was going to come,' he said, head almost scraping the corrugated iron roof, neatly clipped salt 'n' pepper goatee and pointy ponytail indicating rigorous grooming but out of place with his backpacker get-up of singlet, shorts and flip-flops, like it was all an elaborate disguise.

'This is Ronnie,' said Nigel. 'Ronnie, Graham.'

'*Bonjour*,' said Graham, taking the oversized hand proffered and while the handshake was firm, the cold, everywhere eyes spoke of a deviousness even out of place in Bangkok. 'What do you do then?'

'Zis guy's got a sense of 'umour. Do? What should I *do*?' he said with a shrug, which along with the French accent would've been comedic if it hadn't been for the eyes. 'I'm an art dealer. Ow you say… a sophisticate. But I do some work on the side for Mr Paul.'

'Oh,' said Graham, as he felt collective breath exhaled around him, Ronnie's face relaxing, like the deception was complete, though the man's manic laughter was mocking him, the man who'd now finally fixed those eyes somewhere else, Natasha, but even she was keeping a wary distance. 'Drink?'

'Diet Coke, please.'

'Coming right up,' said Graham, though the lame request coming from the toughest looking of men confounded him, it certainly took some balls.

'He's a mercenary, a gun-runner or something, maybe a terrorist. And God knows what he does for Mr Paul. *Petis pois* in a pod those two,' said Nigel into his ear.

Ronnie grabbed his drink and went into full on continental mode, a kiss on either cheek for Von Eil like they were mafioso, giving Paris the once over before she sloped off and the two men engaged in a cosy huddle, an impenetrable conversation.

'Also heard he's got an odd thing for mutilating stray dogs and cats his one piece of trade told me. But the boy was eventually warned off and he's never been seen with anyone since,' said Nigel, nodding over to the pair of them stood by the bar in isolation. 'Lives in a big old house somewhere all alone.'

'What are they up to?' he said, lighting a cigarette with shaky hands.

'I don't know and I don't wanna know. And if you value your balls, you keep this out,' said Nigel, tapping his nose.

'And what's with the Ronnie? I never met a Frenchman called Ronnie before,' said Graham.

'You ask too many questions. I'll let him tell you the story if you dare ask. I'm not going anywhere near it, love.'

'Nige, come on. I need a laugh.'

But Nigel simply but a finger to his lips, then mimicked a

throat-cutting gesture, though something about his expression indicated he wasn't joking.

'Ladeez and Gentelmen, welcome to *Amazing* Thailand and so to the greatest show on Earth…' blasted Nigel's disembodied voice from the speakers, Graham looking out hollow-eyed into the darkness silently popping a Xanax into his palm, swigging the pill back with the remainder of another drink, not wanting to feel.

***

The crowd had thinned out to nothing, which was usual after the show – just Graham, Nigel and their rotting livers left, the guests of honour having gone on to taste the delights of an all-night club in Sukumhvit, appropriately called Apocalypse Now. Natasha had half-heartedly asked Graham to come but he preferred the devil he knew rather than hanging out with the likes of Von Eil and Ronnie, though he was looking forward to meeting Smale again. He could do with a bloody induction into the mores of the so-called tropics and the man had a warmth about him, what seemed like a rare commodity in this town. He closed his eyes trying to still his racing mind, though all he could see were Von Eil's slimy hands pawing Natasha, muscles in his body tensing, pulsating ache in his back a constant reminder of the state he was in.

'Evening, gentlemen,' said Police-General Peeklong, sauntering into the bar, followed by his two goons standing around looking awkward as ever.

'Drink?' asked Graham, as was now customary, reaching for the most expensive malt, thinking in practice the policeman had never really given up ownership of the place, it was just structured a different way, him appropriating a third of the takings every night, with someone else to do the donkey work.

'How's business?'

'A bit better,' said Graham, gently placing down Peeklong's drink but thinking life would be so much better without His Majesty's Constabulary – another expression coined by Chubby Bird – taking a cut.

'Receipts, please,' he said, rolling the whisky around on his tongue.

As Graham laid the bar bills on the counter one by one, like it would make their number seem more, he was almost prompted into laughter by the succession of funny faces Nigel was pulling behind the policeman's back.

'And how are you, Mr Nigel?' said Peeklong, swivelling round on his stool to face Monroe, while colleagues Tweedle Dum and Tweedle Dumber – another Birdism – had lost interest and were sitting in a corner smoking, their radios squawking uselessly. 'Maybe we need to look at the situation re your work permit.'

'Everything's fine,' Nigel said, raising a glass.

'Hmm, it is getting better, isn't it,' said Peeklong, taking his glasses off, peering at the number Graham had written down in terms of total takings for the night.

'Yes, through hard work.'

'And I am hoping it will get even better soon. Beat the competition. Grind them to dust,' he said, banging a gloved fist on the bar. 'That Mark, your neighbour, useless foreigner. He never pays me. Not one baht. Nothing!'

'Another?'

Peeklong produced an outstretched hand for the night's

takings. Money, it was all about the bloody money, Graham seethed as he did what he was told, heart palpitations almost in time to the music, the pills having done nothing to calm him, thinking of Mark getting quietly drunk next door, the Liverpudlian trying to forget, though he'd have nothing to forget soon. He might be a bastard but he didn't deserve what was coming to 'im, no way.

Chapter eight

Murderously hot

'Hi, mate,' said Mark, looking up from behind his desk. 'Hot out?'

'Yeah, you know the usual. Hot in too,' said Graham, dabbing at his brow with a handkerchief, air-conditioning desperately unable to cope in the confined space with the clouds of cigarette smoke the Scouser was neurotically puffing, plonking down the bottle of Scotch he'd brought as a so-called peace offering, his excuse for convening the meet.

His host rattled around getting glasses, then ice and mixers from a small fridge in the corner but Graham could barely look at his neighbour, let alone wanting to go through the charade of having a drink with him, his last supper, gripping onto his chair to curb his shaking, to stop himself bolting right for the door, the Xanax he'd popped before arrival doing nothing to ease the tension jolting through his body.

'How's business? You're dead on time, by the way,' said Mark, sitting back down, pouring the drinks, though the trembly hands meant he missed most of the time, sending booze oozing over his chaotic desk.

'It's fine,' he said, ignoring the 'dead' remark, though he wasn't really listening, certainly not thinking about what he was saying, too distracted, already glancing up at the clock that seemed to be ticking in a horrible kind of slow motion.

'Got somewhere else to be?'

'Not at all,' he said, batting a bead of sweat away, gulping at his drink.

'What's all this about then? You said you had a proposition?'

'Yep, that's right,' said Graham, raising a shaky toast. 'A proposition is what I have, old son. A great proposition. One for the ages.'

'For fuck sake. This is like blood from a stone.'

'The erm… the ah… the proposition is this…' he said, the sweet, sickly unmistakable smell of petrol hitting his nostrils completely destroying his train of thought, words sticking in his crusty throat, praying Mark hadn't noticed the stench through the fug of cigarette smoke, patting his pocket furiously, the key still there.

'You all right, you divvy?'

'I'm not all right. Not at all. I spoke to Nat last night. She told me all about it,' he said, folding his arms, settling back into his chair, needing to hear Mark's defence but having to hold himself back, the urge to lash out pulsing through his body, though how could an admission of guilt justify what was coming next? Who was he bloody kidding?

'All about what? You outta your mind. You come in here spouting all kinds of bullshit. Graham, what's going on?'

'I tell you what's going on, shall I. She says she turned you down one night, that you bloody raped her, that you beat her up, broke her arm. This was years ago. She was almost a kid.

What the hell 'ave you go to say to that, tosser?' he said, leaping up, grabbing Mark by the collar, dragging his neighbour up to face him, colour draining from the Scouser's features, tic under his right eye throbbing manically.

'She was a spoilt bitch. Like a wild fucking animal,' he said, slamming the desk with his hand.

'Did you do it?' he said, having tightened his hold on Mark's collar, the pair nose to greasy nose. 'Did you bloody do it?'

'She's worse than any man. She's a whore,' he said, wriggling away from Graham's grip, sickly smile on his face, slumping back into his chair.

'You did it, didn't you!' he shouted, anger exploding off the four walls, launching himself across the desk, grabbing Mark's skinny, pathetic arm with one hand as he landed a punch with a sickening crack into his right eye, warm blood spattering into his face as the Liverpudlian lurched backwards, toppling to the floor.

'What the fuck?' said Mark, looking up pathetically, a twitching, groaning bundle.

'That's for Nat,' he said behind him, pulling the door shut with a metallic twang, sloshing around in the very petrol he'd smelled, it puddling horribly over his shoes, making his eyes sting, panicked throat constrict.

He grabbed the key, stabbing at the door in the semi-darkness, finally locating the lock, plunging it in where he turned it not once but twice as instructed. It clicked as the deadlock engaged. That word again, *dead*.

'You fucking bastard, let me out! Let me out of here!' Mark screamed, an animal-like howl.

Graham was walking away but the banging on the door drew

him back, right outside again now, fumbling for the key in his pocket, ready to show mercy, he wasn't a killer, didn't want to have that on his conscience, it just wasn't him, no matter what Mark was supposed to have done to Nat. He'd never hurt anyone, never even stood up for himself before Bangkok, a place where he was fighting for his very survival.

'I take over now,' said Daeng appearing out of the shadows, holding out a hand. 'Give me key.'

'Or what?'

'Let me fucking out of here now!' shouted Mark, voice sounding more and more unhinged as though he knew what was going to happen, insane banging on the door.

'Just give me that key,' said the Thai boy at almost a whisper, flash of silver, cold, sharp metal of a knife at Graham's throat. 'Either that or you both die.'

'Scum, you're all scum,' he said, throwing the key to the floor, Daeng lowering the blade as Graham slowly backed away to the bar's exit, the shouts replaced by an awful sobbing sound from the other side of the door, presumably the awful noise someone makes when they know they're close to the end, that there's no escape.

'Mr Mark, Mr Mark, don't worry. We're bringing someone to see you,' said Daeng with a twisted smile as he edged to the exit, lighting an oily rag as he reached the outside, throwing it back into the building where it went up with an explosive blue flash.

Graham ran for the other side of the road, Daeng just behind, and waiting on the pavement opposite Natasha and Nigel. He felt the sheer heat of the blaze searing his skin, belching smoke at the back of his throat, bent double with coughing, like he was going to vomit it all out, the horror of the night as the fire made a mockery of the makeshift wood and corrugated structure of Christie's it so quickly laid to waste. He hugged himself to stop his body jerking crazily around but as he looked frantically from one conspirator to the other all he saw were flames reflected in impassive eyes, flames that shot high into the Bangkok night sky. And despite the roar of the inferno he could imagine the screams coming from inside.

***

Graham was at his usual night-time station – behind the bar – though business had been majorly disrupted by the rather amateurish attempts of the local fire brigade to put out the blaze the night before, which in the end had also taken with it two empty shophouses either side. Empty apparently because their occupants had been warned beforehand, accidents in Thailand seemingly predictable.

'Good evening, Mr Graham,' said Police-General Peeklong, whistling a cheery tune as he approached the counter, his glasses noticeably absent as were his two goons, the officer taking a snatched glance around the empty bar. 'Just you?'

'I'm afraid so,' he said, wishing Peeklong would put his glasses back on, save him from those busy, searching, what looked like black eyes that fixed him with a forensically piercing stare.

'Where is everyone?'

'The towering inferno on the other side of the street isn't exactly good for business,' he said but guessing the policeman wouldn't get the ironic reference to a cheesy 1970s disaster movie. 'I sent me staff home.'

'So no money tonight?'

'Doesn't grow on trees,' Graham said with an exaggerated shrug.

'*Mai phut* [shut up],' said Peeklong. 'Come with me.'

Graham did as he was told, following his unwelcome guest out of the bar and onto the street where the only thing still standing opposite was the signage declaring Christie's Cabaret spelled out in blackened and busted light bulbs. Ground level featured charred, and in places, still burning debris, with everything an appropriate funereal black.

'Come on, let's take a closer look,' said Peeklong.

The officer lifted the flimsy yellow tape proclaiming 'police line', as if this was a professional investigation, and Graham scooted under, coughing as the acrid taste filled his lungs, eyes stinging. He shook, unable to get Mark's image out of his mind, feeling like they were desecrating his final resting place as they clumsily crunched over the ashes, Peeklong occasionally prodding at something with his baton like a naturalist searching undergrowth. They stopped in front of what appeared the bar – where Mark had spent most of his time – only recognisable for the fact a number of blackened bottles hung limply off what was left of a wall, labels so burnt as to be indecipherable. Graham kicked at something bright and sparkly on the floor, bending down only to see it was one of the ornate headdresses worn in the cabaret that had somehow survived, a throwback to more frivolous times, part of a costume probably conceived in a period when the Liverpudlian had hope. They walked a few more metres and stopped by the office door virtually unscathed by fire yet lying horizontal, the structure around it having burned to nothingness.

'Bloody hell,' said Graham, bending over as his stomach burned in pain, panic coursing through him like the rush of puke as he fell to his knees, spewing a second wave with his hands crumpled in the ashes, just blackened dust left.

'Get up. Get up now.'

'Oh, God,' he said, finally able to stand as the nausea eased slightly, wiping the crust from his mouth with a handkerchief, though unable to get the taste from his mouth, the soot from his hands, rid the guilt from his mind.

'One body was recovered at the scene. Is there somewhere we can talk in private?'

'Let's go back to my bar,' he said, hastening his step, Peeklong locking the door behind them both with a click as they re-entered Natasha's.

'Drink, please.'

'My absolute pleasure. Coming right up,' he said, locating the most cheap shit local whisky.

'Long night,' said the Thai, acknowledging the drink with a curt nod, wiping sweat from his brow. 'So I believe you were the last one to see Mark alive?'

'Er, yes but I thought…'

Peeklong held up a warning hand, his notebook open ominously on the counter.

'This is all procedure, Mr Graham, as there has been, how you say, a suspicious death,' the policeman said, licking his lips, settling down on his stool.

'I had a meeting with him at four,' he said, beads of sweat popping out on his forehead, shooting pains in his stomach making him wince, wanting to double up again.

'I see,' said Peeklong, scribbling away. 'So you came back

to the bar...'

'Look, you and I both know what happened.'

'Okay,' he said, slamming his notebook, draining his drink. 'It's on record you were the last person to see Mark alive. But we'll leave it there for now.'

'What?'

'It's not as simple as that. He's a *farang*. When a *farang* die it's headache. Questions are asked. The British Embassy gets involved. I can put them off for now.'

'For now?' said Graham, putting his head in his hands, tears streaking down his cheeks, listening to Peeklong's receding boot steps, the policeman who'd left his words resonating like some terrifying threat, words that echoed through his pounding head, prompting him to reach for the box of Xanax, the bottle of whisky.

Chapter nine

A proposition from the depraved

He was chopping up limes behind the bar, shaky hands just about fit for purpose, though if he wanted something done, Graham knew he had to do it himself. Swigging at a glass of whisky in between slicing, he looked out at the empty seats, the forlorn stage, shoulders twisted in that familiar pain, though for him it was the best time of day, the quiet time before the headache of Nat and her entourage arrived. 'You can't hide those lying eyes,' he sang along to the Eagles' Greatest Hits, trying to outrun the companion constantly with him – anxiety. 'Your smiiiile is a thin disguise…'

'Am I interrupting something, fella? Wow, great singing though. Didn't realise you limeys could do the great American songbook justice. Maybe you can do a turn on stage. Let me see, maybe this'll suit you,' said Von Eil, having strode up behind him, making him jump, twirling around one of the pink headdresses the girls wore, it looking suspiciously like Natasha's.

'What do you want?' he said, wielding the knife, about to plunge it into another lime.

'Man, what kind of way is that to treat your best bud?' he said, depositing a bag on the bar, patting it lovingly.

'I'm not in the mood. You know what happened two nights ago,' said Graham, the American giving him a more than matey pat on the shoulder that shook his shrinking frame, the two almost nose to nose across the bar.

'Yeah, awful business. I meant to pass on my condolences. Poor old Mark, eh. Bet you're gutted. Gutted, haha get it?'

'Von Eil, this might all be a bloody joke to you but some people actually care. Care that a man, a good man, lost his life…'

'No, you fucking listen,' he said, grabbing Graham by his cheap collar, twisting him even closer toward him. 'You need to get off that high horse of yours. I hear you know more than you're letting on.'

'And who you hear that from, I wonder? Keep your nose out of my business,' he said, swiping the Yank's hands away, banging a fist on the bar.

'Business? Funny that, cos that's what I've come to talk to you about. Sorry we got off on the wrong foot,' said Von Eil, backing away, easing down onto a stool, lighting one of his cigars.

'Looks like you're staying. Drink?' said Graham, knocking back the rest of his, needing another.

'Champagne. Perfectly chilled, like me,' he said, pulling an expensive looking bottle from the bag he'd left on the bar. 'I guessed it wouldn't be available in this dump. You should know that's all I freakin' drink. Like Ronnie, I'm a sophisti-cat. Though he only drinks Diet Coke, the pussy.'

'Sophisticate. It's sophisticate. Yeah, that's one word for it.

Champagne. What are we celebrating?'

'Celebrating the future, Graham. I'm taking you out tonight.'

'I've got a bar to run, police-generals to pay,' he said, dusting off a pair of grimy champagne flutes, pouring out two liberal doses. 'I certainly don't have time to go out with you. Like we're mates all of a sudden.'

'You English are so damn reserved,' said Von Eil, clinking glasses, taking a long draw on his cigar before exhaling in a stream towards Graham. 'I've discussed tonight with Nigel and Natasha, you're all mine. You need a bit of fun.'

'Fun? What's fun? My neighbour's just died in a fire and I'm meant to be going out drinking with you. My girlfriend's moaning about living in a shit hole of a hotel and I'm painting the town red. I got his majesty's cunt-stabulary up my arse too,' he said, balling his hands into fists, face reddening, feeling shooting pains in his stomach.

'Ah, that's where I can help,' said Von Eil, patting Graham on the arm. 'I've got a business proposition for ya. I can make all your problems vanish.'

'My fairy friggin' godmother. Oh, yeah and what's in this for you?'

'I'm an investor, that's what I do, man. It's like the stock market. If I see this little sucker going up, I'll lump my dough on it. And that's what I'm seeing here, Natasha's. It's on the up and I want in. Just think you can get out of Paradise. You can move to the right part of town. Nat will be happy. It's win-win,' he said, wiping a finger along the bar, tracing a line in the dust, kicking at a stray dog that had wandered in, making it howl in pain.

'Sounds like this has already been bloody agreed. You might

be able to buy her, you know, but you can't buy me. You can do what you want with your money but I'm not giving up my half of this place,' he said, slamming down the now empty glass, refilling it.

'Let me take you out and we can discuss this properly, like businessmen. Jeez, the way you go on, you'd think I eat people for breakfast. I'm just trying to help.'

'I just don't see you as some kind of Bill Gates figure, helping the poor to help themselves. But we need all the help we can get. I don't want to end up like Mark.'

'Amen to that. Good man. Get your glad rags on. Bangkok here we come,' said Von Eil with a smirk.

'Just don't think we're friends,' said Graham, the American putting an arm round his shoulders, unleashing a horrible laugh.

***

'Where we going?' he said, sinking back into the convertible's soft black leather upholstery, wind in his thinning hair as they drove through the soupy night.

'Let's just say it's a little treat from Uncle Paul. What's known as a sweetener in the trade. This city's rammed full of candy and we're about to gorge ourselves silly,' he said, shaking with laughter.

'I'm not that kind of guy. You may be but I'm not. I don't sleep around.'

'Graham, Graham… stop being so English. Don't you think I've seen the way you look at some of those girls, boys. We all do it. There's so many distractions in this place. But it's just *sanuk*, you know? That's the Thai word for fun. I think they

112

invented it.'

'Yeah, they've always got an excuse for everything here. That's why the country's in such a bloomin' state,' he said, gripping onto the sides of his seat, feeling the urge to run, heart beating with the thump of the trance coming from the car's expensive speaker system.

'Then why are you here? You can't have it both ways, man. Listen, we… I mean we as in me and you, came here following our dicks. As I told you before, get off your fucking high horse, sheriff,' said Von Eil, nudging him.

'I'll try,' he said, as they passed the chichi high-rise shopping malls and hotels of Sukumhvit Road, where Graham knew wealthy Bangkokians came out to play with their friends from the gutter, gleaming edifices so at odds with the greasy squalor of street level where scrawny *soi* dogs and rats the size of domestic cats roamed.

'This is us,' said the American, as he pulled up outside one such building, Red Lantern picked out artfully in neon, a striped canopy stretched out above what looked like the entrance to a vast lobby sprinkled with potted palms.

'Mr Paul, Mr Paul, so good to see you,' said a besuited little Thai opening the driver's side door, looking no older than sixteen.

'Take her to the underground car park. We'll be a few hours. Don't fucking scratch it,' he said, drawing a hand across his throat before shoving the boy a fistful of notes.

'A few hours?' said Graham.

'I told Natasha not to wait up for you. Not that she does early. We have business to discuss. Business, my man.'

'What the hell is this place? Somewhere for sophisti-cats?' he said, looking up at storey after storey rising before him, expensively rendered chrome and glass as far as he could see almost blotting out the night sky, red interior glowing like a warning.

'You'll find out. Oh, you'll find out all right,' said Von Eil, putting an arm behind Graham's back, propelling him to the entrance.

Serene, perfumed, the lobby stretched out before him like a vast marble sea. It was so air-conditioned cold it caused goose pimples to rise up Graham's arm, though he knew it wasn't just the chill as he felt in his pocket for the strip of Xanax that was now always there.

'Toilet… I need the toilet,' he said as Von Eil steered him across the marble towards a reception desk manned – for want of a better word – by uniformed flunkies, his cheap trainers squeaking as they went.

'This is like taking a kid out. The john's down there on the left. Don't get lost.'

He squeaked to the toilets feeling childlike in his shorts and polo shirt, like he was being mocked by the richness of the surroundings, the lobby a huge atrium, lit appropriately enough by enormous red lanterns. The toilet door swished open like something out of *Star Trek*. He shook standing at the gold-plated urinals, taking all his effort to piss, the noise in his head unending, the questions cascading one on top of the other. What the hell was he doing here with someone in another life he would've punched in the head for coming on to his missus? Not that Graham ever fought back before, the 'human doormat' Sheil called him.

'Sir, you like hot towel,' said a man as if appearing from nowhere, breathing into his ear.

'Oh, uh, no, no thanks,' he replied, hurriedly zipping up.

'Neck massage, Sir.'

'I told you once, no bloody thank you,' he said, heading towards the sinks, the massive pool-like sinks, but in a pincer movement the man managed to block him off.

'Cologne, Sir?' he said, indicating with raised eyebrow the vast array of aftershave bottles lined up neatly.

'Leave me alone,' he said, noticing the big bamboo basket filled with condoms as he quickly washed his hands, took another pill from his pocket, knocked it back with a swig of water from the tap, glancing sadly at his beetroot red face in the mirror.

'Hey,' said Von Eil grabbing him by the arm as soon as he'd exited the loo. 'Don't even think of bailing on me. We're here for fun. Remember. And what's the red face all about?'

'Stress, Paul. It's called stress.'

'What's to be freakin' stressed about. There's even a guy in there to massage your neck or more, if you want it.'

'That's exactly what I mean, you can't even have a piss in peace in this town without someone offering their services, wanting paying.'

'Take it easy. It's the Big Mango, take a bite. C'mon there's people I want you to meet,' he said, nodding back over to the reception desk.

'Mr Paul, so good to see you,' said a kimono-clad young ladyboy behind the desk, lashes almost as long as her nails, eager to please smile on her face like she was checking them in to fly on some boutique Asian airline.

'Not as good as it is to see you,' he said, clumsily grabbing her across the gargantuan desk, hands going straight for her

115

ample, obviously paid for arse.

'I see you got a friend?' she said, indicating Graham with the most discreet of nods.

'Oh, yes, I'm so rude. Graham meet Chelsea.'

'Lovely to meet you, Chelsea.'

'A pleasure,' she said but looking at the immaculately turned out Von Eil the entire time. 'How many would you like today?'

'Let's see, can we start off with two. One each. See how he handles it.'

'Age?'

'You know what I like,' he said, throwing a gold card down onto the desk, which Chelsea took in her fingers talon-like, studiously inputting the details into the computer in front of her.

'What's going on?' said Graham.

'First rule of business, if it fucks, flies or floats, you're better off renting,' said Von Eil chuckling, again pulling Graham by the arm as they headed for the lifts.

'Natasha knows I'm here?' he said, staring back into his glum face in the infinite mirrored walls of the lift.

'She used to work here, dumbass,' said Von Eil, laughter uncomfortably filling the confined space as they shot up fifty floors.

'Anything else I need to know?' he said, punching the lift wall, blood coating his knuckles.

'Gray, we're here now. Sort your life out. Remember, *sanuk*, fun. Smile for fuck sake and clean that hand up,' he said, throwing a silk handkerchief at him.

The lift doors opened and in rushed booming sound, strobe lighting making it hard to see what was in front of him in the semi-darkness as he stumbled out, weird chemical smell in the air only adding to the disorientation.

'Where are we?' he said above the thumping beat, eyes adjusting to the gloom, writhing human shapes picked out in silhouette by the flashing lights, what looked like bodies on top of bodies but all moving to the frenetic beat.

'Isn't this awesome? And can you smell that? It's amyl nitrate, poppers, it loosens 'em up,' said the American, moving manically in time to the music, jostling his way through the crowd, dragging Graham with him.

'Why are we here?' he said into Von Eil's ear but he was waved away, the Yank rearranging Graham's rigid features into a smile as he looked frantically at the faces in the crowd for an answer but the blankness, the dead eyes told him nothing or maybe more than he wanted to know.

'*Sanuk*, remember. Smile.'

'*Sanuk*, my arse,' Graham replied under his breath as he continued scanning the semi-naked throng as he was dragged along, looking at the mostly old white men gyrating with their young Thai partners, hunters and hunted.

'Ah, Mr Paul, back again? We've been expecting you,' said another kimono-clad hostess as they reached a bar area partitioned off from the main dancefloor.

It was brighter lit with extravagant chandeliers hanging down in the cavernous space, low slung leather sofas arranged pleasingly around table after table groaning with drinks and edged elegantly with soft pink mood lighting. Graham noticed the sofas peopled with similar clientele to those on the dancefloor, though several of the Thais were reclined so far back they looked like they were asleep but for the fact they were being

117

devoured by their dates.

'What is this place?'

'This, my man, is the Red Lantern. It can make all your dreams come true,' said Von Eil with a wink, the sound from the piano drifting over from the player in the corner seeming to lend the place more sophistication than it deserved as the American let the hostess take him by the hand.

'Four of you tonight, isn't there?' she said, putting a long-nailed hand to her enhanced pneumatic chest, guiding them to an empty table.

'For now. Two bottles of Cristal, please. Let's get this party started,' said the American, sinking back onto the sofa, patting the space next to him for Graham to join as he lit a cigar.

'Who are we meeting?' he said, looking at the empty sofa opposite.

'Relax, man. You'll see. Enjoy this expensive champagne Uncle Paul's ordered in the meantime. Costs more than a night of takings at Natasha's, eh.'

'If I didn't have to pay a police tax, then we'd be fine.'

'T.I.T – this is Thailand. They do things differently but what a place,' he said with a sweeping gesture, indicating the room they were in, the artfully done bar with the backlit bottles of expensive booze, as the hostess returned with four ice-cold glasses, the champagne.

She bent down and said something into Von Eil's ear in a way that showed she'd practised concealment as however hard he strained he couldn't make out a word, again the shooting pains in his stomach, twisting his guts, that knot across his back seizing up his shoulders. What he'd tried so hard to run from, ever since Emmy, the fact he'd felt stuck forever with Sheil,

118

catching up with him again. Graham snatched for the glass of champagne as the hostess backed away from the table with an inscrutable smile, leaving two unfilled flutes on the table like questions marks.

'Cheers,' said the American.

'Up yours,' he replied, clinking glasses but looking around, surveying the room again, locals of variable, if not questionable ages, in various states of undress and he swigged down his fizz like it was water, hostess immediately on hand to refill.

'As I was saying, this place is freakin' amazing. And this is just for starters,' said Von Eil.

'Yeah.'

'That's all you can say, yeah? Ungrateful son of a bitch,' said the American, directing another stream of cigar smoke directly at him. 'You Brits crack me up.'

'Look around you,' he said, jabbing a finger in the air. 'You think this is healthy? You think this is right?'

'Man, there's the door. You wanna walk, go for it. No one's keeping you here, like no one's keeping you in Fun City, the Big Mango, whatever you wanna call this amazing place. I'm prepared to invest my money, my hard won moolah in Natasha's. We'll leave your stake where it is and I'll join forces with Nat and Daeng. You want to get to this level or you want to carry on living in a slum, flogging that piss-stinking hole in the wall?'

'Do I have a bloody choice?'

'I take it that's a 'yes'. Cheers to that,' said Von Eil, Graham raising an unsteady glass in assent.

'Here are your guests, gentlemen. Enjoy,' said the hostess, dispatching two Thais who hovered uncertainly.

119

'Take a seat, ladies,' said Von Eil, patting his knee, indicating the youngest looking of the two sit on his lap. 'Fucking ask her to sit down, you loser.'

'Here, love, sit here,' he said, feeling the bile in his throat as he guessed neither was over sixteen, budging up so there was a polite gap between him and the girl, not wanting to touch, instead feeling the urge to run and never look back, his head swirling with the booze, heart quickening as the piano from before was replaced with the rapacious beats of the trance of earlier.

'What your name?' said the girl, shaky smile, unable to look him in the eye.

'Gray,' he said but he wasn't looking at her or the flesh-baring outfit that was an abomination on her scrawny child's body, eyes instead boring two holes in Von Eil's head.

'Hey, it's not for everyone. Just relax into it,' he replied, turning back to his girl, hands already inside her halter top.

'Bloody hell,' he said as he and his companion sat in silence, pouring the girl a glass of champagne as well as refilling his own for he didn't know what else to do, staring out at his surroundings, a man with a lizard-like tongue on an adjoining table slobbering all over a slight boy and all Graham could do was look down, stare at the floor.

'Thank you,' she said, tapping his arm.

'What's your name, love?' he said, taking her in properly for the first time but it was the eyes, those dark rimmed, sad eyes that felt like a punch to the stomach, like he was winded.

'Em,' she said quietly, barely audible above the thumping music, looking away.

'Em? Like Emma. I can't believe this is bloody happening.'

I used to have a daughter… my Emmy,' he said, arms over his head, sinking back into the sofa.

'You look like you need some of this,' said Von Eil digging him in the ribs, emptying white powder onto the mirrored table, methodically cutting two lines, rolling up a 500-baht note, hoovering one up, wonky smile once he'd done.

'Why not,' he said with a shrug, manically sniffing up the granules, the coke bitter as it hit the back of his throat, feeling the girl's hand on his knee that he pushed gently away, her eyes searching his face, glass of champagne in front of her barely touched, while Von Eil was sickeningly wrapped back around his piece of rent.

'You don't like her?' said the American in a cruel stage whisper, having finally disengaged. 'Man, you can have anything you want. You want a boy? Another girl? Something inbe-fucking-tween? What's your fantasy?'

'They're too bloody young. This is sick. Bloody sick,' he said, kneading his nails into his palms, drawing blood, unable to bring his gaze from the floor, gaze clouded by tears, feeling his heart quicken with the coke, sweat breaking out all over his forehead, moisture dripping down his back.

'The door's there, my man. You can cry about this in your fucking slum. We're gonna take this upstairs,' he said, raising a hand to signal the hostess, leaving a lingering kiss on his girl's cheek.

'What's wrong with 'er?' said Graham, looking at the Yank's companion who'd gone limp in his hands like a rag doll.

'Too much champagne. Goes straight to here,' he said, comically waggling his head around.

'Yes, Mr Paul? Everything okay?' said the hostess bustling

attentively over.

'Everything's wonderful, just wonderful,' he said, patting the girl at his side but her head was thrown back, eyes open though unseeing. 'We're taking this party upstairs. The usual room, please. Two more bottles of champagne.'

'With pleasure,' she said, scrupulously wiping down the table, removing the two empties, smile affixed to her face.

'Let's go,' said Von Eil, roughly lifting the comatose girl in his arms. 'Strong stuff that champagne.'

'What am I seeing here?' he said, following the Yank, grabbing his shoulder, the second girl straggling behind them.

'Listen, prick, they're all here of their own accord. They might be here to sightsee but there are alligators, lions and lizards out to get them. Sexy, beautiful girls and boys, they're just prey.'

'They're just bloody kids,' he said as the four of them bundled into the lift, the bright light illuminating to Graham just what he was a part of, the girl in Von Eil's arms a pallid grey, clothes hanging off her where they'd been torn at and his companion too shy to wrench her gaze away from tattered shoes, skinny arms trembling.

'And you're whiter than white, are you? You basically went out and bought Natasha and you know why? You're the same as all the rest of us. Yeah, they might be a bit younger but they're here cos they wanna be. They all want to bag a rich man.'

'Because they want to be? She's not even conscious. Look at the state of her!' he shouted as the lift came to a halt, indicating the drawl leaking out of her mouth.

'Man, we met before. I'll take care of her,' said Von Eil, leading the way, heading down a thickly carpeted corridor, same ambience as the bar, all mirrors and mood lighting.

'I bet,' said Graham, the second girl pawing at his arm, though again he gently batted her away.

'We're home,' said Von Eil, hurriedly unlocking a door.

Graham's attention was drawn to a table in the middle of a large sitting room laden with the same expensive champagne, costing more than the average Thai could earn in a bloody year no doubt, four iced flutes as if put there by fairies.

'Home? This is just a knocking shop, however you dress it up. It might look like a five-star hotel but it's just a bloody brothel,' he said, taking in the expensive furnishing and fittings, the same music from downstairs being piped through Bose speakers.

'You got that right. Take your pick of bedrooms,' he said, that sickening laugh again, nodding left and right, the girl still frozen in his arms. 'Though mine's the lucky one on the right. Got business to attend to.'

Graham took the girl's hand, sat her down on the edge of the large bed not only designed for sleeping, the mirrored ceiling tellingly above, basket of condoms on the bedside table.

'How old are you?'

'Fifteen,' she said, making eye contact for the first time, hugging herself to stop the shaking.

'Fifteen. Jesus. Look, I'm not going to touch you,' he said, emptying the contents of his wallet on the bed as she immediately started to scoop up the notes, like it seemed she'd done countless, awful times before.

'What about your parents?'

'Parents?' she said shrugging.

'Family. What about your family?'

'Sold me,' she said, eyes fixed to those threadbare shoes again.

'Where you stay?' he said, punching at the mattress.

'Dormi-tory. He drive us here.'

'He?'

'Yes, white man, *farang*,' she said, hands tugging at her hair now, really wrenching like she was going to pull it out.

'Name? What's his name?'

'Won.'

'Won… Ronnie? That bloody scumbag. Is he tall?' he said, putting a hand a foot or so over his own head.

'Yes, yes. He has hair, like you know?' she said, pointing to the back of her head.

'Okay, Okay. You just go. Go now. Please take care of yourself,' he said, that eye contact again, almost hope there, Graham feeling like he'd just become that sliver of hope but flinging the bedroom door open, watching as she slunk sadly away to God knows what.

'What the hell just happened tonight?' he said barging into Von Eil's room, the girl stricken on the bed, the American menacingly above her in just underwear, his shirt flapping open.

'You don't fucking get it, do you?' he said, wheeling around, jumping off the bed, hand around Graham's throat, jamming his head against the wall. 'Don't come across all Mother Theresa. We're all in the same boat here. We're going to hell.'

'You bastard. Look at her, just look at her. She looks like she's bloody dying. What have you done?' he said, wrestling free from the American's grasp, pointing at the prone figure on the bed, her glassy eyes rolling back, little dress pulled up around her thighs.

'It's just GHB, get over it.'

'GHB?' he said, still looking at the skeletal girl, completely statuesque, then back at the bulk of the gurning Von Eil.

'Yeah, GHB, retard. It's odourless, colourless, an amazing freaking concoction. You better watch out, it can be slipped in anyone's drink but this never fucking happened. You got that?' said the American, pointing a finger in his face. 'Get out now while you can. I'll bill you for the champagne, shall I?'

'You're sick, you know that, sick in the head. I'll never, ever respect you after this. I may have to work with you but it's just bloody business. It's all a transaction from now on,' he said, looking into Von Eil's uncomprehending, blank eyes like he was the crazy one, shrinking from them as he ran and ran.

Graham didn't stop before reaching the pavement way below, crumpling to the ground, quaking at what had happened, first Mark, now this place, this confounding city.

Chapter ten

Fighting back

'Why the bloody hell are we meeting here?' said Graham breathlessly, wiping away the sweat from his forehead, sitting opposite Smale.

'Patpong in the daytime isn't a pretty sight, I know, dear boy, plus it's rather hot out. But I wanted you to experience some of the old Bangkok, before the place was beautified.'

'Beautified? Mike, beautified is not a term I'd use to describe this… this hellhole.'

'Awful now, is it? Don't become one of those *farangs* constantly complaining. You know why you're here. You've got to turn a blind eye to certain things or you'll go mad.'

'Yeah, mad like poor old Mark. I still can't believe it,' he said, leaning back in his chair, digging fingers into his thighs, feeling just bone, like he could afford to lose more bloody weight. The damn stress of it all.

'Look, you're in deep but we all are. That's why Aunty Smale agreed to meet at such short notice. I know you need a shoulder to cry on, even though we barely know one another,' he said, as a waitress left a large bottle of beer and two glasses on the

126

filthy chequered tablecloth. 'A shoulder to cry on and a beer to cry in, of course.'

'Thanks. I know we only met the once but I don't have anyone else to turn to. You also talked about getting my induction, so I'm taking you up on the offer,' he said, banging a fist down on a baby cockroach zig-zagging its way across the table. 'You weren't kidding about the old Bangkok, were you.'

'Ha, no. This is Mizu's Kitchen. Been here since the Vietnam war. Great food, Wagyu beef is the speciality but just don't inspect anything too closely,' he said, holding up a smeared glass, polishing it on an immaculate sleeve.

'Seems to be the motto of the whole place. Don't look too closely. But I was there, I helped do away with Mark. I'm not sure I can live with it,' he whispered, face crumpling, unable to look Smale in the eye.

'Listen,' said the professor, placing a hand on Graham's. 'You're a good man. I don't know all the details about Mark but Nigel…'

'Nigel, what? He told you all a bloody 'bout it?' he said, flicking the hand away.

'Graham, listen for fuck sake. It's a small town, word gets around. Nigel's not like that though. Believe it or not he's got your best interests at heart. He told me you might need some help, that's all.'

'Well, as I said, I was there. I could've stopped 'em but I didn't,' he said, still studying the tablecloth, arms trembling, taking a shaky chug of his beer but it didn't do anything to wet his parched mouth.

'You can't do anything about it. This is a jungle, survival of the fittest and all that. Nat and Daeng wanted him out the way.

You were a pawn. But you can't expect it all to be easy here. Think why you're here, what you did to get what you want. You were married, right? There must be a very good reason you gave all that up.'

'A thousand bloody reasons. But I still have morals.'

'Morals,' said Smale, throwing his head back and laughing so hard his grey mane quivered. 'Then sign up and become a missionary or some such. Don't make a home in Bangkok. Morals my arse.'

'I didn't expect you to understand. Why would you?' said Graham, stabbing at the air, eyes blazing, cheeks glowing red.

'It's not me you should be getting pissed off with. I'm on your side.'

'I know, look I'm sorry,' he said, turning away, gazing down at the table again. 'I need to blame someone... for what happened before I moved here, for what's happening now.'

'For what happened before you came here?'

'Mike, not now okay. I'm not going there. I'm trying to live in the moment. That's what my counsellor told me. Not sure it's working,' he said, letting out an unconvincing laugh, draining his drink.

'You were getting counselling?'

'Not now, as I said, I'm not going there. Not today. Mark's gone. I've gotta get my head round that,' he said, fishing about in his pocket, pulling out the Xanax, needing to banish the tightness that felt like it was gripping his whole body.

'Drugs now?'

'Anxiety like you wouldn't believe,' he said, swallowing down a pill with a swig from a second bottle of beer.

'They don't help, dear boy. They destroy one's libido as well,

128

which really won't do here in the tropics,' he said, clapping his hands with an unnecessary flourish. 'Now how about that steak? I do love prime beef.'

'I'm really not hungry. There was Mark and that's hell, Daeng putting a knife to my throat and those eyes… but what I saw last night, somehow it's worse. You might think you can't survive here by having morals but I'm not giving up everything I believe in. I can have both,' he said, looking Smale in the eye, easing back in his chair. 'I'm not like all the rest, the Peeklongs, the Daengs, the Ronnies, the Von Eils.'

'The Natashas?'

'She's not completely lost. I think I'm getting somewhere. I've got to keep that evil scumbag Von Eil away from her. But that's why I'm really here, last night.'

'Pray tell, what happened last night? See if I can be shocked.'

'Von Eil, he took me to the Red Lantern…'

'You're taking the moral high ground but you were at the Lantern last night.'

'You know it? I needn't ask, right. Anyway I did go and I was disgusted. They're just kids. Em, the girl he bloody set me up with, she was fifteen. She's a child.'

'Oh, spare me the liberal leftie hand wringing. It's awful but there's a market for it, it goes on. You bought Natasha and now you're complaining about what goes on here. Newsflash, you can't have it both ways,' he said, tapping Graham on the side of the head.

'It's not hand wringing. They were drugged. She's just a kid. She's old enough to be…'

'Your daughter, yes, I know. Stating the bleedin' obvious. And you know those kids, as you call them, come from impoverished families. This is a way out of poverty and, I'm not going to lie, they can't all meet their knight in shining armour but some of them do get rescued.'

'Yeah but most get raped by Von Eil and his cronies. Drugged and raped. And I'm sure that's the least of it.'

'What the fuck do you want to do about it?' said Smale, finger in Graham's face.

'I want Ronnie's address. Don't tell me you don't know it,' he said, slamming the table, setting the drinks wobbling.

'Ronnie? You have no idea what you're getting involved in. You're so outside your comfort zone it's not even funny. They eat little boys like you for breakfast…'

'Look, I've given up caring about my own safety. If I did, do you really think I'd own a bar in Bangkok. Look around, look at this bloody place for a start. We're in the land that time forgot, there are no laws but it doesn't stop me trying. I wanna save Em, that girl, the fifteen-year-old-girl.'

'Yes, Mr Mike,' said a waitress, responding to his signal.

'A pen please, my love,' he said, taking it from her, scribbling an address on a napkin, handing it go Graham.

'Thanks,' he said, giving it a cursory glance before pocketing it but computing exactly where it was, how long it would take to get there.

'You're a brave boy. I think you could do well here. But, Graham, please be careful.'

'It's not brave. I've seen brave and this isn't it. But I owe it to Em.'

'Why?'

'My daughter, Mike, she's just like my daughter, Emmy,' he said as he got up from the table, unsteadily navigating his way out of the restaurant through a mist of tears.

***

It wasn't far from Mizu's to Natasha's, a short stroll through the grime of the city's red-light district. At night the tacky neon and glitter lent it a certain allure but it was disgusting in the daytime, Bangkok revealing the face of the so-called developing world unadorned. It was so filthy Graham felt his shoes sticking to the grease slicked pavements, pinching his nostrils as unspeakable smells wafted up from one of the numerous open drains he passed. When he'd decided to give up everything, do a runner from his previous life, this is not what he'd imagined. He'd filtered out all the realities, the dirt, the X-rated scenes but now he was living it and in some ways it was more frightening, though he was proud of what he'd done, knew he'd had to run, Emma had told him to. There was no way he was giving it all up now, he wasn't giving in either, unprepared to just kowtow to the amoral.

'No bloody way,' he said to himself, pouring himself a lunchtime whisky on reaching his empty bar scorching in the afternoon sun, taking the crumpled napkin from his pocket, spreading it out on the burning Formica top, scanning the address again.

He looked across the street at the charred, jumbled remains of Christie Cabaret, thinking of Mark as the booze seared the back of his throat, slid down his gullet. His tensed muscles finally relaxed, Graham breathed out heavily, feeling under the bar for his emergency pack of fags.

'It was them, mate. It wasn't me. Mark, I didn't have a choice. Whatever you did, you didn't deserve this. I'll make it right in

131

some way with that bastard Von Eil. He's behind all this. Rest in peace,' he said, raising his glass, wiping frantically at his eyes.

He felt the phone vibrating in his pocket, took it out. Nat calling. She was probably worried, he hadn't been home since the Red Lantern, wandering those early morning streets in a kind of numb fury before meeting Smale. But he let it ring and ring, he didn't want to talk to her right now, couldn't, knowing she'd try to talk him out of what he was about to do next, still shattered by the fact she'd engineered Mark's death but it wasn't death. Only one word for it – murder.

'God,' he said, throwing the tumbler to the pockmarked concrete floor, it shattering into pieces.

Graham rifled through the receipts from the previous night and it had seemed to have picked up after he left, though of course the money in the strong box didn't tally with the amount on the bills. He imagined the rotund, pig-like Peeklong sniffing around late on, drunk patrons oblivious as the policeman dipped his hands in the till, protection racket Thai style. And he felt the pain across his shoulders, like they were being twisted by an external force, the pressure running from his forehead down behind his eyes. Discarding the receipts, watching them fritter away on the breeze, he snatched up the napkin from the bar, headed out into the street, hailed the first passing cab.

'Where you go, man?' said the driver, offering him the requisite crooked-toothed smile, then pulling his mouth open and wiggling his tongue around in a crude approximation of cunnilingus. 'You want sex show? Lady? Ladyboy?'

'No thank you,' he said, hesitating at the side of the road, no desire to be whisked off to some dive bar in the shadows where he could be robbed or worse.

'You like *man*?'

'No, look, I want to go to Soi Nantha, just off Sathorn Soi One. You know?'

'You like massage?'

'No, Soi Nantha, please,' he said, waving a 500-baht note at the cabbie, knowing it was ten times the going rate, needing to get there.

'Okay, we go,' said the driver, nodding for Graham to get in.

He slid into the backseat, jaunty, upcountry Thai folk music on the radio, like all the drivers seemed to prefer as it reminded them of their simpler lives in the rural northeast, he guessed, but to Graham it was so at odds with his jittery mood, as he balled his hands into fists. Pain stabbed at his stomach and he felt almost seasick amid the dizzying whirl of concrete and movement as far as the eye could see, Bangkok bubbling with life from the clogged pavements to the roads glinting with a metallic sea of cars – the massive billboards towering above selling everything from Pepsi to Lexus. The smell, the heat, the light permitted no refuge from the intensity, nor did the thoughts of Emmy.

It was his daughter that came to mind when driving the morose drunks back from another day's slog in the City in his cab on a grim winter's night, the fact she'd made him promise he'd leave Sheila as the wife was so vicious towards him. 'Get a life, Dad,' she'd said and he wiped away a tear, one of what had seemed like an endless stream not so long ago. Sheil's unsmiling, sneering face so often came back to life despite the distance between them now, her vile abuse still stuck on a loop in his brain. The illogical shouting, the pinching, the slapping, the sheer hate just for something as inane as intruding

133

on her favourite telly programme, that's what made him run, not look back.

'Sir… Excuse, Sir, we're here,' said the driver, turning around and tapping Graham on the knee.

'Oh,' he said, rummaging in his pocket for the money, handing over the 500-baht note.

'*Kup khun krub* [thank you].'

'Thanks,' he said, nodding as he got out, offering up a smile, having basically been robbed but avoiding the far worse fate of being dropped off at a sleazy bar in the shadows where no doubt he would've been shaken down, feeling in his own small way he'd won.

That was life in Bangkok, the need to revel in small victories. He remembered Smale telling him about the Thai epithet of 'keeping a cool heart' and Graham realised if he could stick to that principle, however hard, then he at least had a chance of not ending up like Mark and Nigel. Too many foreigners lost their hearts, then their heads in Thailand but looking at the expansive wooden house in front him, perfectly pitched behind lush foliage in a tropical garden with an adjacent tennis court that heart was hammering in his chest, palms greasy from sweat, horribly metallic, dry taste in his mouth. He checked the napkin again to make sure it was the right place but it all added up, though somehow it shouldn't have but Graham knew this is what selling sleaze bought in a city like Bangkok, just look at Von Eil. He thought back to the fifteen-year-old Em of last night, then looked at the elegant facade of the colonial-style house with its canopies and shutters, its grand terrace where expertly mixed G&Ts were no doubt served in the welcome shade of early evening.

'You arsehole,' he said, surveying the eight-foot high locked gates, finally locating an intercom, depressing it.

He looked up at the gates again, wondering if he could climb them, wondering whether his skinny, unconditioned frame could take them on when a pair of big dogs bounded over the manicured lawn. The rottweilers poked their noses through the gate, inches from his trouser leg as if they'd just been let out and were looking for an early dinner.

'Ronnie 'ere,' a voice said finally over the barking dogs via a crackly speaker, like it was miles away.

'Ronnie, listen, it's me, Graham.'

'Gra... I don't know any Graham. I'm busy right now.'

'No, look, Ronnie... Ron. You came to my bar, Natasha's. I'm a friend of Mike, Mike Smale's.'

'Ah, Smale. *Oui*, yes. But what do you want?'

'I've got a little something to discuss, a proposition for you,' said Graham, hopping from foot to foot, finger white, throbbing from keeping the intercom depressed, sweat forming a great ugly patch on his shirtfront.

'Be my guest, a friend of Smale's is a friend of mine' he replied as the gates rattled open. 'Don't mind the dogs. They don't bite unless they're 'ungry.'

'They look angry,' he said.

'*Hungry* not angry,' said Ronnie as the intercom clicked off.

Rather than not minding them, the dogs formed a dervish of gnashing teeth around him, inhibiting his progress to the house every step of the way. Graham impatiently kicked out, sending one of the hounds skittering off to the side, though the other sank its teeth into his hand, pointed enamel piercing skin, causing him to yell out in pain as he looked down at the blood leaking from an inch-long wound, staining the neatly clipped grass crimson.

'I said don't mind them. You shouldn't be kicking them,' said Ronnie, standing at the door, furiously clapping his hands as the dogs finally turned their attention away from Graham, slipping sleekly back into the house from whence they came.

'So?' he said, holding up a bloody hand, stood on the threshold, having to look up to Ronnie, the tall, skinny streak of piss, fuzzy beard growth, flip-flops and singlet like he was some extra from *The Beach*, not lord of the bloody manor.

'So what? I guess they took a disliking to you but I can't be too careful, you know. I take it zis is not a social visit. You've not come for a game of tennis,' he said, thumbing at the court, laughing at his own joke.

'You think this is bloody funny?' he said, shaking a fist just in front of Ronnie's protruding nose, shoulder barging him as he entered the hallway, the shadowy, parquet floor lined hallway, smelling faintly of lilies, of wealth.

'Hey, hey, where you think you're going?' he said, grabbing Graham roughly by the arm with a hand the size of a bunch of bananas.

'Get your bloody hands off me,' he said, turning around, pushing Ronnie in the chest, sending him flailing backwards.

'Sir, Sir, you okay?' said a boy running into the hallway.

'Fuck off, I can deal with this shit,' Ronnie said, big frame bent over panting but having regained his balance, fast closing the space between him and Graham with big strides, airily waving the lad away.

'I was at the Red Lantern last night. I saw how you treat those girls. They're just kids. Kids,' he said, leaping up at him, hands clawing pathetically at the singlet, banging his fists on that chest but they simply bounced off.

'Zat's the problem with people like you, you come 'ere with all your ideas, your dreams but you don't get it,' said Ronnie, eyes searing into Graham's, wiry frame uncoiling with power, like they'd just been play fighting before, twisting his arm so hard it felt like it would snap in two, backing him up against the wall, a wall hanging with exquisite works of art. 'This place Bangkok is shiny on the outside but it's a *toilette*, a cesspit. The meek shall inherit the earth? *Non*, it's the most corrupt.'

'You're proud of it? You're sick. Sick! You lock up little girls, you sell them to be drugged and raped. Em, she's fifteen. Fifteen years old!' he screamed, aiming a fist at that nose, which bent with a sickening crack, like a branch snapping.

'Fuck,' he said, putting a hand up to his nose, the Gallic like beak slightly less protruding than before, dripping blood.

'Come on,' said Graham, his fists raised, ready to go again, invincible as the heat of adrenaline coursed through him, all too easy but Ronnie's elbow slamming into his throat sent him flying back into the wall, pain pulsing from the back of his head.

'You come into my 'ouse and do this,' he said, pointing at his nose, spitting in the prone Graham's face.

'No,' he gasped, backed up as far as he could go, massive hands around his neck, fingers tightening their grip, air pushed from his throat, a blackness around the periphery of his vision as the pressure intensified, the pain in his head, through his whole body at a level he didn't think possible and it was as if he was shrinking, collapsing in on himself, folding up into the wall.

'You fuck. Tell me why you think you should live?' said Ronnie, finally letting go, Graham bent over and greedily breathing lungfuls of air, almost at the feet of his tormentor.

'You're bloody evil...' he said, still gasping but looking up, staring at the Frenchman's face, steadying himself as he put hands on his knees.

'*Merde*!' said Ronnie, throwing up his hands. 'What do I have to do to get rid of you?'

'Then I'll be on your conscience as well,' he said, standing up straight, them eye to eye again.

'Fuck you,' he said, face contorted, hands around Graham's neck again, though the knee to the groin sent Ronnie tumbling backwards, slipping on the parquet in his flip-flops.

'It's my daughter. My bloody daughter. That's why I'm not giving up. She was just seventeen when she died. I blame meself as I got her driving lessons. She was out driving one night and someone drove into her, head on collision. Boy racer on the wrong side of the dual carriageway. Emmy, she didn't stand a bloomin' chance,' he said, sliding down the wall, sprawling over the floor. 'I can't see another young girl's life wasted. Not someone I can save.'

'What the fuck do you want? You can't change the past,' Ronnie said quietly, kneeling next to him so they were eye level again.

'I'm here because of her. I wanna do something worthy of 'er. You know I watched her on a life support machine, she was a fighter, such a fighter. I had to ask them to switch off the machine. I'm a bloody joke,' he said, looking away, blinking back yet more tears.

'What have I got to do with this? *This*?'

'It's when I saw Em last night. It brought all the feelings back. This young, vulnerable girl. I just wanted to help 'er. I want to help her,' he said, kneading the wooden floor.

'And what, I'm meant to feel, how you say, guilty as sin?'

'Just let her go. She told me they're all kept in dormitories. If you can't let them all go, then let her out.'

'You know, sometimes birds are kept in cages so long, you open the door and they back further into the cage.'

'Bullshit. You know that's not true. I saw how much she hates that life. It's in her eyes.'

'Where will she go? Her parents sold her. Where's she gonna go?'

'Ronnie, if you've got any decency left, if you've listened to anything I've just said, you've got to let her have that chance. I'll give her some money to set herself up. Please, give her one more chance.'

'You're *ting tong*, as they say in Thai, crazy. A real *ting tong farang*. You barge in here like you're not even scared, don't know what you're dealing with. It's formidable,' he said, patting him on the knee.

'I'm not scared. I've got nothing left to lose. But I'm taking it that's a 'yes'?' he said, still breathing hard, hands at his bruised neck.

'*Oui.*'

'One more thing. I've never met a Frenchman called Ronnie,' he said, amazingly trying to hold in a laugh after everything.

'Don't push it, man. But if you really wanna know, my mother loved Ronald Reagan. That's the actor, not the president. *C'est la vie.*'

***

139

'Look at my fucking nose, eh. It was bad enough before,' said Ronnie laughing as they walked out of the house, down the pleasant tree-lined street.

'My hand,' Graham replied, holding up the bandage, the wound having been almost lovingly tended to by his former enemy.

'You kicked the dog. They've not so much as barked before. Ask the postman.'

'And my neck,' he said, displaying the red, bruised skin.

'War wounds. We've all got them.'

'Yeah,' he said, patting Ronnie on the back. 'You know I don't agree with what goes on at the Red Lantern but I'm grateful for this.'

'For zis?' he replied with an almost comic shrug, in keeping with the continental accent.

'Yes, zis. You know, agreeing to let Em go,' he said smiling, thinking all Ron needed was a string of onions around his neck, a stripy T-shirt.

'Shush, not a word of this to Mr Paul. Von Eil to you. You got it?'

'That arsehole.'

'I'm warning you. You and me, we've kissed and made up for now but don't push your luck. Today is between me and you.'

'Fine but what's Von Eil got to do with all this?'

'Graham, don't be a bloody hero, you know. Keep your nose out of 'is business.'

'But he wants part of mine.'

'Then you don't have much choice. Just say *merci* and be grateful. He's a better friend than an enemy, believe me. Now follow me,' he said as they reached a dilapidated apartment block, gaggle of street dogs yapping outside, having gnawed through some rubbish bags, nosing at a mound of rotting, stinking food.

Graham looked up at the flats, like something out of an old Hong Kong movie, the blackened facade, the bars up at the windows, washing poked out haphazardly at every conceivable angle as if to catch the sun's rays but it was arranged courtyard style so one flat looked in on another and all was gloomy, in constant shadow. It was just yards from the serenity of the Frenchman's house with its parquet flooring and antiquities but it felt a world away, going from colonial splendour to slum in a Bangkok minute.

'What is this place?' he said as Ronnie fiddled with a large rusted padlock at the building's entrance, holding in place two pretty formidable looking steel doors.

'Welcome to the Monkey House,' said the Frenchman, turning around and offering him a smile as they entered a dimly lit corridor.

'She's here, isn't she. This is where you bloody keep them. It's a prison. A bloody prison.'

'Yes, Sherlock 'Olmes,' he said, throwing open a door but putting a hand to his lips.

'Jesus,' he said under his breath, air thick with cheap perfume, cigarettes but something horribly human too, sweat, like too many dirty bodies stacked up in one place, evident as his eyes became adjusted to the weak light filtered through the rags at the windows – girl abutted girl in row after row laid out on the hard floor.

'This is better than what they've come from.'

'Yeah, you're Mother Theresa. At least we know who the

141

next Nobel Peace Prize is going to. This is absolutely bloody disgusting,' he said, turning away, wanting to run, that pain twisting at the muscles in his shoulders again, feeling a familiar weight pressing down on the back of his neck.

'Come here,' he said, moving towards a girl at the end of one of the rows, each in an almost identical bundle in the foetal position and Ronnie shook her roughly.

'Won?' she said bleary eyed but bolting upright, flinching from his touch.

'It's all right, love,' said Graham, bending down to her level, Em's face grey, hair lank, eyes lifeless. 'We've come to set you free.'

But smiling at her elicited no response, the word 'freedom' not meaning a thing as the girl stared out beyond him into nothingness.

'Get your things, we're going,' said Ronnie, dragging her up, filling the holdall next to her with a pitifully small pile of cheap clothes.

'Here,' said Graham, as she stood, tears visible in those dead eyes, pushing a big bundle of notes into her hand, 10,000 baht.

The three of them left the room, Ronnie hurrying Em down the hallway ahead of him. At the entrance she finally looked at them both as if for the first time, glancing from one to the other, but Graham pointed off out into the distance.

'You go,' he said, again waving her off, and she looked at him even more quizzically before walking out into the street, past the mangy dogs, but he realised she was just a frightened animal being asked to leave her friends, four walls that were not only a prison but had become a home and he felt guilty all over again, guilty and useless like he'd been when he held that vigil for his daughter at the hospital not long ago.

Chapter eleven

Tears for a daughter

As he travelled to the airport, the almost infinitely tall towers of Mammon on Sukumvhit Road mocked the poverty of the slum he was living in, the threadbare state of the chipboard and corrugated iron lean-to he called a bar and worse, much worse, the blackened, scarred landscape opposite Natasha's Cabaret that had once been Mark's domain – a constant reminder of what he'd got himself into. The night at the Red Lantern just underlining how he'd done a deal not just with the devil but several of his best mates as well. He popped another happy pill as the future shock unfolded outside his window flummoxed as to why he couldn't be part of this prosperity, this new Asia – a miracle they called it. Graham was going to England at Natasha's behest to finalise his divorce, not letting him forget it was about money, always about the bloody money. Peeklong had taken pleasure in disabusing him of the idea of just 'disappearing', the Thai talking murder charges and extradition if he didn't come back to pay his dues. Not that Graham could face going back to a life where he was barely existing. No, he was experiencing life in all its gory glory and he wasn't about to lose that.

Arriving at departures he absently picked up a copy of the *Bangkok Post* as he sat down for a quick coffee to recover from the now ubiquitous hangover. Leafing through, as there was never usually anything to hold the attention aside from the ongoing red versus yellow shirts soap opera, he stopped suddenly at page three: '*Bar owner found dead after blazing inferno.*'

Rapt, he read on past the headline: '*Bang Rak area police have revealed the body pulled from a mystery blaze at the popular Christie Cabaret in red-light district Pat Pong was that of 41-year-old bar owner Mark Smith. The foreigner from England was identified from dental records. The cause of the fire last Wednesday is unknown but police have not ruled out arson. Area commander Police-General Peeklong said, 'The case remains open'.*'

'Bloody Peeklong,' Graham said, loud enough that people started to look at him, quickly flicking the page over as if not wanting to be found guilty by association, disbelieving the police-general was even haunting him from the pages of the *Post*.

He flicked through more pages of filler, filler he knew Mike Smale edited five nights a week before he came to the bar, now a regular. Creepy though he was, he'd replaced Nigel in his affections as the archetypal English gentleman abroad – all the panache of Monroe, none of the desperation. For instance, it was always a G&T, never a 'ghastly' whisky and soda, for whisky was always Scotch, foreign, to Mike. The irony was in England Graham would've run a mile from a man like Smale but in Bangkok he found he needed him. He was a reminder of home in such an alien, baffling place and the professor's refusal to be even a little intimidated by it all was the thing he found so attractive. The way he'd given up Ronnie's address showed whose side he was really on.

He got to the lifestyle section of the paper where '*Chubby Bird was all of a twitter*' and there accompanying the very first paragraph of his column was a thumbnail picture of Graham pouring one of those ghastly Scotch and sodas.

'*I advise the denizens of the Silom area to take heed of a new watering hole in Patpong called Natasha's Cabaret. The demi-mondaines – if that's what they are as poor Chubby has difficulty telling the difference these days – are buxom and lovely. Tweet! Tweet! Sundowners are two for one making this the perfect vantage point for pre-dinner cocktails. Owners Graham and Natasha make a fine couple and I am sure he'll do the decent thing and take her up the aisle soon. Tweet! Tweet!*'

'Jesus,' he sighed, neatly folding the newspaper and slipping it into the pocket of his hand luggage, two paragraphs all his crazy gamble warranted, the sacrifices he'd made, the blood on his hands.

He shook as Mark's face came to mind, as it did all too regularly, the searing ache across his shoulders, acidic backwash from his gurgling tummy just a constant reminder of his guilt. Graham so on edge that the sudden ringing of his phone made him jump, cheap Nokia mobile sounding shrill in the departures lounge.

'Nige, for what do I owe the pleasure?'

'Daeng's not pleased. Thrown 'is toys out of the pram, my dear,' he said, the mixture of Cockney and upper class like something out of a *Carry On* film.

'Thanks for making my day. The little bastard's never happy.

145

What is it this time?' Graham replied, so loudly the woman in the oh-so Far East chic elephant emblazoned safari suit sitting next to him tutted.

'Well done for the piece in the *Post* but he took umbrage at you and Nat being described as the owners of the bar.'

'For God's sake,' he said, accompanied by another tut, thunder thighs in linen reminiscent of Sheil, so glad he was out of it. 'Did you see page three? The *Post* not *The Sun*.'

'You know I'm really not into those type of titties,' said Nigel with a laugh that morphed into a wheezing cough. 'Yes, I did see it but it's all bluster from Peeklong. They will leave it be. Just don't upset the *gendarmerie* again.'

'What the hell is a *demi-mondaine*, by the way?' said Graham, provoking the loudest tut yet.

'I think it refers to a 'lady of the night', another Birdism.'

'Thanks for that Nigel, I knew you'd know, but I really must, as you'd say, 'dash orf' as there's an elephant in a trouser suit next to me eavesdropping on every word.'

'How dare you!' she screeched.

But Graham just walked off chuckling to himself because he could, since despite his responsibilities, he was now totally irresponsible. He also had far more important things to worry about, he thought, popping another pill that came too readily to his trembling hand.

'Screw the future,' he said under his breath as he headed for the always open airport bar, needing to silence the noise in his head. It was 9am.

***

Landing at Heathrow it wasn't so much 'fuck the future',

however, as 'fuck the past'. The drab monochrome that greeted him after the glorious Technicolour of Thailand was so numbing. He'd never really seemed to notice before when people said everyone on public transport looked depressed but glancing about him on the train back to Sutton, the scummy south London commuter town he once lived – though he bloody knew it wasn't really living – *everyone* did look depressed. There was no buzz, no spark, the sky a lifeless grey. The lack of colour, the lack of noise, the absence of any kind of stimulation of the senses made him feel repressed, cowed. He also got the impression other passengers were staring disparagingly at his Bangkok bar drag, shorts, T-shirt and cheap loafers out of keeping with the uniform shirt, slacks and sensible shoes of the commuter brigade. The very brigade he'd ferry around pissed and snarly in his cab on a Friday night when they were trying to obliterate another working week and he was just trying to forget.

Having dumped his bag in the drab, provincial Holiday Inn down the road, resisting the pull to get absolutely hammered, he turned into Alexander Avenue, as in Alexander The Great, but it was really far from that. The dreary street of washed out terraced houses sprouted satellite dishes, as though the inhabitants wanted to be anywhere but there. Graham arrived at No 49 billed proudly as an 'end of terrace' when they'd bought it but the place looked somehow lonelier, more woebegone without another house to its left, just a filthy alleyway separating it from the next row of grimy pebbledash edifices.

He rang the bell, setting off the inelegant chimes of the *General Lee* – reminiscent of a US cop show from the 1980s – something he'd installed as a bit of a joke in lighter times but now felt part of another, sadly forgotten lifetime and he realised they'd been living in a time warp. Standing on the doorstep, he could see how his life had stopped in the middle of their marriage because not only had he fallen out of love with Sheila, if it had ever existed, he'd fallen out of love with life.

'You better come in,' she said, opening the door after an impolite pause, like she'd almost had second thoughts about answering.

Graham noticed she looked gaunt, slow and decrepit in her movements, seemingly so much older than forty, like it had all taken a terrible toll. Pathetically he was holding a bottle of wine in one hand, stiff envelope containing the divorce documents in the other as she showed him into the front room, once *their* front room, wishing he'd never bought the cheap peace offering, wondering what to do with it but she simply grabbed it off him, like how could a bottle of plonk pay for what he'd done. Instead of sinking into the comfort of his usual armchair, he perched himself awkwardly on the edge of the sofa. The television was on in the corner and the old gas fire was hissing away, everything as normal, as though nothing had changed, but the atmosphere betrayed the fact it all had.

'Tea?'

'Please, Sheil,' he said quietly, looking away, no longer able to bear the scrutiny of her judgmental stare, the room feeling so claustrophobic, restrictive, prison-like, leaving him wondering how they'd coped all those loveless years.

But as he heard her banging about in the kitchen, having left the room unannounced, he dared to look around, to see if she'd rearranged anything. Worryingly she hadn't. Pride of place on the mantelpiece was a photo of them, the three of them, him, Sheila and Emmy, and he wanted to put it face down, tell her to stop hoping. It seemed even though she hated him, she'd have him back for the sake of habit, so they could play act through another twenty years, at least to the outside world.

''Ere's your tea.'

'Thanks,' he said, shakily taking the mug, placing the envelope on the armrest, it sitting there like an awfully weighty, unanswered question.

'I'd still 'ave you back even now, Gray. All you bloomin' put me through. We could start over, start again,' she said with a sigh, easing her bulky frame onto the chair opposite, alternately eyeing him and the envelope.

'You always hated me. How was the last twenty years about love? Twenty bloody years. You never touched me and when I tried to get close to you, you turned your back. I feel something now and I've been numb for so long. I actually feel,' he said, looking at his shoes, those cheap, filthy Bangkok loafers rucking up the carpet, treading Third World dirt into the neurotically pristine house, everything smelling of furniture polish, the whiff making him queasy.

'You still with her, *it*?'

'Oh, come on. It's always insults with you. Haven't you said enough? Look, I'm…'

'Don't you dare tell me you're sorry again. I don't wanna hear it. You've ruined my life. Our life. How about I tell your parents you're a shirtlifter, eh? You always were pathetic but this is disgustin', just disgustin'.'

'There are the papers,' he said, rattling the stark white pages out of the envelope, laying them on the seat next to her, trying to ignore her blubbering, so many crocodile tears after the years of abuse he'd suffered. 'It's the divorce petition and like I said,

149

you need to sign it.'

'I'll bloody sign it all right,' she said, sniffing back her sobs, making to get up.

'I got a pen,' he said, fishing it out of the envelope, handing it to her, having made it all as easy as possible. 'Sign where the crosses in pencil are.'

'You with your pathetic nerves, your whingy voice, your toilet breath. You bloomin' repulse me. No wonder I haven't touched you for so long,' she said, peering over Pound Shop glasses at the papers, though giving them only a cursory glance before scribbling down her signature and throwing the documents back at him.

'One more thing before I go,' he said, gratefully scooping up the scattered papers, double checking she'd signed in all the right places, depositing them neatly back in the envelope despite his trembly hands. 'I need to see her room. I wanna remember.'

'Just a minute,' she said, hauling herself up, scrabbling around in one of the drawers of the sideboard, retro piece of furniture that had been a wedding present. 'Here, she would've wanted you to have this.'

'Bloody hell,' he said, as she placed the gold pendant that spelled out 'Emmy' in his sweaty hand, the necklace he'd bought his daughter for her seventeenth and as Sheila looked into his eyes it was as if she was still playing a game, still trying to get under his skin, change his mind.

'What would she have thought about all this, eh?'

'She wanted me to go,' he said, curling his fingers tightly around the necklace, looking at his wife's face, the soon to be ex, but it was blank, devoid of emotion, set in that typically hard expression he hated and as he turned wordlessly for the hallway and the sanctuary of his daughter's bedroom he was on the verge of letting out a little cheer as Graham knew he'd done the right thing.

He stopped at the bedroom door for a beat, like he always did, would've politely knocked but finally stumbled awkwardly in. There was a horribly musty, stagnant aura about the little box room, when before it had been full of Emma and her vibrancy, a time when the air was infused with her favourite perfume, pop songs playing on the little radio Graham now eyed sadly in the corner unused, gathering dust. Even the posters of the popstars she'd once lovingly affixed to the walls seemed to have a sadness behind their eyes. He sat on the side of the bed, its familiar old creak in his ears liked she'd just turned over in her sleep as he'd kissed her gently goodnight, putting his head in his hands as he rocked back and forth.

Graham had no idea how long he'd sat there but it was dark as he made his way down the rickety staircase. He silently let himself out of the house, clutching all that was left of their marriage, the divorce papers, in the other hand the necklace, all that remained of… No, he didn't want to think about that but still the memories came as fast as the tears falling in big blobs on the pavement.

Chapter twelve

Cheated

Standing in the drive of the suburban semi, archetypal gleaming Japanese motor adjacent to manicured lawn he felt intimidated by it all, what most people aspired to but something Graham knew he could never live up to. He'd taken a huge gamble instead and his mum and dad certainly weren't gamblers, frowned upon anything that deviated from the norm or their version of what that was – the job for life, the gradual move up the property ladder, the comfortable retirement in a faceless suburb. His mum peeping out of brilliant white net curtains broke him out of his thoughts and by the time he'd got to the end of the drive she was there with a smile and a hug.

'Good to see you, love,' she said.

'You too,' he said as she held him at arm's length but he noticed that look in her eye. What was it? Disappointment? Disapproval? Both?

'Hello, son,' said his dad, wresting his head from the *Daily Mail* as he followed his mum into the immaculately tidy front room, the old man standing up, shaking his hand but stepping back with a polite, passionless detachment.

'Lovely to see you.'

'Cup of tea?' said his dad.

'Please,' he said with a tight smile, the first real words they'd spoken for months and that was so one of them could leave the room, further abdicate their responsibility, Graham thought savagely.

'Graham, you're not coming back are you?' she said, hands writhing in her lap.

'I don't think so, no.'

'Poor Sheila. And why there of all places?'

'Bangkok, you mean. Mum, I know what you mean about Sheil, but sometimes these things don't work out. Bangkok… I don't know… it's different. I need space.'

'Is there, you know, another, er, woman?'

'I'm getting to that. The real story is I saw an opportunity and took it. Selfish, yes, but I had to do it.'

'Business good, son?' said his dad, handing him the tea.

'Yes, the bar's going well. Bit of a sticky start but we're making money…'

'We are?' said his mum.

'I went into business with two other partners.'

'Thais?' said his dad.

'Yes, as it happens.'

'You got to watch these Far East types in business.'

'Well I happen to be with one of those Far East types, Dad.'

'Happen to be with?' said his mum.

'Mum, you don't have to repeat everything and, yes, her name's Natasha, she's a transsexual.'

'Sorry, son, I've got to get on with my gardening,' said his dad, laboriously hauling himself out of his chair, shaking his hand with a solemn finality.

'Dad?' he said, watching as the old man slowly turned away in silence, left the room on unsteady legs, no doubting the bloody sentiment.

'Oh, Graham,' said his mum, eyes wet with tears.

'What's the matter with you all? She's a woman essentially, if it bothers you that much. I could've lived with Sheila another twenty years, carried on lying to her, you, myself. Is that what you bloody want?' he said, forcing his knees together to stop them knocking, heat moving from his chest to his neck, face burning hot.

'When you called us to say you were staying there I had my suspicions. First you leaving and now this. I can't take it all in. So you're gay?' she said slapping a hand down on the sofa.

'She's basically a woman, as I said. How can I be gay?' he replied, pain throbbing across his shoulders, pinprick of sweat growing under his armpits.

'I don't know, boy. I just don't know anything anymore. That poor wifey of yours.'

'Mum, I'm going to go now, you've got dad. I don't know... I just can't talk to you.'

He stood up to leave and she stood too, her hug feeling cold, empty, just like Sheila's always had. As the front door slammed behind him and he was enveloped in the cold he smashed a palm into his forehead, the fact he was telling half-truths even to himself, after all this, after everything, who was he bloody kidding? Nat was no woman but if he couldn't admit to himself what that made him how could anyone else bloody accept it?

***

It was ridiculous, he knew, but despite having mocked and rejected his parents' life there was something about its safe, pathetic dullness that seemed so attractive amid the chaos of his own existence. And yet... and yet... the tropical heat, the ready sex, the sitting behind a bar for a living was an addictive cocktail that had lured Graham and dozens of others away from a life of dull conformity. He'd long seen through the illusory Land of Smiles schtick – Peeklong among others had set him right about that – but he was heading back for more, having cut short his trip to London, nothing to keep him there anymore, bonds broken. Not just broken, snapped in two. He was going home to Natasha, though she didn't know he was en route.

'You reckon you'll ever come back then, Gray?' said Art, his oldest friend, a former schoolmate, who was driving him back to Heathrow.

'The sixty-four million dollar question,' said Graham chuckling but the query made him uneasy, lips twitching, like they had a life of their own, unsure whether Art had got word courtesy of Sheila about the fact he was 'shacked up' with a ladyboy because there was no way he was going to confess, admit it. Couldn't.

'Well?'

'Nah. I don't think so, sunshine 365 days a year. Cheap booze. What more could you want?'

'Yeah'.

'Yeah,' he said, filling the silence, familiar nervous pain wracking his body.

'I love Thailand, don't get me wrong, but I couldn't get my head around living there full time.'

'No?'

'I mean I've got to put the kids through university, we've got Jen's parents to worry about, both getting on. Me old girl might need to go in a home soon. Sorry to mention the kids, uni, I know you're still hurting…'

'Art, it's okay, I've gotta try and live. Emmy would've wanted that,' said Graham, holding on to his daughter's necklace in his hand, gripping it so tight it ached. 'I'm gonna look after my parents though, they don't have to worry about that. When the bar takes off we'll be rolling in it. Rolling in it.'

'I'm sure. Right, me old son, this is us,' said his friend as they pulled up beside the terminal.

'Cheers. We'll be sure to get that drink next time. It's all been a bit of a rush,' said Graham as he got out, watching for a long time as the car's rear lights disappeared off into the distance.

***

He arrived in the white heat of a Bangkok morning – burst of relentless light and heat a huge contrast to the grey and cold of London, the city's brutalist concrete face looking even more stark in the unforgiving glare of the tropical sun. The taxi driver babbling the usual nonsense about 'Man You-nited and Chelseee…' but Graham had learned to tune it out, despite the runaway beat of his heart, beads of sweat popping out all over his forehead, he smiled benignly in the back seat like some Buddha, knowing he'd perfected the art of creating an aura that said 'I know where I'm going'. It avoided the way he'd been led astray by cabbies when he first arrived. Not engaging meant not getting riled as the driver's words foundered on silence, Mr Taxi's answer turning up the radio full blast.

The silence drowned out by loud music seemed indicative

of the distance between him and Thai people as a whole – unbridgeable and that was an unbelievably lonely place. He'd already seen for all the Land of Smile nonsense they were not open to foreigners, at least those hanging around longer than their allotted two weeks and in some ways he could hardly blame them for what was his real motive? And Nigel's? And Smale's? And Chubby Bird's? And Von Eil's? So there was guilt on his side to complete a very toxic relationship but that didn't stop him being in love with it all with an addict's craving.

'Paradise, mister,' the cabbie shouted above the radio.

'*Kop khun krup* [thank you].'

'Room number, Sir?' said the lad behind the hotel desk.

'Six-one-ohhh.'

'No one in six-one-ohhh,' he said, faint mimic in his voice, dangling the key towards Graham with a self-satisfied smile.

'Thanks,' he replied, swiping the key, mulling over the fact Natasha obviously wasn't around despite it being morning, normally time to catch up on her beauty sleep.

Opening the door just confirmed his fears as he saw the perfectly made bed. He moved to the mini-bar and despite the earliness of the hour cracked open his first beer of the day. Pacing the room he dialled her number but tellingly it went straight to voicemail. Graham didn't leave a message, not wanting to spoil the surprise she had coming. He slumped down at the window sipping distractedly at the booze, dozing on and off with the jetlag.

The booming of an atypically sleek black vehicle turning into the car park jolted him out of his slumber, its clean, expensive lines so out of place with the surrounding clone-like Japanese tin boxes. Guts twisted, heart turning hammer-like in his chest, he focused in on the registration number – EVIL. Despite the blacked out windows he imagined Natasha sitting in its plush interior with a hand on Von Eil's knee or worse. After an agonising pause out she stepped, still in her trashy evening gear, though the figure-hugging shiny outfit he loved, watching as she leaned back into the driver's side, swallowed up by the car's airy interior as he guessed she gave the American a long, lingering kiss goodbye.

He could hear her footsteps echoing in the concrete hallway, envisioning her tottering along on those cheap platforms, lipstick smudged from kisses, face pallid from another long night out, reeking of cigarettes and booze.

'Surprised to see you, Gray, but receptionist told me,' she said, whisky-tainted breath all over him, slender arms around his puny shoulders.

'Where you been?' he said, brushing her off.

'Ah, I went to Spicy, you know the club on Sukumvhit. It was my friend's birthday.'

'Then how come I just saw you getting out of Paul bloody Von Eil's car?'

'Darling, he was there. He gave me a lift home.'

'Enough of the darling, you've been gone all bloody night,' he said, aiming a kick at the revolving electric pedestal fan in front of him, which exploded into plastic pieces, his body convulsing into shakes.

'I didn't do anything,' she said, palms raised skyward.

'Don't... lie... to... me,' he spat, banging a finger into her chest with each word, backing her up against the wall, hot breath in her face. 'I saw you lean back into the car and give that bastard a kiss. Wish him a good day at work, did we? Or whatever the hell he does for a living.'

'Fuck you!' she shouted, pushing Graham away with all the power coiled in her strong arms.

He fell backwards cracking his head on the sharp side of a block-like chest of drawers and putting a hand to just above his hairline felt blood, it soon coating his palm, dripping in big worrying globules on the shiny linoleum.

'What the hell have you done?'

'I'm so sorry, baby,' she said but hauling him roughly to his feet, grabbing a towel and dabbing at the wound.

'Nat, I don't know whether we can live like this anymore.'

'We can work it out.'

'Can we?' he said, resting a throbbing head in his hands, hyperventilating in the tiny room, tense with the urge to just run but London was lost to him, finished, what about Bangkok?

'I only want you. I love you,' she said, doleful eyes like they were pleading with him. 'Remember time we went out clubbing. It was so amazing. We can live like that.'

'I want to believe you,' Graham said, collapsing into those arms because it was easier but what other options did he have? He had to bloody trust her.

Chapter thirteen

End of a friend

Six months later...

Graham was walking past one of the gleaming coaches, one among several, in the car park, the car park that had once been Christie's, the ultimate desecration of the site of Mark's death. He ran his hand along the coach to make sure it was all real, but it was all too real, so real Natasha had instructed him to 'get rid' of Nigel that evening. Graham didn't have a choice but to actually agree the red-faced, trembly old drunkard was no longer in keeping with the slick operation the club had become, the new anodyne, family friendly incarnation catering to coachloads of tourists. But where did that leave the other red-faced, trembly old drunkard? Nigel was from the era of T&A and it was one Graham still hankered for, what had brought him to this point in the first place. Tears welled in his eyes because in a city of strangers, Nige was his mate, his only friend next to Smale.

Beside the coach was Von Eil's Merc, looking dark and brooding in the street lights as if it possessed a personality similar to that of its owner, while the little sign in front of the vehicle

'Reserved for directors' was an indication of what had changed over the last six months. It was an unwelcome reminder of how the balance of power in the business had shifted even more in Natasha's favour, the nominal fifty per cent, everyone knew it was really the fifty-one per cent controlling share, now owned jointly by Natasha, Daeng and Von Eil. The Yank had demanded his share as a reward for investing in the business.

Walking into the artfully lit interior, the new Natasha's, open about a month, literally sparkled. The guests, not punters as in the past, now sat on row upon row of velveteen banquettes. He let out a sigh as he surveyed the scene, feeling several pairs of eyes on him, trying but failing to blend in with his cheap jacket and slacks combo, looking out of place among the dubious but expensive smart-casual of the tourist throng. He longed for the days when he'd been able to slink into the dimly lit, threadbare Natasha's of old in his Bangkok bar drag of billowy shirt, shorts and flip-flops, a week of beard growth on his chin and pour himself a liberal dose of whisky that would be totally unaccounted for. Now with besuited barmen in place almost umbilically tied to a new computer system nothing could be misappropriated, Graham not even permitted to go behind *his* bar.

'Hi, Nige,' he said, sidling up to his old friend, the spot-lit dazzle of the place illuminating how ancient old Monroe looked, picking out his desperate expression, tattered clothes, no longer afforded the anonymity of the shadows for there were none.

''Ello, dear,' he said, skeletal frame perched uncomfortably on a sumptuous leather bar stool, as though if he eased back he'd be swallowed up by its luxuriousness.

His greeting was followed by the loud strains of Thai folk music negating further conversation, heralding the start of the show as if it was some important cultural experience bound to the very fabric of the country, a show Nigel no longer had any input in. Suitably cowed, he barely looked up from his glass, sense of mischief long gone from his eyes as what fun was there to be had in the new Natasha's, thought Graham.

'Look at all this,' he said finally, shouting above the din, nodding to indicate the cavernous space the club had become, mostly due to the Yank's money but with a helping hand from his own divorce settlement. 'Strange this is all we ever really wanted.'

'Is it?'

'You know it is,' said Graham, indicating two more drinks to a pretty, well-groomed barman, no more ladyboys playing suggestively with beer bottles, service of a different, more wholesome kind. 'We did want this but now I'm not so sure…'

'Who's all this we? I'm no longer a part of this,' he said, slamming down another empty glass on the chrome counter.

'You're still being paid.'

'I know they want me out. You want me out,' he said, offering up an accusatory, yellow-eyed stare, the first time their eyes had met that evening, the drink Graham had bought for him left completely untouched.

'Well, er, that's what I've come to talk to you about. Afraid you're right. Daeng, Natasha and Von Eil don't want you around.'

'Don't want me around? Don't fucking want me around? So you've bled me dry, plundered my little black book of contacts, nicked my show,' he shouted, so loudly customers were turning away from the performance on stage to look at the commotion.

But as well as anger Graham saw the tears in Nigel's glassy eyes, eyes that were downcast, as though he didn't have the strength to fight, knew he was beaten, the wits that had got him so far finally failing him. The city, bloody Bangkok, like with scores in the past and surely many more in the future, taking everything he had.

'I'm sorry, Nige.'

'Sorry? You are fucking sorry?' he said, picking up the peace offering and drenching Graham with it, soaking his expensively acquired shirt as Daeng appeared right on cue.

Nigel didn't even have time to resume his rant as the Thai boy was on him, bulky muscles against skin and bone and it didn't take much to bundle him to the door. A small stand-off ensued at the exit but the traditional throat-cutting gesture was finally enough, the Englishman walking away from his life without a fight. Graham sensed with a shiver the knife the boy had put to his throat just a few nights ago wasn't too far away, that he'd have used it if necessary. The threat was enough. Poor Nige, like Graham, was completely aware of what the bar owners were capable of.

'You see him again, you tell me straight 'way,' said Daeng in his rapid-fire babble.

'You didn't have to do it like that. Don't you have any bloody feelings at all? He was a friend. A friend. Do you know what that even means?'

'He not my friend. You don't tell me what to do. I listen to Natasha and Mr Paul, so fuck you,' he said just a centimetre or two from Graham's face, vile chilli-tainted breath all over him.

'You know what, you used to scare me. But I don't care anymore. This bar's mine as much as it's yours. You won't get rid of me as easy as that. You might 'ave done at one point but I've wised up. I'm not going anywhere,' he said, stabbing a finger at the stool Nigel had been sitting at, now a yawning space. 'Tell that to your buddies.'

***

Padding through the two-bedroom apartment bought in his name – well he'd insisted but knew it was all probably meaningless anyway like his fifty per cent stake in the club – he opened the front door and grabbed the *Bangkok Post* from the mat. Passing back through the flat he grabbed a can of Diet Coke from the fridge, his usual breakfast, and took his traditional spot on the balcony. Slurping from the can, enjoying the cool chemical concoction in the heat, unfolding the paper, he dared to let out a sigh, hoping, as he often did, things would somehow get miraculously better, that he could slide into a groove of living that would allow him to just be, rather than the constant battle for survival. He looked out from the balcony, out into the blinding light but there were no answers, the slum directly below blunting his good mood, as did the luxury apartments looming way off in the distance towards the river where the likes of Von Eil resided in palatial splendour, their own bubbles hermetically sealed from Third World filth. Finally, looking down at the paper, it was the first thing he spotted, and as he read on it was another one of those all too common mornings where he wished he'd never got up.

'*Foreigner throws himself from Rama IX bridge*' was the headline, rereading it to himself numbly, desperately trying to compute the details.

'*Long-time Bangkok resident Nigel Monroe, 66, was found on the banks of the Chao Phraya river last night, after hurling himself off the Rama IX bridge, according to eyewitnesses…'*

'Jesus,' he said, shaking his head, banging a fist so hard on the railings he feared he'd broken a bone but he really didn't feel it, the pain was all in his head, unanswered questions shouting back at him in his crazed mind. Did he really go straight from the bar to the bridge? Wasn't it too neat the report had appeared in the *Post* the very next morning? Who were the supposed eyewitnesses? Was Daeng involved some-how? Natasha? Von Eil?

'Aargh,' he growled, animal-like, shaking with sobs, think-ing this place, Bangkok, had made him paranoid, the lies, the duplicity, familiar pain arcing through his body as he grabbed for the pills.

'Good morning, baby,' she said from the balcony door.

Her sudden appearance startled him. 'Is it?' he said, already swallowing back a Xanax, looking away from her grinning face and back out at the city, a city that despite everything always seemed to wear a smile on its face but those myriad smiles were beginning to look more and more sadistic.

'What you mean? Always a question with you.'

'It's Nigel,' he said, Natasha moving to his side, tangle of bird's nest hair like she'd slept the sleep of the dead, hand on his shoulder that felt freezing cold despite the relentless tropical heat.

'What the old man done now?'

'He killed himself apparently.'

'Suicide?'

'He threw himself off a bridge… apparently,' he said and while she may not have got the sarcasm, Natasha certainly

165

understood the gesture of a newspaper being thrown at her.

She scowled at him but it was if she knew better than to engage as Graham pushed past her and into the living room, the kitchen, rooting around in the fridge for a beer, anything to blot it out. As he took his first swig, he listened as the bedroom door clicked quietly shut.

***

'Dear boy, good to see you. Sad circumstances though,' said Smale, standing in the expansive doorway of his luxury apartment, as though it was the entrance to some English palace. 'Come in, come in.'

'Thanks,' Graham said, lifted by the vigorous pat on the back as he was guided over the threshold, the professor looking tanned, healthy and unruffled in tweed.

'Oh, you shouldn't have,' he said, grabbing the cheap bottle of wine Graham had been limply holding, leading him into a huge living room, patio doors running the length of one side.

'This is, er, very nice,' said Graham, shivering under the cold blast of the air conditioning, though cowed by the opulence, shelves groaning with books, *Dynasty*-style sheepskin rugs in abundance only hinting at something a little more racy and he felt scruffy amid the burnished perfection, awkward among the order, realising this was exactly how Smale wanted his, no doubt, regular young visitors to feel.

'G&Ts on the terrace?' said his host, throwing off his tweed jacket, even that seeming to land neatly on one of the gargantuan white leather sofas. 'I was told not to get white, damn nuisance if you spill any coke. That's cocaine, by the way, not the pop.'

'Too right.'

The gentle shade afforded by a patio umbrella, cool breeze wafting around them from the river far below should've made it the ultimate spot for Graham to just breathe as he sat down in a wicker armchair but he was jolted as just in the distance were the huge dimensions of the Rama IX bridge.

'You like the view?' Smale cried above the stiffening breeze, throwing an arm out to indicate the wonderful panorama, temples glinting in the light, river almost turned golden by the tropical sun. 'Best view in the city, apart from the one I saw last night haw, haw. Or whore, whore!'

'It's so fresh up here,' he said, but writhing his sweaty hands around under the table, thinking how Smale's insulated, gilded existence was another world away from what had been Nigel's sad little life and its awful bloody end.

'The view's good from down there too,' said the professor, pointing to the riverbank. 'Early evening you get the boys from the slums bathing, barely a stitch on.'

'Smale, I've come to talk about Nigel.'

'We need a drink first,' he said holding up a hand, punching a number into his mobile. 'Tong, be a love and bring drinks to the balcony… yes I've got a guest… No, no, boy, you fucking listen, I'm not asking, I'm telling.'

'Trouble in paradise?'

'No, gawd bless him, he's my house boy. Needs to learn how to take orders though,' Smale said, swiping around an imaginary cane as if on a miscreant's arse.

'House boy? You really have it all worked out.'

'He cooks, cleans, rolls over. What I say goes. I don't do relationships.'

'Hello there,' said Tong with a high-pitched whine, tray of

expertly iced and sliced drinks in his hands.

'Graham meet Tong.'

'Nice to meet you,' he said, shaking the bony hand on offer, skinny, hairless body advertising the fact he was barely eighteen, though the provocative hot pants and singlet combination spoke sickeningly of sexual maturity, like he was selling something and knew exactly what he was worth.

Graham was mesmerised by the pretty, boyish face marred only by hard eyes, hit by an unwanted flash of recognition as he'd seen that expression before – Natasha. What did that make him? The blokes in his local coming to mind again, their faces contorted in hate, the bile in his throat rising, gulping it back, silence swirling around them like the breeze.

'You okay, dear boy? You've gone so quiet, white as a ghost you are,' said Smale, patting Graham's knee as Tong slipped away.

'I don't think Nigel killed himself,' he said, swigging back his gin and tonic, trying desperately to focus, avoid having to talk about what he was really feeling, something he'd perfected.

'What? Graham, stop with the conspiracy theories. You saw the paper, plus Nigel, gawd bless 'im, was always liable to do something silly.'

'Silly? You call that bloody silly?'

'No, no, Graham, look, you know what I mean,' Smale said, placing a hand lightly back on his knee. 'I knew the old man a long time, a lot longer than you. He basically had nothing left. He should've gone back to England years ago but some people, I don't know, they figuratively miss the boat. By the time they realise, it's too late. They lose track of friends and family, sentimental thoughts of home are replaced by regret, guilt… fear. Withering away in the tropics alone is not a good place to be.'

'Is that meant to be some kind of warning?' Graham said as he drained his drink, staring out of Smale's ivory tower into the filthy river below, the little brown slum kids now in the water wriggling and splashing around but maybe looking up at the building and wondering, wishing.

'It's not a warning. You have a purpose, a business.'

'I was there last night when Daeng threw Nigel out of the club. It's too much of a coincidence.'

'Listen, love, remember when I talked about keeping a cool heart? That old Thai saying. If you want to survive here, you've got to turn a blind eye here and there.'

'A blind eye? A bloody blind eye to murder? I've done that once.'

'Quiet,' said Smale, bringing a finger to his lips. 'We don't know that and we may never know. And even if we did, then what? Are you going to march in there and take out Von Eil? Daeng? I loved Nigel as much as you but he wouldn't have wanted that. You've already got yourself tangled up with ze bloody Frenchman.'

'You 'eard. Word gets out fast in this place,' he said, clinking Nigel's raised glass, smiling for the first time that day, first time for too long.

'Aunty Smale's very proud of you but please be careful. You're playing with wild animals. Sometimes you've got to know when to stop.'

'So I just let this go? Am I that pathetic?'

'You're not pathetic, far from it. You chased your dreams. There's not always a fairy-tale ending or a fairy's end but you've got to choose your fights wisely. Stay and fight for what you've

169

got,' he said, suddenly reaching into his pocket, placing something on the table that glinted in the sun, nodding at it for him to pick up.

'What's this?' said Graham, taking the weighty slab of cold steel in his hands, pearl inlays either side, and pressing a raised button he ejected a long silver blade that flashed menacingly in the light.

'That, dear boy, is protection. An old family heirloom. Been to a world war and back. I've been meaning to give it to you. I won't need it where I'm going.'

'You're leaving?' he said, hurriedly placing the knife back onto the table, though unable to keep his eyes off it.

'We're here to talk about you. Now be a good lad, fold that up and put it in your pocket. As they say in the Boy Scouts, be prepared. I always like a good Boy Scout,' said Smale with a laugh.

'I want to fight. Believe me I'm ready,' he said, breathing out, taking the knife gingerly from the table, replacing the blade with a click, shakily slipping it into his pocket, it heavy against his thigh, wondering if Mike knew something he didn't.

'Well done. Remember the fight's about the club, Natasha. Everything else is superfluous. Here's to Nigel,' said Smale, raising a glass.

'To Nige' he said. 'Nat's asked me to meet her parents, by the way, like organising an audience with the Queen, so I'm getting somewhere. But what about you?'

'All in good time but Graham, look at this, look around you, I have means,' he said, whirling his tanned hands about. 'I can leave at the drop of a hat and set up anywhere. That's the difference, I'm not trapped.'

Chapter fourteen

Meet the parents

He was back at Natasha's, and the multi-million baht vision in gold leaf and chrome it'd become, space extended five-fold with surrounding shophouses colonised by the ever-growing empire. Where once they'd sold sex, they were now 'selling dreams', according to Von Eil and his marketing spiel. But sinking into the deep-pile carpet, Graham longed for the anonymity afforded by the gloom of the old, where his attire of shorts, crusty T-shirt and flip-flops reflected the sleaze on offer. Now uncomfortably suited and booted he arrived at the bar with barely a nod of recognition from the staff, most of the new employees hired by Natasha and Von Eil, professional performers lured from the show across town that the American had cannibalised, the performers of a different kind from the past long gone. Before it had been camp, bawdy, off the cuff, replaced by a slick money-making machine that he had little say in, though he was intent on bloody changing that. Whatever it took.

'Drink, Sir?' said one of the impeccably dressed, well-educated boys behind the bar, seemingly oblivious to who he was.

'Whisky, please. Double,' he said above the pop trash, at least some things never changed, but bereft at the fact there was no grizzled foreigner to his right or left, the place didn't attract lonely white men any more apart from the loneliest bleedin' one of all.

He should've felt comfortable sinking back into the well-upholstered leather-clad stool sipping his drink, watching the expectant crowd. It just wasn't him though, he thought, kicking the side of the expensively rendered bar, imagining star of the show, Natasha, backstage somewhere being feted by all and sundry, the Yank close at hand, her hand.

'Ladies and gentlemen, welcome to the greatest show on Earth…'

'For God's sake,' said Graham mumbling into his drink, looking crazy, unhinged, as Nigel's voice assailed him from the speakers, a voice from the dead.

The cast appeared on stage, Natasha at the centre, but they were just figures to him now as he was forced to turn away, looking out instead over the darkened auditorium.

'Good crowd tonight,' said a voice directly into his ear, the firm pat on his back forcing him to look up and into the face of his tormentor, Von Eil.

'What about Nigel?'

'You've always got to look at the flipside. Be fucking happy, man. Look at this place.'

'Don't you even give a shit? Didn't you hear Nigel doing the introduction?' said Graham, banging a finger into Von Eil's chest to emphasise every word he spat, body spasming, other hand caressing the cold steel of the knife that was always in his pocket now, imagining how good it'd feel to plunge it into the

Yank, maybe that would bloody enliven his constantly blank expression.

'I'll tell you what…' said Von Eil, grabbing his new business partner by the lapels, lifting Graham off his stool. 'I don't give a fuck. He was a wino, a loser. He didn't contribute anything. We can't afford passengers.'

'I hold you all responsible for Nigel. Even if none of you were there when he jumped. You won't get rid of me,' he said, slumping back as the American finally let go, the sweat sliding down his face.

'Look at the state of you. Just have another fucking drink,' said Von Eil, summoning the barman with a click of his fingers, stalking off.

It wasn't as though he could even go to the police regarding his suspicions about Nigel's death, Peeklong looming in his washing-machine mind, a world that was constantly spinning. He knew the police-general was far too cute to come to the club anymore given how conspicuous he'd look in the new surroundings but surely abreast of what was happening on a nightly basis, while being furnished with a very generous stipend to keep him sweet.

'Cheers, Nige,' he said, gesturing to the empty space beside him, the yawning person-shaped void, glad of the darkness, the darkness that hid the tears in his eyes, concealed the fact he'd just popped another happy pill, though that was a complete misnomer. 'I can't do this tonight, be here. It's like you never even existed, mate.'

Polishing off the drink he made sure to pass right in front of the stage on his way out, show still in full swing, hoping Natasha was witnessing his walking out as he knew she always felt it a personal sleight when people left in the middle of a performance. It was a feeling ingrained right since the early days when one walkout could make the difference between profit and loss, whether they could afford that month's rent or not.

In the car park again and past the gleaming coaches, he crunched over the site of Mark's death to the street, the grime a horrible contrast to the gleam of inside but more in keeping with the way he felt. A taxi drew up, like they typically did outside Natasha's now, cabbies knowing the drunks of old with barely enough money to get back to their flophouses had been replaced by whole families bound for luxury hotels, wallets bulging, heads full of wonder, wanting to make a difference to those worse off than them. To Graham, Natasha's, what it had become, was Eastern promise wrapped prettily for Western consumption, but he wished they could actually see the truth, behind the illusion, like he had.

'Where you go?' said the cabbie, having drawn up beside him and already thrown open the near-side door in anticipation of another decent tip.

'Soi Cowboy,' he said as he slid into the back, destination the street of tacky neon-lit, lean-to beer bars where Natasha's had taken its original cue from, the concept that had brought him back to Bangkok in the first place and of course where they'd been fatefully reunited, though it hadn't really been fate, he'd been damn well looking for it.

Getting out the cab, a barrage of catcalls from the desperate girls that circled the bars like vultures hit him but he was already such a veteran he managed to tune it out. He marched into his usual watering hole, as Chubby Bird would have termed it, a quieter, even more down at heel place than most of the rest. It didn't even have a name, adding to the feeling of transience. He sat down at the bar without being hassled, such a regular the girls knew his habits, that, unless he said otherwise, he was basically there to drink, more importantly that he didn't pay to be entertained.

'All right, mate,' said some chancer sitting at an adjacent stool. 'Where you from?'

'England,' he said, shaking an outstretched hand but looking away, sensing another foreigner desperate to have a conversation other than the childlike dialogue to be had with an uneducated Thai bar girl.

'Heaven, innit,' said his new neighbour.

'Heaven? This?' he said, wheeling around to look the man directly in the eye, fresher of face, the latest adventurer to have found paradise, he thought as he banged a fist down on a large cockroach crawling along the bar top, squishing the hard brown shell into an off-white pus, its spindly legs still jittering.

'It's not bad compared to back 'ome.'

'Let's see, my best mate's just been offed, I don't own me own bar and I've got an American business partner that likes little kids. But I'm in love,' he said, signalling for a drink, turning away again, not wanting to listen to a confessional about another man's naïve love for Thai whores – Nigel, Mark etc the names were interchangeable but their fates the same.

He listened as his neighbour scraped his stool back, saw him throw some notes on the bar out of the corner of his eye. By the time he'd turned fully, there was another empty space, a half full bottle of beer on the counter.

'You bad for business,' said the bar girl with a scowl, waggling the bottle of Chang at him.

175

'I don't bloody care,' he said, lighting a cigarette, having plundered his stash again, thoughts cascading through his brain, always needing another drink, having to get out of his head.

***

'Remember to *wai* [bow] to my father,' said Natasha.

'Yes, Madam, anything you say, Madam,' Graham said and they both laughed, an unusual but welcome sound in their household, feeling the love that he'd talked of in the bar to that complete bloody stranger bloom inside him again.

He knew this was a big deal for Nat, as family was everything in Thailand. The fact her dad had beaten her, thrown her out when he discovered she was a transsexual still seemed to be an open wound, he could sense that, even though they'd since kissed and made up. How could you forgive someone that? What did it do to you? In a typical irony around Thai morality, however, her parents owned a brothel so who were they to bloody judge? But still he felt honoured to have been asked by her to go along, though at the same time the shame gnawed at his insides, the fact they were a real couple. It was something he was determined to get over but he didn't know how.

'How do I look, Daddy?' she said, spinning around.

'Hot,' he said, eyes glued to the little black dress accentuating all her curves, certainly not 'mum and dad attire' but very Natasha, the lust flooding through him, chasing the negative thoughts away.

'*Pom rak khun* [I love you].'

The words breathed so quietly into his ear he wondered afterwards whether she'd actually said anything at all but he was happy to let the feeling linger, along with the warmth inside.

At that moment Graham looked out of the window and saw the myriad lights of the city blinking back, this city of angels and demons, which not merely co-existed but too often merged into one another in a baffling but exhilarating way.

'What you thinking?'

'I'm thinking I wish it could always be like this. I'm thinking despite Mark, despite Nigel…'

'Shush,' she said, snuggling up to him. 'I already told you about Mark. He was bastard. Nigel, look, I know he your friend but it wasn't me. He old man. He could've stayed forever. It wasn't my decision.'

'Decision? It was a bloody decision? By who?' he said, eyes blazing, grabbing her arm, in her face.

'Von Eil,' she said, tears rolling down her cheeks.

'So Von Eil did away with him?' he said, still holding her arm taut.

'Did away with…'

'Killed him, Nat. Did Von Eil kill Nigel?' he said, disengaging, head in hands.

'He choose,' she said.

'Bloody hell,' he croaked, rocking with sobs, her hands pawing all over him, lips nuzzling his ear and Graham didn't want to shake her off, needed her, wanted to feel safe from the nightmare just outside the window.

'Baby, you think too much,' she said, springing up, pouring him a drink.

'Think too much? Think too bloody much? How can you not! That damn Yank. Promise me you won't have anything to do with him. He's just a business partner. It's just bloody business,' he said, thumping the sofa, really pummelling it.

'I promise, Daddy,' said Natasha, grabbing his arms to finally still him, stroking his hair, taking him in with soft eyes.

'Not that I need any more worries but I'm worried about tonight,' he said, knocking back his drink, unable to get Von Eil out of his head, Nigel.

'Gray, just be. If you embarrassed by me, I'm going to be embarrassed by you.'

He sank back into the sofa, rolling her words around in his head and it all made perfect sense. He just needed to be. But he couldn't escape the concern of how they'd all look at the Marriott Hotel's swanky New York Steakhouse, recommended by a certain Von Eil, suspecting he'd already taken Natasha there on a number of occasions – he'd even booked the bloody table to ensure they got the 'best seats in the house'. Taking a swig of his drink, bitterness in his mouth, as well as in his heart, he was pissed off that every which way he seemingly turned there was a problem, normally with a six-foot tall American attached to it.

Still, he swallowed down the rest of his drink, along with his pride, something he'd become worryingly good at. Excusing himself to the bathroom before they left, Graham looked at the thinning hair straggly on his scalp, the bags under his eyes, the sports jacket that failed to hide his very unsporting paunch and he worried again about the forthcoming night, that him and Natasha would look exactly what they were – a transaction, one concluded in a sleazy bar. But he smiled at the fact Nat said she loved him, God that was a weird concept after his marriage.

'Come on, we're going to be late.'

'Making meself look beautiful,' he said to her playful giggles through the door.

***

The lights of the Marriott lobby were unforgiving and Graham felt all eyes were on them, calculating exactly what they were, computing how much it had cost him, an ugly sheen of sweat forming on his brow.

'Can I help you, Sir?' said a uniformed flunky approaching, ushering them to the side of the lobby, as if out of view, Natasha's heels clacking conspicuously on marble.

'We're here to meet friends.'

'Take a seat, please.'

'Friends?' said Natasha with a frown.

'I'm not going to say I'm meeting my future in-laws,' he said reddening, sitting on the sofa as directed but Graham was too tense to ease back into the luxurious leather, instead perched on the very edge, jumping as Natasha placed a hand on his knee.

'There they are,' she said.

'Pleased to meet you both,' said Graham, affording the little bow to her parents like he'd neurotically practised in the mirror.

'Good,' said Mr Chinawat, seemingly as economical with language as Natasha was non-stop, while his wife stood mute, immovable and hard as her helmet of hair, no doubt coiffured in one of the city's most expensive salons.

'Have you been here before?' said Graham, jaunty tone disguising fear, Chinawat's dumpy appearance failing to blunt the brothel owner's edgy aura, looking every inch the mafioso with his slicked back hair, shiny jacket and 'impress me' stare.

'No, we don't go to *farang* places.'

'*Poh* [Dad], it's very good. I been here many times,' said Natasha.

Von Eil may have termed them the best seats in the house, as they were led through the airy, brightly lit restaurant to their table, but for Graham they were the worst – sat right at the centre of things. Chinawat head of the table, mum and daughter to his left, Graham to his right in ridiculous wing-backed chairs perfectly suited for Bangkok's answer to Tony and Carmella Soprano, he thought. The ostentatiousness of the setting only underlined the poverty of their conversation, chemistry, as they sat in virtual silence.

'Drinks?' said a camp, pretty waiter.

'Four ice waters,' barked Chinawat.

'Four *iced* waters,' said the boy, turning smartly from the table.

Natasha was now deep in conversation with her mum, *so she did speak*, he thought, while Graham noticed Chinawat eyeing him like he was some animal in a zoo, unsure whether he was expected to perform or just remain dumb.

'So...' said the Thai man finally, flexing his shoulders in his jacket, continuing to fix his eyes, like two black marbles, on Graham. 'Do you like Thai lady?'

'I love your daughter,' he said but the old man waved a dismissive hand, as if to indicate what? That the two of them couldn't possibly love one another? Graham felt the tension coiling through his body, wanting to grab at the jowly neck, rip at that wrinkled throat. 'Yes, Mr Chinawat, I love her.'

'Gray...'

'No, Nat. Let me speak,' he said, feeling all eyes on him, even having the mum's attention as an expectant silence descended, taking a long swig of the iced water that had just arrived, palms slick with sweat despite the coolness of the restaurant's air conditioning. 'Natasha and I, we're together, a couple, we love one another. It's natural… as natural as you and your wife, Sir.'

'Yes, natural,' said Chinawat, throwing his head back in laughter, banging the table lightly with his hand, wife looking at the floor.

'It's about here,' said Graham, pounding at his chest, his heart, staring at Nat, her hand grabbing for his under the table, squeezing it tight, so tight he felt like it could be forever.

'Aha,' he said, waving that pudgy hand again, one discoloured with age, rheumy eye winking at him. 'You should come to my bar. Many lady there, beautiful Thai lady.'

'I'm not sure it's my thing.'

'One day a man… *farang*… came to my bar…' Chinawat said.

'Go on,' he said, heart reverberating in his chest, wanting to run but needing to hear, wondering if this mean bastard would make the decision for him, for both of them, holding even tighter to Nat's hand.

'He sat there getting drunker and drunker, redder and redder, then him, my son, very naughty boy…' he said trailing off, indicating Natasha, steely expression disintegrating into a frown.

'Yes?'

'Natasha… She… he was only about eleven at the time, just came and said 'hello' to the man and then ran off. Next time the man orders a drink, he says, 'How much is the boy?' I say, 'Finish your drink and we agree a price after.' He finishes his drink, I say '2,000 baht', he says 'okay', handing me the money and I direct him upstairs. My eldest son was waiting up there with a big surprise. A piece of broken piping. Beat his head

181

into a watermelon shake. Watch yourself.'

'We're going,' he said, forcing his chair back with a squeal, other diners turning around to look, Natasha on her feet too.

'I can't believe you. Do you hate me that much? I your own flesh and blood!' she screamed, launching the glass of water she'd been fussily cradling all over her old man, before turning away, collapsing into Graham.

'Come on, it's just the two of us now,' he said, placing the faintest but most loving of kisses on her cheek, wrapping his arms around that slender waist as they walked out of her parents' life.

Chapter fifteen

Knife crime

Natasha was sick, had come down with something after the chilling meeting with her dad. Graham had agreed to do the 'meet and greet' at the cabaret in her place, which amounted to nothing more than standing on the door with a supercilious grin on his face as the jolly wives and their supposedly grumbling husbands brought up the rear like they'd been dragged along, like he'd done once. But so often he noticed a hungry look in the men's eyes when confronted with the pneumatic optical illusions in front of them, though guests barely made eye contact with him, a contrast to the cabaret's colourful creations in his drab suit, nervy hands desperately craving a drink. As the last of them were shepherded in like passengers on an imminently departing cruise ship, all silly smiles and strong drinks, he headed for his perch in front of the bar, where a besuited boy, at last seeming to twig who he was, got him his usual. A new intro – recorded by Smale, who'd once had theatrical pretensions, unsurprisingly – began to boom out, still promising 'the greatest show on Earth', completing the ruthless airbrushing of Nigel from the club's history. Another of Bangkok's characters gone and forgotten, thought Graham, chewing at nails that had become just a pulpy mush.

Taking his first swig of the day, always the best one, he worried about Nat back home, knew she'd been in no mood to turn up, in fact he'd encouraged her non-appearance. Her bloody dad was an arsehole and her tears after had flowed like the Chao Phraya but they'd never felt closer. The way she'd whispered into his ear that she loved him was the best thing anyone had ever said to him, something he needed to hear after existing so long in what he thought was a loveless world. No, she deserved a duvet day but even as he smiled to himself, there was a nagging in his head, the nagging that never seemed to go away.

'Have you seen Von Eil?' he said to the barman over the opening strains of Britney's 'Hit Me Baby One More Time'.

'Mr Paul not here,' said the boy, waving a hand dismissively in the air.

'I know that but is he not coming tonight?' Graham said with a sigh, nagging in his head getting that little bit louder.

'I don't think so, Sir.'

He scrutinised the little area of seats in front of the stage reserved for directors and their admirers but the bulky silhouette of the Yank was conspicuously absent. Ordering another drink, Graham told the barman he was going for a walk and would be back shortly, careful to slink away as the first performance of the night began, away from the alert eyes of Daeng, acting on a hunch, feeling it in his gut, knowing instinctively he was right. And he wished he'd acted on such feelings more often, though at least Bangkok was teaching him that, to trust his instincts, as he stepped outside and immediately flagged down a passing taxi. His phone began to ring as the cab pulled away, seeing from caller ID it was Daeng, like Natasha's eyes and ears when she was otherwise engaged, presumably wondering why he wasn't at his station in the club, the Thai already onto him.

'Shit,' he said as the phone continued to ring, the cabbie looking at him eyebrows raised in the rear-view mirror in that judgmental Thai way, like he was some foreigner jilting a Bangkokian lover, no clue it was usually the other way bloody round. Amazing Thailand, eh?

'Okay, man?'

'Just drive.'

Pulling up outside their apartment building, his and Natasha's, a sleek black Merc came darting out of the car park at speed, tinted windows masking the driver but the EVIL number plate made the camouflage redundant, causing Graham to punch the back of the seat, the fact he'd been damn right all along. Hurriedly shoving money at the driver, not waiting for his change, he sprinted into the block, past the security guard probably sniggering behind his trashy newspaper, well aware of what was going on, delighting in watching another foreigner's life unravel no bloody doubt.

He ripped open the door but she was already in the hallway as if to fend him off, like she'd been forewarned of his imminent arrival.

'He was here… why the bloody hell was he here?' Graham said, a couple of inches from her now.

'Who?'

'I saw the bloody Merc!' he shouted, nose to nose, spittle flecking the front of what looked like her hastily rearranged

185

bathrobe.

'I sick, darling. He came to see how I am. I didn't wanna tell you as I know you be mad.'

'Sick? You're sick in the head, yeah. You liar,' he said, accusation reverberating menacingly around the claustrophobic hallway, bursting into the living room, needing to get her out of his sight before he did something with those tightly coiled hands, so tight they ached.

But she stuck her pretty little head into his face. 'You crazy *farang*. Why you shout? Why you say stuff like this?'

'Yeah, of course I'm the crazy one. It's always *farang* this, *farang* that. I want you gone. Pack your stuff and go. Last night you told me you love me and now this? Now bloody this?' he said, having to turn away, looking out of the window, overheating with the blood coursing around his body, heart banging in his chest, but the tinkle of knives ringing from the kitchen drawer made his whole body tense, guts twist, legs throb in readiness to run.

'I'm not going,' she said, manically waving a machete under his nose.

'Natasha, what the hell...' he said, silvery glint of the blade almost blinding him but brushing past her, arms raised in surrender, breathlessly entering the bedroom, hyperventilating, pulling out the large holdall he'd packaged his whole life in when he moved to Bangkok, throwing items in as fast as he could, grabbing them from the shelves with shaky, slippery hands.

Wrestling with the zip, sweat coursing from his brow, all senses on alert he heard her rattling about in the kitchen drawer again no doubt replacing the machete as if nothing had happened. For her, if it was out of sight, it was out of mind it seemed, like her unfaithfulness. He couldn't pretend anymore though and lugged his bag into the hallway where she was stood sobbing, the great little actress.

'What about how I stood up to your dad and his bloody homophobia. I told him that me and you are just like the pair of them, that we're a couple. Do you know the hell I've been through to be able to do that, accept myself and what I am and this is how you treat me?' he said, eyes clouded by tears, shakes spasming through his body and as Graham barged out of the bedroom he looked into her eyes as if for an answer but they appeared chillingly blank. Like what? She didn't care? Was in shock? Just what the hell was she playing at? He thought he was getting to know her but she was a complete stranger.

'I not care. You don't shout at me. You don't understand me.'

'Understand you? No, I don't. I'm bloody sick of your lies. Your bullshit lies. That's all you're good at,' he said, slinging his bag down in the hallway, backing her up against the wall. 'I'm not scared anymore. Do what you want. You might think you got everything you ever wanted now but I ain't losing this, Natasha, any of it. Half of it's mine. The flat, the club. You remember that when you're shagging Paul bloody Von Eil.'

'Gray, listen, I'm…'

'Not sorry again. I can't listen to it. But I'm not gonna give this up. I've already given up everything to get here. You better work out how this turns out because Natasha's is fifty per cent mine,' he said, watching as she slid down the wall, her awful wailing still in his ears as he headed out the door.

'Taxi?' said the guard in the lobby.

'Please,' he replied, managing a sheepish smile.

'You okay? I heard noise... shouting.'

'I'm fine, just fine,' he said, pumping a fist, not having realised he was a fighter but now he had something to fight for, the apartment, the club, the fact he was making a life rather than just existing, at last he was actually feeling something.

'Where you go?' said a cabbie through the open window.

'Paradise,' he said, thinking it couldn't be much further from the truth as he slid into the back seat with his bag, imagining Natasha looking down and wondering where he was headed, though did she even bloody care?

He still owned half the club, the bloody apartment but questions were racing through his head as frequent and blinding as the stream of headlights passing them in the opposite direction on the forever frenetic Bangkok roads. Christ, thought Graham, her and Daeng had been difficult from the off but throw in Peeklong and Von Eil too and it was understandable where he was.

How fitting as they pulled up outside the Paradise that he was back down in the dirt, the dilapidated, brutalist breezeblock square of a building with its attendant prostitutes loitering expectantly outside symbolising his descent. The Yank and his gilded life popped into his head, the fact he seemed able to rise above it all, an insulated existence with access to tender young flesh and Graham kicked out at the door of the cab, knowing he had to do something.

'Why you hit my cab?'

'Sorry, I'm a *ting tong farang* [crazy foreigner],' he said, handing the driver a placatory tip as he got out.

'How long you stay?' said the hotel receptionist.

'I'll be here at least a month,' he replied, grimacing as he looked around at the various transactions going on in the lobby, the very human transactions usually involving old white men and young Thais.

After dropping the bag in his room, he hastily headed back to the street and hailed another taxi, not yet done for the evening, not by a long way.

'Ban Chao Phraya,' he said, prompting an odd look from Mr Taxi, along the lines of, 'What business does a scruff like you have at one of the city's most luxurious apartment complexes?'

And they were luxurious, Graham had heard, home to a crown prince, along with the city's more colourful, ie corrupt, politicians, while Smale's finely appointed ivory tower was just next door.

'I've come to see Von Eil,' he said to the guard in the palatial lobby, who waved Graham through after giving him a brief onceover with sleepy eyes.

He rounded a corner from the reception desk, cheap trainers squeaking disconcertingly on marble but relieved to be out of the guard's eyeline as he entered a stairwell and began to jog down, faster and faster, finally reaching a door at the bottom. He exited into a brilliantly lit underground car park smelling vaguely of petrol and emitting an electric hum. Looking frantically around, the place littered with virtually identical gleaming, expensively imported cars, in a far corner he spotted the black Merc, sparkling in the brightness. 'Evil,' he mumbled under his breath as he read the number plate back to himself.

Graham thrust a hand in his pocket, prepared as Smale had advised him, the pearl handle welcome in his fist. And as his shadow loomed over the shiny piece of German engineering he ejected the flick knife, plunging it into one of the fat black tyres with a satisfying whoosh, repeating the action again and again and again, the car not sitting so elegantly on the tarmac once he'd finished. Leaning heavily on the bonnet with his blade he jumped as the vehicle's alarm sounded claxon-like, booming in his ears but he wasn't bloody done, grinning manically as he scratched off the paintwork in great screeching, whirling flakes. Stepping back to inspect his handiwork, he laughed at the 'SCUM' scrawled across the front of the once pristine motor.

He about-turned and headed to the stairwell amid another burst of the alarm, then fast approaching engine noise and headlights, a car speeding down the ramp towards him. The driver slowed, winding down his window, possibly seeing the Merc's flashing lights, hearing the beeps, Graham knowing he would have to stop. A place as civilised as this probably meant people were expected to pass the time of day, maintain the illusion, he thought, luckily having managed to fold the knife into his trembling fist.

'Okay?' the Thai asked, nodding towards the Merc in the far corner.

'Bloody car alarms,' said Graham shrugging, looking at the older man, the luxuriant hair speaking of money as did the Porsche, all one and the bloody same.

But satisfied, the Thai nodded again, gave a terse smile and drove off. Engine noise gratefully receding in his ears as Graham reached the confines of the stairwell, taking the steps two at a time. The security guard in the lobby was face down on his desk as he squeaked back across the marble and out the front door. He breathed in great greedy lungfuls of air as he stood doubled up on the pavement outside.

'Who's the freaking loser now?' he said, convulsing into laughter, imagining the look on the Yank's face.

Chapter sixteen

Deadly low

Sitting on a lumpy bed back in the Paradise, the half-satisfied yelps of cheap sexual encounters reverberating through the paper-thin walls, Graham was trembling, new box of Xanax unopened next to him, though he'd been popping them like Smarties. It didn't make any difference to the sleepless nights, the shaky red-eyed days, he thought, checking his phone for the umpteenth time but there was what seemed like an ominous silence from Natasha and Von Eil since the car incident a couple of nights before. He'd fought back but who was he really fighting?

The jarringly loud knocking at the door meant his fretting was the last rational thought in his mind, a mind shattered into shards of different scenarios zig-zagging through his head but tinged a funereal black, like there was no way out of what-ever came next. Despite his legs feeling leaden, he somehow managed to get up, looked out the window, peered into the darkness of the car park hoping it would give him a clue as to who was at the door, the knocking becoming ever more insist-ent, aggressive, so forceful it was bowing inwards.

'Okay, okay,' he shouted, hearing splintering wood, not having a choice.

The commotion was replaced by rapid-fire voices in the corridor, finally descending to a low mumble. He fumbled with the lock and opened the door, which hung limply on its hinges after the battering, a suited Von Eil filling the whole frame, eyes searing into him. Just visible behind his menacing bulk was the bloody Freak, Ronnie, so tall he was almost touching the ceiling. And Graham stifled a nervous laugh as he looked at the Frenchman's protruding Gallic beak that was now twisted roughly to the right after their little contretemps amid the antiques and fancy paintings. Then as now his hair was scraped back so harshly it made the pale skin on his face appear frighteningly taut like he was some kind of ghoul. They ambled into the room, Ronnie in the role of Von Eil's goon, roughly locking the door behind him, what was left of it.

'*Bonjour*,' said the Frenchman, casually stifling a yawn. 'I should 'ave finished you off when I had the chance. Even your little Em flew back into her cage. You know, two nights ago she begged me to come back.'

'You bloody pigs. Do whatever you want with me but please, leave her be,' he said, having trouble keeping jittery arms by his sides, wanting to dig into his pocket for the knife, lash out but knowing he'd get whatever back treble because how could he be prepared for this?

'She got reacquainted with a nice fiftysomething gentleman. Slapped 'er around a bit. But she loves zit...'

'You arsehole,' he said, lunging at Ronnie but he was too quick for Graham this time, grabbing the offending arm, twisting it behind his back so hard the pain burned through him.

'I'm not gonna waste my breath on you this time. It's the boss's turn,' said Ronnie, letting Graham's arm drop, turning to Von Eil

'I think that's what they call in your parlance a cunt's trick,' said the American quietly, pushing him onto the bed.

'What... what do you mean?'

The Yank, towering over him, eyes an unremitting blank, laughed and laughed, the loud bellicose sound filling the room, Ronnie joining in but it seemed totally forced, almost comical coming from someone that always looked so serious, someone said to stamp on kittens for fun.

'I mean what you did to my fricking car. Not to mention getting involved in my business at the Lantern. Letting my girls off the leash. Who do you think you are!' he screamed, face flushed burning red.

'Like what you did to my bloody girlfriend, you mean.'

'Your so-called girlfriend asked for it,' said Von Eil, hauling him up by his collar.

'Piss off,' he spat, trying to wriggle free but caught in the stronger man's grip, the two face to face, Graham tasting the bitter, cigar-tainted breath.

'Let's cut the crap. No one fucks with me. Got it?'

Silence... time expanding, space contracting.

'Get what? What I don't get is what you were doing with Natasha.'

'As I said, she fucking asked for it. But this is non-negotiable. You don't fuck with me,' he said again, letting go.

Graham slumped backwards only to be grabbed by the arm with such ferocity he yelped as he was pulled to his feet and dragged to the door.

'You bloody Yanks are all the same. Everything's a commodity. With Nat you'll just use her up, then spit 'er out. The club is the same, a new plaything to you. See we're different. I loved Nat, I love my club. It's worth fighting for.'

'How very noble, loser. The difference between me and you is I always get what I want.'

'Cos you buy it all, you tosser.'

'Fuck you,' he said with a shrug, pulling Graham to him with such force it sent the top two buttons of his shirt flying off, cascading onto the floor.

'You don't scare me. What's left for me to be scared of? Is this how it ended for Nige?' said Graham, the two eyeball to eyeball again, American panting with the effort, something unreadable passing across those usually blank eyes.

'Ronnie, shape the fuck up. We're going,' said Von Eil.

Graham listened to the door being unlocked, like it was all part of some plan, wrestling with the American despite his body being riven by shakes. Short, shallow breaths sounded desperate in his ears, heart thudding against his chest, sweat coursing down his forehead but he was determined to not leave the room, thinking if he could just stay put then no harm would come to him, fearing what could happen if he was dragged off into the dark recesses of the sprawling city. But Ronnie had other ideas, ripping at his other arm as he was dragged roughly to the lift, too cowed even to shout.

Out in the car park he was hauled not to the offending Merc – probably in the repair shop, he thought still managing a smirk – but to a dusty 4X4 that Graham guessed Von Eil used for his dirty work, number plate EVIL2, like he'd finally found a sense of humour. Ronnie manhandled him through the passenger-side door and shoved him across the bench seat so he would be wedged in the middle, Von Eil at the wheel. Trance filled the cabin with its thudding beat, musical choice at odds with the driver's persona but then Graham supposed he lurked in too many bars and clubs for it not to rub off, reminding him of the crap that was playing at the Lantern, Em and her fate springing chillingly to mind again.

The music so loud it made conversation impossible, not that Von Eil or Ronnie were great conversationalists as they sped along in silence, even lighting up cigarettes virtually on cue as if coordinated. His teeth chattered in the icy cold air conditioning, sweat soaked clothes hanging limp and he gripped the seat so hard it hurt, rough vinyl against his hands like he was hanging on, simply hanging on. The Frenchman rolled down a window, Graham gratefully gulping in the soupy air as the streets of the labyrinthine city flashed by. It was a part of the huge urban sprawl he didn't know, bleak and deserted compared with the colour and vibrancy of central Bangkok, and it felt hostile, alien, like the mood in the truck. Still the beat pounded, still they smoked, still they drove…

The gargantuan stabilising cables shot up into the night sky on either side as they reached Rama IX bridge, the six-lane carriageway eerily devoid of cars, while there was darkness beyond the tonnes of concrete and metal, just inky darkness. Graham had only ever viewed it warily from a distance, the majestic structure that was named after a king. The truck perceptibly slowed as they got halfway across, stopped, his trembling now uncontrollable, chattering teeth audible as the music was silenced, finally 100 per cent certain of Nigel's fate and realising his.

196

'You don't fuck with me. I fuck back,' said Von Eil as he turned to face Graham with those dead eyes, wrenching him from the vehicle.

He tried to say something to save himself but it was hard to form words in his desert dry mouth, staccato mutterings frittering away on the fierce wind, the breeze swirling in his face, taking his breath away. Ronnie was at the other arm now and they shoved him against a protruding steel railing at the edge of the bridge, forcing the remaining air out of his lungs like an explosive punch to the stomach, head pounding, he retched, like all was bloody lost, like they weren't going to stop. Graham used the last remaining shred of energy to twist his head out of their grip, staring into both men's faces, pleading with his eyes but with a sickening snap he was bent double over the fence, making out the river 150-feet down, sheer drop where the concrete and steel simply ran out, the water's dingy brown such a long way below.

'Nice view, look,' shouted Von Eil into his ear, forcing Graham's head further down.

Then letting go of the back of his neck, the American transferred a large hand to one of his legs, Ronnie simultaneously grabbed the other and in one swift movement he was manoeuvred over the railings, the blood rushing to his head, the vileness of his bowels erupting, wind smashing into his face, thoughts screaming in his mind. Above the breeze he made out the swish of a car's tyres but knew it couldn't save him as he dangled there, eyes wide to what was below, and then what he thought was a shout from Von Eil but as he listened harder it wasn't that at all, it was laughter, mocking bloody laughter. Was this damn well it?

Chapter seventeen

Bangkok's burning

He felt his laces being undone, shaking violently as one shoe then the second was ripped off, both spiralling down and down where he watched captivated as white spume splashed up out of the darkness as they hit the river and then disappeared, gone without a trace. Spinning desperately around in the pitch black, first one way, then the other, Graham was enveloped in a gloom he felt he might never emerge from.

'You could be just another suicide, another Bangkok casualty,' Von Eil shouted down to him.

'Like Nigel,' he croaked, craning his neck, desperate to catch his tormentor's eye again, a final chance, he thought, to change the course of what was about to happen, head screaming at what a fool he'd been picking a fight with the two biggest bullies in town but he hadn't been ready to just give up.

The Yank was looking directly over the railings at him but his eyes never registered a thing and he knew it was hopeless, even through his dizzy, befuddled mind, vomiting the remains of his stomach, pain jolting through him like an electric charge from his head to the tips of his toes. Graham sensed their grip loosening, body totally wired into any slight variation in the pressure applied, as they began swinging him from side to side like a pendulum. He wasn't sure how long he was hanging there as a numb kind of serenity came over him, like an acceptance of his fate, not able to fight or flee. And it wasn't the cliché of a life flashing before his eyes but regret – the regret of the mad gamble that had disastrously failed, though some small part of him was proud he'd chosen the path he had, having lived more life in the last year or so than in the preceding forty. He had started to be true to himself, as Smale so bluntly put it with the tough love he'd needed, had begun to thrive.

'The only reason you didn't get a beating, we didn't let go… Natasha pleaded with me not to,' said Von Eil, having finally pulled him trembling and soiled back over the railings.

'Natasha…' he said breathlessly, dry heaving, having to turn away from the American's forensic stare, looking back out into the darkness, wondering, disbelieving at what the hell could be coming next.

'Shitting your pants will be the least of your worries next time, believe me,' said Von Eil turning away to light a cigarette, Ronnie already back at the pick-up, like they had somewhere more important to be.

'There's nothing left of me to take. Look at what you've done. Just look at what you've bloody done,' said Graham panting as he sank to the floor, crumpling to the asphalt, punching the concrete, knuckles grazed and bleeding.

'Make your own way home from here, I don't give rides to losers,' said the Yank as he jumped into the truck, the Freak smirking from the passenger seat, as if they'd won.

'Dunno about Ronnie Reagan, more like Ronald McDonald.

You're both bloody clowns,' he shouted after them, using up the remaining air he had left in his lungs.

'Loser,' mouthed Von Eil, gunning the engine, the Frenchman sticking up a middle finger as they pulled away.

'It's not over,' said Graham, struggling back to his feet, touching the knife in his pocket that somehow hadn't come dislodged, watching as EVIL2 receded back into the darkness. 'Whatever it takes, Nige. Whatever it takes.'

**

It was late at night but still the cars came as he walked on, the city of never-ending rivers of traffic. From his vantage point he saw a blur of red taillights going in one direction, bright white headlights in the other – perpetual motion but Graham was shuffling along shoeless, violated. Some cars slowed on seeing him but when illuminated in their headlights as a white ghost no one stopped, regarding him with what seemed the Thai default setting outside the cosy tourist enclaves – studied indifference or, on occasion, downright hostility. If it'd been a Thai at the side of the road in obvious need of help he guessed it may have been 'little brother' this or 'uncle' that but he knew he stood no chance, another foreign scumbag, *loser*, as Von Eil had put it. He carried on because he wouldn't be beaten but felt the burning weight on his shoulders, the familiar sting of tears in his eyes.

As he continued putting one foot tentatively in front of the other, not taking long for the roughness of the Bangkok pavement to shred his socks, invasive swish of traffic in his ears, Graham remembered the naïve love for the city on his first visit, feeling a sense of rage at how far he'd been taken in.

Then he'd marvelled at the sense of nationalism, togetherness that saw people rise for the king before every cinema screening, the hordes standing to attention at 6pm every night for their monarch but now he knew for a bulk of the population it was a lie, that one half despised the other. A nation divided, ideology signified by what colour shirt people wore said it all really.

And in the grey light of morning he was fixated by a red orange glow in the distance, not the tropical sun for that was usually shrouded in smog, but an inferno, as if something had stirred, the hatred exploding between the red and yellow shirts – the former supporting nouveau riche ex-prime minister Thaksin, the latter traditionalists who proffered undying love for the king. Thoughts swirled in his head, an ache as though his skull was cracking, matched by a cacophony of police sirens, the clattering of helicopters above as if the very city was facing its denouement, the day where everything was falling apart.

'Bastard, that American bastard,' he repeated to himself like a mantra, winding himself up, keeping going, despite blundering along in his own shit.

'*Farang*! Hey you! *Farang*.'

The shout pierced his thoughts and he turned to face his accuser for the way it was being said, *was always said*, like he was guilty of something. The chubby cop's face protruded out of the window of the police car beside him, red light flashing on top like he was Bangkok's most wanted. Bloody typical, Graham thought, they had accosted the innocent party, wondering if Von Eil had put in a call to round him up, complete his humiliation.

'What?' he said through parched lips, knowing by the policeman's sceptical expression, the way he eyed his shit-stained trousers, he'd receive no sympathy.

'Get in car,' he said, directing Graham to the back seat with a nod of his fat head.

The cop unleashed a grating cough as soon as he got in, opened all the windows, black, beady eyes viewing him suspiciously in the rear-view mirror. Graham looked away, writhing his hands that had become sore with fiddling, biting his filthy nails, rocking back and forth, needing to be outside, in the park, or on a beach, anywhere but there. They drove through a seemingly endless parade of streets, brittle light of early morning having caught up with his night and lending it all a grimy sheen, offering no prick of recognition, no comfort.

The police station was small, box like, harshly lit throughout as if to compensate for the fact there were no windows. The officer led him through to the back of the otherwise empty station, into a small ante room lit by a bare bulb, a plastic water butt in one corner filled to the brim, a ladle on top.

'Wash,' said the policeman, nodding to a prison-type boiler suit hanging off a wire hanger on the far wall, a starched white towel – what looked like the only clean thing in the room – draped over it.

As soon as the officer left, he discarded his clothes leaving them in a shameful bundle on the floor, ladled water all over his body in a frenzy as if to cleanse himself both mentally and physically, tears mixing with the run-off as it sloshed down the blackened drain, dirt finally coming from his feet to reveal the bloody cuts, raw, open wounds as tender as he felt. He fanatically scrubbed and scrubbed, only halting when there was a heavy knock on the door.

Graham quickly dried himself, put on the boiler suit, which

felt scratchy and cheap against his skin, slipped on a pair of flip-flops that had been left by the door as if they'd been waiting for him. Exiting the shower room he stumbled along on unsteady legs. The policeman was sat behind a desk, head lolling like he'd just woken up and he only just about had the wherewithal to nod him towards another door.

He entered another windowless cell, what looked like an interview room, strip lights in the ceiling forensically illuminating his every pore, a table and two cheap plastic chairs in the middle facing one another and on one of those chairs, epaulettes glinting in the brightness, Police-General Peeklong. He motioned with a hand for Graham to sit, sunglasses firmly in place like some tinpot dictator.

'The red shirts… they've burned down Central World department store. Bangkok's burning and you! You!' the officer shouted, sweat springing to his brow in the airless room, rapid-fire words making Graham jump, taking all his effort just to sit still.

'I…'

'Don't speak,' he said, whipping the stubby revolver from its holster.

He felt the cold metal of the muzzle against his temple, a sickening click reverberated through his head, rattling around in his frazzled brain as Peeklong pulled the trigger, hugging a body ruined by spasms, second near-death experience of the day. 'You bastard. I'm not letting you win. What more can you do?'

'You'd be surprised what we can do to *farang* like you. I've spoken to Mr Paul, Ronnie, this is your last chance. It can get worse, a lot worse.'

Chapter eighteen

'What a bloody city'

'Amazing Thailand,' said the taxi driver, mimicking the seemingly catch-all tourist board slogan.

'Yeah,' he said, manically chewing at red raw nails but allowing the hint of a smile, still kicking after his near-death experience on the bridge.

'Where you from, mister…'

Not wanting to engage with the familiar banter, he looked out the window, the city its usual dizzying whirl of concrete and movement as far as the eye could see. But there was something else now, Graham felt a tension in the air so electric it virtually crackled. Yesterday's skirmishes having escalated to the inferno he'd witnessed, razing part of the city's most exclusive shopping district, protesters gunned down in a hail of bullets. The playground spat had turned into a bloodbath, yet he was travelling far away from the slaughter of downtown, state sponsored murder outside the likes of Dolce & Gabbana and just yards from a Buddhist shrine, for he was headed to Smale's riverside apartment. His friend had mentioned 'the bloody charade' on the phone, belittling a conflict claiming dozens of lives, seemingly unaffected as ever but Graham thought that probably summed up the feelings of the expat community, as long as it didn't affect their comfortable existence then it was business as usual, not that he was a part of it.

'Dear boy, come in, come in,' Smale said at the door of his palatial apartment, though the usually ebullient voice at least an octave or two lower, normally perma-tanned features an odd ashen colour, even the regulation cravat seemingly askew.

His gaze focused not on Graham but on a huge TV dominating one wall. Even though the sound was turned down low it was the carnage unfolding on the screen that gripped him too, streets he recognised, the gunfire crack crack-ing through the Bangkok air.

'What's happening?'

'Army are moving in. Red shirts have been given a deadline to leave,' Smale said, the screen turned an inky black by smoke, military calls for surrender chillingly audible, sirens still sounding their hysterical lament in the background.

But as Graham turned from the screen, he looked out the window and all he saw was the relative calm of the Chao Phraya river glinting a majestic gold in the afternoon sun like nothing could possibly touch them, though the Rama IX bridge loomed menacingly in the distance. Returning his gaze to the room he suddenly noticed the place was conspicuously empty, having been distracted by the TV when he'd first arrived. It had always been somewhat minimalist but gone were Smale's precious artefacts, mementoes of many adventures, what looked like packing cases neatly lined up against one wall. Where was the houseboy with the requisite G&T?

'You moving?' he said, nodding at the boxes.

'Ah,' said Smale, finally turning from the screen. 'Yes, Sherlock, I'm leaving.'

'Leaving?'

'Listen, forgive my rudeness,' he said, muting the TV. 'I've sent the boy home, upcountry, too dangerous here. So you'll have to make do with one of my concoctions. We drink, then we talk. You really need to tell me what happened, Graham, you know you look…'

'I know,' he said, avoiding Smale's piercing stare, looking out the window again where angry flames appeared like a gash on a once pristine horizon, Bangkok burning.

'For fuck sake,' said Smale, letting out a sigh as he came back into the room with the regulation G&Ts, closing the blinds with a snap, shutting it all out.

'So you're leaving Thailand?'

'No, we need to talk about you first. We need to sort this. Aunty Smale wants to know you'll be okay. You've invested everything in this. Everything.'

'They, er, Von Eil and 'is bloody henchman…'

'They what?'

'I thought they were gonna kill me,' he said, having to place his glass down on the immaculate coffee table as his hands were shaking so badly, again averting his eyes from another questioning gaze.

'Oh, Graham,' said Smale, edging closer, putting a consoling hand on his arm.

'I really thought that was going be it. But I'm not letting that Yank arsehole win, there's no bloody way. Even if I lose Nat, I'm not giving up the club.'

'But what on earth happened?'

'They hung me over the bridge. The Rama IX bridge. The same bridge they chucked Nigel off,' he said, slamming his drink down, running to the toilet, scrambling into the gargantuan marbled bathroom, bent over the bowl, vomit cascading from his knotted stomach, the shivers running up and down his back, sweat coating his forehead.

'You okay in there?' said a voice softly through the door.

'No, hang on a minute,' he said, getting to his feet, splashing his face with cold water, luxuriating in the coolness but whatever he did Graham couldn't get the images of last night out of his head and he wanted to make someone pay, he wasn't running anymore, what was the point?

'Come on now,' said Smale as he came out the bathroom, guiding him back to the sofa like he was an old man.

'Sorry, I'm still so shook up.'

'Nonsense, nonsense. Shook up? They bloody tried to kill you, you silly sod. Anybody else would've run for the hills by now.'

'What are my options?' he said, sitting back down, shakily taking the box of Xanax out of his pocket, popping another pill.

'You need to give that rubbish up for a start. That's not making you better.'

'It makes me numb sometimes. Which is better than feeling. This feeling.'

'Listen, you came here because you wanted to feel something. Now I'm not saying you should stay but if you do, you need to think about that.'

'I think of England and all I remember is greyness. And the cold. That bed was so bloody cold.'

'Wasn't just the bed, eh? As for options, well you either stay and try to patch it up with Natasha or you take a seat next to me on the first flight out.'

'I kind of know it, I just need to hear it…'

'Fuck it,' said Smale. 'You got no claim in Thai law on any assets as she has a majority stake in the business, she occupies *your* apartment and I doubt any of the papers you've signed legally stand up. She's also best friends with a police-general and a psychotic American with an even scarier French sidekick.'

'Right.'

'If I were you, I'd get on that first flight out. If you want to live that is. That's Aunty Smale's advice, for what it's worth,' he said, swirling ice cubes around in his empty glass. 'Refill?'

'Yes, please,' he said, looking around the room as Smale poured, taking in the grandeur, imagining Von Eil the bloody Second in a nearby apartment laughing his head off at his fate, probably shagging Nat on a sheepskin rug, biting down onto his tongue, not wanting to think anymore.

'Here you go, it's a strong one,' said the professor with a wink.

'I know all you're saying is true but I can't go back to England with nothing. I've got to at least fight for what's mine. As you say, I've sunk everything I have into this.'

'You go, girl,' said Smale smiling. 'You're a brave man. Don't let anyone tell you different. And how about your trip to Cambodia? Phnom Penh's great this time of year. Lovely wildlife, if you know what I mean. You got Vincent's number I sent? He's a love, the archetypal laidback Canadian.'

'Beats a highly strung American or the French Freak. It's a visa run but I need to get away for a bit, thought I'd tack on Phnom Penh. Vincent took a while getting back but yeah, we're gonna meet. He said he'd show me the sights.'

'Oh and what sights. Enjoy. Do send him my love. He's still bashing away at the old *Phnom Penh Post*. Be careful though. You think Bangkok's wild, you ain't seen nothing yet. Don't do anything I would do'

'You mean anyone? But, Mike, seriously, what about you though?'

'World's my lobster, as they say. Don't worry I'm not going just yet. I want to hear all about your travels on your return.'

'I won't spare you the gory details,' he said, clinking Smale's glass.

'Talking of gory details, I've been a complete fool. Oh, you know, I never believe all this 'land of smiles' bullshit but I thought money, my standing, *my fucking standing* haha, insulated me from all this,' he said, viciously pulling up the blind, rapping on the window to indicate the blackened horizon. 'How can they be expected to even like us when they fucking hate each other?'

'Amazing Thailand,' said Graham and they both laughed.

'Sorry to say it but this fantasy, the illusion, took me in. I even believed for a while the boy loved me. Do you know what though, that boy fucking hates me,' said Smale, no longer transfixed by the images on the TV but by those just outside his own window, tears in his eyes. 'I overheard him talking on the phone to his friend and that was almost word for word what he said. Oh, he's a great actor, I'll give him that.'

'Christ,' said Graham, head in his hands. 'Sorry, I don't really know what to say. Bangkok… what a bloody city.'

Chapter nineteen

Bordering hell

He was sat inside the sweaty, inadequate office of No 1 Visa Run – a company that specialised in making Thailand's expat waifs and strays legal by ferrying them across the border and back again, allowing the likes of Graham to live off three-monthly tourist visas. He hated the trip to the dirt poor Cambodian border town of Poi Pet, where he'd witnessed girls as young as eleven or twelve, blackened faces brightened by garish make-up, luring foreign sex tourists, their cheaply colourful clothes only heightening the look of desperation and poverty.

He couldn't stop the perspiration running down his brow in the small space, a brutalist concrete box in the heart of Thailand's own Prostitution-by-Sea, Pattaya. The dust-caked electric fan on the cluttered desk in the office only displacing the hot air, hot air he knew would come out of the mouths of his fellow visa runners, expecting the usual motley assortment. He hated them too because it was like holding a mirror up to himself – the whiff of alcohol in the morning, the giveaway cheap shoes, the slovenly beard growth unable to hide the too twitchy mouth which hinted at the dishonesty and irresponsibility that effectively came from being on the run. It was how he felt, constantly on the move, looking over his shoulder.

Himself, these men, all around his age should have had homes, wives, careers – and maybe they did once – but he wondered what they, he, had given it all up for, the stifling, claustrophobic space only compounding his feelings as did the whiff of shit on the breeze from the town's creaking Third World infrastructure. Oh, they talked a good game, sounded happy, but there was no more unedifying site than a middle-aged man cracking open a beer at ten o'clock in the morning when the rest of the world was earning a living, yet that's exactly what one of his travelling companions had done as he'd blundered into the office. He realised the main reason was not wanting to think, an abdication of responsibilities and of that he was partially guilty too, though at least he had a business, a life after the lifelessness of London. But being away from Natasha – someone who'd finally said she loved him – was like a physical pain, an ache that wracked his body. That bloody American had so much to answer for, having cruelly taken it all away. With the Yank no doubt in her ear, she'd even stopped his monthly salary, it failing to materialise in his account at the allotted time, though maybe there was something behind her passive aggression, did she want him to come running back? But needing to stop thinking, hoping, Graham popped another pill, grinding what was left of his nails into his palms.

'All right, mate,' said the man, waving the beer can in his general direction in sorry salute, the regulation scuffed shoes, billowy shirt, sad slacks combination.

''Ello,' he said but looking away, wary of another newbie

wanting to regale him with tales of paradise, or an old hand who despised everything about the place but couldn't say why they were staying put.

'Bloody hot, innit?' said the man, cracking open yet another beer.

'Sure is,' said Graham, cringing at the grating London accent but mopping his brow in sympathy, though not wanting to engage, dreading the tenor of another loser's story, thinking the weather was completely lame as an opening conversational gambit in Thailand – when wasn't it bloody hot?

'Beer?'

'No, you're all right. Do you know why nothing's happening?'

'You've obviously not been on many of these beanos. A few of the other lads went out last night. These trips never leave on time.'

'Oh, don't you worry, I've been on one too many.'

'Right you are. You not based in Pattaya? Don't recall your face.'

'Nope, I'm from Bangkok.'

'I wouldn't give a thank you for that place... crazy. Dunno how you guys do it. Nasty business too with those whatsisnames?'

'Red shirts,' said Graham sighing, thinking it pathetic most expats had hardly any grasp of what was happening in their adopted country, frankly didn't care as it never touched them, though if it got too uncomfortably close they'd just up sticks and move elsewhere ala Smale.

'That's the ones, yeah. Evil bastards. Can't trust 'em, can you?'

'Who?'

'The Thais.'

'Been burnt have we?' said Graham, looking at the wry smile on the man's lips, as though he'd uttered an incontrovertible truth, rather than a racist bloody slur.

'Too many fucking times. You?'

'Bloody incinerated,' he said, turning away again, not wanting to engage in any more barroom chat, had heard enough as he walked outside but couldn't help thinking of the inappropriateness of his comment as Mark's charred corpse came to mind, shivering uncontrollably despite the incessant, cloying heat.

'Hello, mate, I'm Pete from No 1 Visa Run,' said a short, grizzled figure through a mouthful of cigarette as he returned to the office – the man's West Country burr just about discernible in an otherwise generic English accent.

'Graham,' he said, receiving the obligatory handshake.

'That there's Mr Incinerated,' said his tormentor from earlier.

'Eh?' said Pete, brushing a hand – the hand he wasn't furiously smoking another cigarette with – through the few straggly grey, almost translucent hairs that were scraped back pitifully across his scalp, forty-odd going on eighty.

'I said, 'have you been burnt by a Thai?',' said the man. 'And he replied, 'incinerated'.'

'Very good,' said Pete, letting out a forced laugh, though a frown remained on his face. 'Graham, old son, I know the feeling. Listen, the other lads are on the way. Sorry there was a bit of a booze up last night. We'll be off shortly.'

'Oh my head, man,' groaned a burly Geordie, sizable frame filling the doorway, at the head of a large phalanx of similar-sized gentlemen – Pete and the other man laughing presumably in reference to the hangover as they too held their heads as if in sympathy.

Graham was introduced to everyone but forgot their names almost instantaneously, as he suspected they did his, trying hard to tune out their spiel, which had been much the same as his earlier encounter, just a different intonation. He happened to overhear one of them say he owned the British Bulldog pub, a Pattaya hangout known for 'football hooligans', though the very term seemed dated and made him think how these men in their XL shirts advertising Newcastle, Chelsea and the like needed to grow up, accept some responsibility, but the slackers' symphony as one after the other cracked open their beer cans said otherwise, it being just ten-thirty on a Tuesday morning.

He made sure to sit up front – Pete on one side, mute Thai driver on the other behaving as if he wasn't really there, in his own world, one Graham wished to inhabit but already encroached on by beer fumes and inane chatter.

'So, Mr Incinerated, what's your story? I hear you're going on a little detour. Phnom Penh, eh? We normally come straight back across the border,' said Pete turning to him, unleashing the sweet, high smell of the morning's nip of whisky.

He sighed, a long, heartfelt exhale, but there was something about Pete, maybe his non-threatening, rounded vowels, or the fact he looked even more hopeless than most of the visa runners, that made him want to confess.

'That there was a long sigh,' Pete said chuckling.

'I just need a break as well as getting the required stamp. Though I've heard good things about Phnom Penh but yeah, long sigh, long story,' said Graham, the boisterousness of the group behind them lending their quiet conversation an air of intimacy at a time when he just wanted someone to listen.

'We got time on our hands. Cigarette?'

'Please,' said Graham, tingling sensation of needing nicotine, booze, anything to shut his brain up, shut the world out, reneging on yet another pathetic attempt at kicking the habit causing him to bite his lip, metallic taste of blood in his mouth.

As Pete lit one, then two, with noticeably shaky hands the driver turned to them, faintly comical in fake Prada sunglasses but no longer mute, unleashing a torrent of Thai, indicating his distaste at the smoking.

'Shush' said Pete, putting a finger to his lips but at least winding down the window in some form of compromise.

'What did he say?'

'Buggered if I know, I only live 'ere,' he said, causing them both to laugh. 'So you were saying, it's a long story.'

'Well… I was married, forty, going nowhere really. There was no love in that marriage, okay we said we loved each other but if that was love, it was joyless, colourless, odourless, everything-less.'

'Tell me about it. I've been there, done that.'

'I had no interest in myself, life, I'd given up. Wife, mortgage… but I got to the stage, took me a long time to admit to myself… bloody scary… I got to the point where I said in my mind, 'I don't know whether I can do another twenty years of this.' So I moved here, set up a bar.'

'Kids?'

'Pete, I can't go there now,' he said, gaze affixed to the window, not wanting to admit the tears in his eyes, that unending, massive, infinite sorrow dragging his heart down to his stomach.

'Okay, mate, okay. Life's hard,' said Pete, patting him on

the shoulder.

'I'm getting there. Slowly, slowly but I'll get there,' he said, finally looking at his companion again, managing a weak smile.

'And your mates at home are still doing it, right? Not living but existing. You ever notice how mates at home of a certain age, been married as long as we have, go quiet when you tell 'em what you've done and that's jealousy, that is, plain and simple. They haven't got the balls to do what you've done. You're an adventurer,' said Pete, throwing his cigarette out of the window.

'It's complicated though.'

'Mate, it always is. T.I.T… this is Thailand. Complicated is the name of the game,' Pete said, resting a hand on Graham's shoulder. 'You can't afford to regret, you gotta push on with the adventure.'

'I'm in deep,' he said and couldn't help but notice the tremor in his own voice.

'But you came on the visa run. You could've just quit, packed up and pissed off back to England. The amount of times I've nearly done it but I've stayed and fought through it.'

'But as I said, I'm in deep, balls deep. I'm…'

'I don't want to know all the gory details, just trying to give you the benefit of my experience.'

'I never realised I was wearing a T-shirt saying 'Bangkok virgin' on it,' he replied, causing both of them to laugh again, 'Cambodian border 100km' flashing past.

Yes, an adventurer, he thought, trace of a smile at his lips, not the loser Von Eil and the Freak had him down as. Not a chance. He'd also become a fighter.

He accompanied Pete as they got off the bus, the other Englishmen thankfully shuffling along at the rear having bonded over beer and Thailand troubles as they walked to the checkpoint. Graham sweated along as filthy dust swirled around him in the breeze, sticking to the moisture on his face, which he frantically rubbed at with a handkerchief that quickly became smudged with the colour of poverty – a shit brown. He eyed several groups like theirs, plus the usual backpackers trying to ward off evil by desperately clinging to *Lonely Planets* and bottles of water, as the walk of shame continued. All this for the privilege of being able to stay in Thailand for another three months – a total charade with the money to be paid out likely to end up in some corrupt bloomin' immigration officer's pocket.

'You got my number, so call if you have any problems getting back in,' said Pete as they reached the Thai checkpoint, frantically mopping sweat from his brow with one hand, smoking with the other.

'Why? What can you do?'

'Fuck all, mate, absolutely fuck all. I just wanted to make you feel better,' he said with a wheezy laugh.

The Thai officer stamped him out with the regulation demeaning look, face fixed as though he hadn't smiled in all his fifty odd years, the noise the old-fashioned stamp made like the crack of a gun or another figurative nail in Graham's coffin, passport filling up with so much incriminating evidence.

They marched over to the Cambodian side with a sheaf of Thai money tucked into their passports to avoid any awkward questions, Pete had said, and it was here along a muddy track that any pretensions of a border town fell away. There were no buildings as such, just squat Portacabins for immigration purposes, while beyond them a number of lean-to structures containing rails of drab clothes and the like seeming to signal some kind of market. There were food stalls deluged by swarms of flies dotted about and tended by unsmiling, gaunt women, the desperate face of poverty, thought Graham, as he crunched through the endless dirt in flimsy loafers, batting away the insects crawling up his nose, into his ears, the futility of it all making him want to run and not stop.

'Ever been to Cambodia, mate?' said his tormentor from the No 1 Visa Run office, breathing hard, having jogged to catch him.

'I hear it's wonderful this time of year.'

'Cheap booze and birds,' he said with a smirk.

'Hey, mister! One dollar! One dollar!' was the cry that came from a group of children suddenly clustered around them.

Graham was jolted by the forlorn faces as filthy and black as the dirt beneath them, looking so much older than their years, for they didn't have the expectant look of the innocent but the hard, calculating eyes of the desperate. A girl as young as twelve, lurid face having been amateurishly daubed in make-up, winked at him, then provocatively stuck out a tongue and he could only turn away, sickened there were other men who exploited such a situation. Quickening his pace, he looked back only to see the man who'd been so eager to extol the virtues of Cambodia moments ago now deep in conversation with the gaggle of kids, hands everywhere, that twelve-year-old girl the centre of his depraved world. He wanted to run back, drag him off her, break his stupid, fat bloody face but knew it could be him being dragged off to a Poi Pet jail, eyes misting up, Em forever in his head, heart.

Chapter twenty

Khmer rogue

'Hi, you must be Graham. This feels a bit like a blind date. Vincent,' he said, holding out a bony hand.

'Yeah, though I'm guessing I'm not your type,' he replied, shaking the proffered hand, small holdall dangling in the other, blinking in the blaring sun of the Phnom Penh morning outside their allotted meeting spot of the Foreign Correspondents' Club.

'Haha, not really no. I like my men... how should I put this, brown.'

'Mike did warn me,' he said, whiny North American accent rather grating compared to the tonal sing-song he'd been assailed by on the hellish overnight bus ride from Poi Pet.

'Oh, yeah, Mike. How is the old bugger? Hear he's leaving the 'Kok. Never would've seen that one coming, man.'

'He always falls on 'is feet. Think he'll be just fine. All the stuff going on in Bangkok, it's like a war zone,' he said, looking at the Canadian properly for the first time, Vincent shiftily hiding behind sunglasses, hair greasy and lank but greying at the temples, jeans, long-sleeve tie-dye and flip-flops combo like he was some hippie gone native not the professional journalist Smale had painted him to be.

'I'm so glad they threw me out. So, so relieved,' said Vincent, laughing for what felt an awfully long time.

'Yeah?' he replied, dabbing at his forehead with a handkerchief.

'Another time. Shall we?' said Vincent, a friendly hand on Graham's arm, leading him to the FCC's shady entrance. 'It's a bit hot. Hot and hotter here.'

'Yeah,' he said as he followed up a pleasantly cool staircase and onto a breezy veranda overlooking Sisowath Quay and the glinting Tonle Sap river.

'What do you think?' he said, sitting down at a table overlooking the view, immediately lighting up, throwing the pack of cigarettes to Graham. 'Two Angkors, please.'

'Angkors?' he said, watching the smiley waitress that had come instantly over now receding.

'Beers,' said Vincent, palms outstretched.

'Right, right. Good plan,' he said, looking up at the clock above the bar, it was nine o'clock, beer drinking in Phnom Penh permissible even earlier than in Pattaya it seemed.

'Where you staying?'

'The River View,' he said, taking a drag, letting the sweet smoke fill his lungs, filthy habit he just couldn't kick but needed right now, whole body tense from the bus journey, familiar throb behind his eyes. 'It's not is it?'

'Not what?' said Vincent, finally removing his sunglasses but seemingly unable to make eye contact, looking everywhere but.

'Waccy baccy,' he said, sticking the fag under his new friend's nose.

'Man, no. They're clove cigarettes. They're local. Cheaper

220

than Marlboro's. That's why I smoke 'em. But what do you want? You want ganga, coke, heroin? What's your favourite tipple?'

'It's okay, I really don't.'

'It's fine, you're among friends here. I can get anything you like. You think Bangkok's Disneyland, you ain't seen nothing yet,' said Vincent with a lopsided smile, clinking Graham's bottle, gulping back the beer as if it had life-giving properties.

'Do you know the River View?'

'Oh that, yeah. It's doesn't feature a river and it hasn't got a view. But it's cheap, clean. Think they had a little problem with backpackers overdosing a while back but happens all the time here.'

'Sounds wonderful,' Graham said, chugging his beer too, indicating for another, on holiday after all.

'Guy, listen to me, you Brits and your irony. We're not like Americans, we get it. But this is a great place, you gotta give it a chance. Give peace a chance. It's twice as cheap as Bangkok, twice the fun,' he said, stubbing his cigarette out, lighting another.

'I need some fun,' he said, tension slowly easing from his shoulders as the alcohol kicked in, the booze as it so often did in Asia also loosening his morals, looking around the bar to see what was on offer, trying to forget Nat but missing her with a dull ache that never seemed to go, a constant reminder.

'I tell you what, I gotta leave you at some point this morning and do my editing shift at the *Post* but I'll park you at the Blue Chilli.'

'The Blue Chilli?' said Graham, twirling absently with a lighter, drumming the fingers of his free hand.

'It's a gay pub. Don't worry, Mike clued me in. You like boys, right?'

'Er, yeah… as long as they're over eighteen,' he said, trying to hide a blush.

'Graham, it might be Phnom Penh but we're not all paedos here. And listen, don't get hung up about being yourself. No one's judging you. We're all in Southeast Asia for a reason.'

'What's yours?'

'You should know never to ask that. Didn't anyone ever tell ya? Mike, for instance. Anyway, it's not that interesting. It was a boring life in the Canadian cold. Everyday's summer here. Look,' he said, turning to take in the view.

'Is this it though?' he said, pointing to the near empty roads of the capital, just the odd Honda Dream streaking noisily along, Monday morning rush hour Phnom Penh style, Graham thought as he took another sip of his Angkor.

'Don't get me wrong, we do have monster jams here. But on a day like this, that's what grips. The languor. Nowhere else like it,' said Vincent, luxuriating back in his chair. 'What else do you need?'

'Yeah. Can you speak the language?'

'I can say 'no', which has come in very helpful. No to girlie bars and no to kids. Plus I don't do shootin' ranges. Other than that, we're all good,' he said, emitting that laugh again.

'It's 'yes' to everything else then?'

'You got it. You planning on doing any sightseeing? Consider yourself solo for that. Not my thing.'

'Yeah, definitely. I've even got the bloody *Lonely Planet* in my bag. You not been to Angkor Wat?' he said, face scrunched up.

'Always end up partying when I'm there. Keep meaning to

but the hangover the next morning's always too bad for ruins. I'm one big ruin. Know what I mean, man?'

***

'This is Graham, by the way. Like Gray and ham but drop the 'h',' said Vincent, sitting him down on a wicker chair in a shaded spot outside the aforementioned Blue Chilli.

'Nice meeting you, Mr Gray Ham,' said the young woman he'd been introduced to, now busily wiping down his already immaculate table in the empty bar, it not being even lunchtime.

'Just call me Gray, like me hair. What's left of it. Everyone else does.'

'Okay, Mr Gray,' she said, laughing shyly, turning her pretty, petit features away from his gaze.

'Enjoy. I'll pick you up at the River View at 10pm,' said Vincent, patting him on the shoulder before he strolled off.

'Drink?' said the girl.

'Yes, please. Angkor.'

'Small or big?'

'It's gotta be big.'

''Scuse me?'

'Oh, sorry, big. Please,' he said, laughing, cheeks reddening.

He lounged back in his chair, the tension having subsided further, breeze from the nearby river cooling him as he looked across at the National Museum. It was a fiery kind of red, late morning sun giving it an otherworldly glow, tiled triangular roofs and pointed turrets speaking of something so foreign yet so alluring. It was as though he'd eased into the city's quiet, slumbering rhythm as the girl poured his drink and gave him that wide Khmer smile and Graham thought maybe Vincent was right, he was already in its grip.

'Don't worry, my brother come soon,' she said, shooting up a hand to cover her mouth.

'It's fine. I'm happy,' he said, sipping the ice-cold beer.

'Sir, Sir, you want *Post? Phnom Penh Post*. One dollar, one dollar,' said a boy, grabbing his arm, thrusting the newspaper under his nose.

'One dollar?' he said, fishing about in his pocket, bringing out some Thai money. 'I got 100 baht, okay?'

'Okay,' said the boy nodding, taking the money with one hand, giving him the paper with the other.

'Thanks,' he said, scanning the headlines screaming about the Japanese journalist that had been shot dead by the Thai military as the protests in Bangkok became bloodier and bloodier, red shirts being obliterated into surrender, though instead of reading on he instinctively turned to the sports pages at the back and the latest results from one of England's best exports – the Premier League.

As he read, he lit another cigarette from a packet kindly left behind by Vincent, though thoughts of football dredged up with it sad memories of home, those days with Emmy at Selhurst Park when he'd taken her to watch Crystal Palace and she'd get so excited her face would come out in a rash, her voice hoarse afterwards with shouting. Sheil would cut them both dead when they got home. 'Stupid bloody game,' she'd say.

'Bitch,' he said under his breath, chucking the paper aside.

'Can I have back?' said the boy who'd sold him it in the first place.

'Back?'

'To sell again, boss,' he said, putting his hands together as if to mimic a prayer.

'You just got 100 baht,' Graham said laughing.

'He bothering you?' said a good looking, well dressed young local man approaching.

'No. Here have it,' he said, the boy grabbing the paper, smoothing down the creases, scooting off.

'Gray Ham, I believe. According to my sister. Sorry about her English,' he said in a crisp accent.

'Call me Gray,' he said, looking at bright shining eyes, that same smile he'd seen earlier, obviously genetically ingrained, he thought, the open collar linen shirt hinting at a toned chest, fashionable sandals showing off elegant feet.

'I'm Kitcharoen. Roen for short,' he said, putting his hands together and bowing ever so slightly, the traditional form of greeting.

'Lovely to meet you,' he said, looking the youngster up and down, disappointed his legs were disguised by shapeless fisherman's pants, imagining underneath, drumming the table again.

'Welcome to my bar. Another?' he said, indicating the empty beer bottle with a little nod of the head, clearing it from the table.

'Please. Will you join me?'

'I'd loved to, Gray. I just need to put the shopping away.'

'Great,' said Graham, watching as he walked back into the bar, Roen turning around and catching him, just a hint of something in those almond-shaped eyes.

'So,' he said as he returned, placing a large beer down and two glasses.

'Yes?' said Graham as Roen sat, the Cambodian eyeing him, making him shift in his seat, look away.

'Don't worry, I don't bite,' he said laughing. 'You have a girlfriend? You married?'

'Ah, long story,' he said, looking out across at the museum, fiddling with the lighter, all he could do to stop from flinching with the electric thrill of the Cambodian patting his hand.

'We got time, mister. So, this is how you found me, ah?' said Roen, fingering the copy of the *Lonely Planet* guide on the table. '*Southeast Asia on a Shoestring*. What's a shoestring?'

'Just on the cheap. Cheap like me,' he said and they both laughed, Graham finally having the confidence to look into those warm, brown dancing eyes. 'But actually, no, Vincent brought me here. Friend of a friend.'

'Oh, Vincent,' he said, smile morphing into a grimace.

'What's the matter?' said Graham, still trying to get a handle on the myriad facial expressions of the East, amazed how the mood could change in the literal blink of an eye.

'Nothing, nothing. Just some of these foreigners...'

'They're what? What about us?'

'Nothing,' said Roen sighing. 'Tell me about you.'

'Me? It's not that interesting, really.'

'Gray, you're so shy. It's like you're scared to be yourself,' he said, refilling their glasses.

'It's not that, I'm just not used to... not used to this,' he said, staring at the floor.

'This?'

'Going to gay bars.'

'Look around us. It's just you and me here. Don't worry. No one's going to make you do anything you don't want to.'

'I know,' he said, grateful for Roen's hand squeezing his, not wanting him to let go, looking into that boyish face and only seeing hope there and he'd been such a long way from that recently.

'Seems like you're having a hard time, mister.'

'I've gone through bloody worse but yeah, it's hard. Thanks for this,' he said, getting lost in those eyes, drinking them in, Roen leaning towards him, their lips grazing, suddenly locked in a kiss, a high flooding through his body, gripping tighter and tighter to the hand, all the pain drifting away.

'Maybe you're not that shy,' said Roen, finally disengaging, laughing softly. 'You want to go upstairs?'

'I'm sorry, it's all so fast. I've got things going on in Bangkok too…'

'Shush,' he said, patting Graham's hand. 'Don't explain. Let's just enjoy our time together. I like your company.'

'We only just met.'

'I know but it's not like a lot of the other foreigners that come here. They just have one thing in their eyes. And they think they can own me, you know. They think everything's for sale here, *everyone*,' he said, his lively eyes having turned watery, tan face taking on an almost grey hue.

'Sounds like Bangkok.'

'No, no. It's worse here. I come from a good family. I don't need anyone's money but my weakness is foreigners. I was with a man, a long time, an American man, one of Vincent's friends but he only had one love and I could never compete,' he said, thumping the table.

'What was that?' said Graham, grabbing Roen's arm, looking at the tears streaking down his cheeks.

'Heroin. That fucking filthy drug. Be careful, please. It's everywhere here.'

'Don't worry, I wouldn't touch the stuff. I only love this,' he said, holding up his beer, drying Roen's eyes with his handkerchief, wiping the tears away. 'Well, I do have other loves as well.'

'That's good but enough drinking. I'm going to take you somewhere this afternoon. You can't just see the inside of a bar. This is a holiday after all, right.'

'Right,' he said smiling, lighting up a cigarette, handing it to Roen.

'Oh, clove cigarettes. You're like a local already.'

'Actually, they're from Vincent.'

'Oh dear,' he said, stubbing it out.

'He's that bad?' said Graham, throwing his hands up.

'We go, come on. My motorbike's out front.'

They left the bar, Graham mesmerised as a crowd of saffron-robed monks glided along in front of the National Museum, another moment that felt straight out of the pages of the *National Geographic*, a snapshot that seemed timeless and already made him feel like he didn't want to leave. This was the Southeast Asia he'd dreamed of after the first trip to Thailand that had changed everything and grabbing Roen by the slender waist as he clambered on the back of his Honda, it was like he'd finally found it, the youngster flashing him a smile before they set off. Though he also knew he needed to make it work with Natasha, he was desperate to make it right or fight for what was his. It would be easier to go off grid and do a Vincent but he wasn't ready to lose it all. He wanted to beat Von Eil. The old, pathetic Graham, the one Sheil abused, now long bloody gone.

***

'So this is a school?' said Graham as they pulled up outside a series of buildings with what looked like a playground out front studded with palm trees, bougainvillea spilling over white-washed walls of surrounding houses, a suburban scene.

'No, no. It was a high school once but this is Tuol Sleng where the Khmer Rouge tortured their victims,' he said, guiding him to the entrance, handing over money as they shuffled into the grounds with a gaggle of other tourists.

As Graham looked around, the silence all encompassing, the grisly aura hit him, commentary next to the images detailing the torture that had taken place. But commentary wasn't really needed – the bloodstains on the floor, the rusted bedsteads with shackles attached, the row upon row of thumbnail photos of too numerous victims in their Sunday best, hair immaculately combed, faces an unreadable mask and all diligently recorded by their torturers the Khmer Rouge said more than enough. The men, the women, the children had all been headed for one fate, bodies crammed in together like cattle in trucks, lives wiped out at the end of a gun barrel, babies slammed against trees to save on bullets, body piled upon body in the Killing Fields, read Graham.

'I'm sorry,' he whispered, eyes misted, as they walked from one horror to the next.

'Don't be sorry. Just look,' Roen said, grabbing tightly to Graham's hand, not letting go this time.

Finally reaching the exit, he breathed out, grabbed for his handkerchief, realising he was sticky with sweat, sticky and stinking, the genocide museum having even numbed him to the fiery heat of a Cambodian afternoon. His hand gently shook as he dabbed at himself with the hanky, looking at Roen but not having a clue what to say. What could you say?

'Let's have iced tea,' said the boy.

'Yeah,' he said, needing something stronger, the picture post-card Phnom Penh having morphed into something far darker, like he'd suddenly woken up.

They sat in a little garden café that was just across the road from S21 but with its tropical trees all a riot of colour and its dainty tables and chairs it felt like a different world. Graham reclined, grateful for the shade, the gentle breeze, thankful for Roen squeezing his knee, that smile was back, the dancing eyes.

'Those foreigners don't come here. People like Vincent. The guy I was seeing. Cambodia, it's all an amusement park to them. All they hear is 'one dollar, Sir, one dollar'. They pay up and shut their eyes or expect others to keep them closed.'

'I know,' he said, sipping his ice-cold tea, thinking he wouldn't want to be anywhere else and it was a long time since he'd felt that way. 'You're alone now?'

'Alone cos I want to be. A lot of men come to my bar, an army. But I'm not interested, you know.'

'Sorry to hear it.'

'Mister, you're always sorry. I brought you here because look at those photos. They were people that didn't fit in. They didn't do what the Khmer Rouge wanted. They were teachers, lawyers, doctors, they didn't want to just work in the fields like Pol Pot wanted.'

'He was evil. Like any dictator...'

'Yes, yes he was. But what I'm trying to say is they didn't fit into society. We're lucky now, so lucky. You might not think you fit in, you were so shy coming to my bar, like you don't know what to be but nowadays we can be anything. We can actually be who we are. Pol Pot's just in your head, your mind.'

'Then I'm gonna tell Pol Pot where to go.'

'Where to go?'

'Yes, I'm going to tell him to piss off,' he said and they both laughed, laughed so hard other customers in the café began to turn around but Graham didn't care.

'Funny man.'

'Roen, thanks for today. I really needed this.'

'My pleasure. What you doing tonight?'

'Ah, I promised I'd go out with Vincent. I'm leaving on a bus for Poi Pet tomorrow afternoon,' he said, grimacing with the thought of returning to Bangkok, his life.

'With Vincent? Oh,' said Roen, sad-faced. 'Would you like to meet tomorrow morning? I want to see you before you go. Breakfast? Please be careful tonight though. Stick your number in there.'

'I will be careful. I'd love breakfast, by the way. Would kill for it,' he said, carefully inputting his number into the shiny new Nokia he'd been handed, a contrast to his crusty antique version, going over the digits again just in case.

'Kill for it?'

'Just a little joke,' he said, patting the boy's knee. 'I dunno, it was like we were meant to meet.'

'Funny man. My funny Englishman.'

***

'Mummy's very well connected, so when I left Oxford she said this would be just the thing for me. My uncle's patron of the VSO, you see. I didn't even know where Cambodia was on a bloody map,' she said, emitting a braying kind of laughter,

231

once silken blonde hair defiled by dreadlocks, eyes dulled from drink or worse.

'And what is it you do again?' said Graham, rearranging an ageing frame unused to sitting cross-legged on the floor, though they were on the most comfy of cushions, breeze from the nearby river gently kissing them on their expansive rooftop perch.

'I basically clean bat poo off the city's monuments. Mostly at the National Museum. It's been there donkey's years, the poo I mean. And I get to live in this lovely house,' she said above the music, playing with her ridiculous hair, taking another sip of her drink, greying face in contrast with her obvious youth.

'There's people starving and you clean up shit? Nice work if you can get it. And you can afford to live in this bloody place?' he said, looking around at the wooden deck littered with other similarly wasted youngsters, all presumably doing similarly very important jobs cadged via Daddy or his well-connected friends.

'I'm broadening my mind,' she said, though her thousand yard stare indicated the girl wasn't seeing Graham, in her own world completely.

'Hey, man, I see you're well acquainted with Hannah here,' said Vincent, thrusting a beer in his hand.

'Yeah, she was just telling me what a great job she's doing,' said Graham, gratefully taking the bottle, pleased to see a familiar face, more at home with the Canadian journalist scraping a living than these leeches living off the old boy network, scraping shit off antiquities.

'They think they're saving the world but they can't even save themselves. Isn't that right, Hannah?'

'Yeah, yeah,' she said, glassy eyed now, lolling back on the

232

cushions.

'Come on, let's take a look at the view,' said Vincent, pulling Graham to his feet, leading him to the edge of the rooftop, fenced in pleasingly by little wooden balustrades strewn with fairy lights.

'I like this,' he said, looking out into the blackness, centre of town but only a few pinpricks of light, speaking for the lack of development, the poverty but there was also something raw about it, vital, stars shining brightly above as they weren't competing with the normal Third World neon.

'I told you this place grips, didn't I? You feelin' it?' said Vincent, putting an arm round his shoulders.

'Yes, I am. But what about all them back in there, they're like zombies.'

'They're young. Just let them do what they gotta do. I hear you had a little rendezvous with Roen. Seems he's smitten, you old lothario you. Didn't know the Brits had it in 'em,' he said, poking him in the ribs.

'Yeah and he told me to be very careful around you. Wonder why.'

'Cigarette?' he said, handing one over already lit. 'Let's see, this is your last night in Phnom Penh. You've got a piece of ass back in Bangkok. What's that little shit got to do with your life, or mine for that matter?'

'Hey, who you callin' a shit?' he said, waving the cigarette away. 'He just happened to be very kind to me. I haven't had that for a long, long time. Do you have a partner here, a boyfriend?'

'Graham, don't get me wrong. I'm sure Roen's a very nice boy but they always want to control you and they always want something, usually dough.'

'*They*? You're just being a racist. He told me about the foreigners here and I've seen it in Bangkok. Not saying I'm perfect but white blokes want their cake and eat it here,' said Graham, feeling the throb behind his eyes.

'Racist? I'm not fucking racist, man. No way. Take it fucking back,' he said, gently shoving him, though his eyes were not so soft as he stared accusingly.

'There was a time when I would've done but I'm saying it as I see it. And if you don't have someone, you may wanna think why. There are some lovely people here. I've seen it with me own eyes. Sorry,' he said, turning his palms skywards.

'Wow. You stand your ground. I'll give you that. Okay, let me apologise then, I'm sorry about the *they*. Journalism 101… I shouldn't generalise. And Roen's perfectly lovely, it's just we have history.'

'I'm sure. Look I don't want to know. We've enjoyed each other's company. As you say, let's enjoy my final night in Phnom Penh.'

'Hopefully not ever. Cheers,' he said with a laugh, clinking Graham's drink.

'Cheers to that.'

***

'What was the deal with that lot in there?' said Graham, as they reached street level, could finally hear himself think after the booming noise of the party, looking at his watch, digging nails into his palm, calculating he only had just hours left in his new favourite city before time ran out and he had to face up to Natasha and that shit Von Eil, needed to find a way to

234

wheedle his way back in, take what was his.

'As I was saying, just youngsters doing what youngsters do,' said Vincent, hailing a passing *tuk tuk*.

'When I was that age, I was working for a living.'

'Chill for God's sake. You okay, my man? You're looking tense, so preoccupied,' he said, throwing an arm lazily around Graham, guiding him into the confines of the *tuk tuk*.

'I got a lot on my mind. Going home tomorrow. It feels like the night before the first day at school,' he said as Vincent babbled something in pidgin English that he assumed was for the benefit of the driver.

'You Brits, love your descriptiveness. No wonder you got so many great writers there.'

'I'm not really a writer but I love crosswords, that's my thing. Help keeps me calm. Where we going, by the way?' he said, feeling in his pocket for the Xanax, relieved it was there, just in case, enjoying the warm breeze in his face, watching as night-time Phnom Penh unfolded – the quiet, the calm kept him rapt and the snapshots of gilded temples, cosily lit bars tucked away in the shadows, the elegantly adorned Khmers wandering by all hinted at the place's potential, providing glimpses of the exotic, erotic.

'We're going to the good ole Heart. Straight for the heart,' Vincent said, manically thumping his chest Tarzan style.

'The Heart?'

'Didn't you check your fucking guidebook, man? Heart of Darkness, talking about great writing.'

'My local pub used to be The Sydney. Now I'm hanging out at the Heart of Darkness,' he said laughing as they pulled into a street lined with bars, swarming with people. 'Ah, so this is where everyone is.'

'Yep, Uncle Vincent knows where the action's at. You got money?' said the Canadian, *tuk tuk* pulling to a halt.

'Yeah,' he said, sighing as he handed the driver a 100-baht note.

'Don't worry, I'll pay you back. In fact, I'll more than pay you back,' said Vincent, skirting the long queue outside the aforementioned Heart, name picked out in pink neon. 'They know me here.'

'Ah, Mr Vincent. How you doing?' said the doorman as if on cue, waving them both in.

Graham followed his lead into the dark, echoey space throbbing with music, though maybe it was too early as mainly young local men stalked the side of the dancefloor with hard stares, most furiously smoking cigarettes, the place having a feral, hunter and hunted feel. The air was fetid with the tobacco, whiff of beer and something more human, like unwashed bodies but it was sexually charged and smiling he recognised the sleazy allure that had brought him to Southeast Asia.

'You look happy,' shouted Vincent above the thump, thump, thump, turning to him on the edge of the dancefloor.

'Not sure I'm happy, just feel at home. This time last year I was probably at a quiz night at my local, trying to escape the wife.'

'Right,' he said nodding. 'I must come visit. To Bangkok, I mean.'

'Vince, don't even go there. I'm not sure what's going to happen. I need to enjoy tonight.'

'You sound like a condemned man,' he said with a nudge.

'Ah, it's not that. Not sure whether Smale's let on... Mike to you and me. But I got in with the wrong crowd. They wanna kill me. This bloody Yank and his sidekick. The Freak. I haven't got a clue what I'm in for,' he said, running a hand through the sparsity of his hair, sweat running uncomfortably down his forehead, heart beating in time to the frenetic music, like it was going to burst out of his chest, breaths coming faster and faster, body trembling.

'Okay?' he said, grabbing his arm.

'It's anxiety,' Graham said, face contorting, shoving one pill, then another into his mouth. 'I don't think I can take much more of this.'

'Gray, listen to me, listen. Drink this down,' said Vincent, shoving a beer into his shaking hand. 'I don't know what the fuck's happening over in Thailand but you can do it. Believe in yourself. Sometimes you mope around but you gotta hold that head up. I've got a little something that can help you tonight. Come on.'

'Okay,' he said, following Vincent back across the dancefloor, even though his legs felt incredibly heavy, an effort just to lift them but he needed to get out, escape.

They were on the back of a motorbike taxi this time, flying through the shadowy streets, Graham's ears still ringing from the music, looking on at the swooping bats visible in the dim flicker of the street lights, it feeling incredibly late, almost too late but he knew he was in for whatever happened next. Bangkok, the fear, was thankfully receding in his mind like the city in the driver's wing mirrors.

'We're here, my abode,' said Vincent as the motorbike stopped, again taking Graham by the arm, pulling him into a grey coloured apartment block.

'Classy,' he said, wrinkling his nose, the reek of disinfectant failing to disguise pungent food smells, stale sweat, cockroaches scattering in front of them as they made their way down a hallway.

'That's what I get for my hospitality, jeez,' said Vincent as he unlocked a rickety old door, thrust it open.

'What we doing here?' he said, the ammonia like stench hitting him first, putting a hand to his nose, taking in the box-like room lit by a bare bulb, bed in the corner, takeaway boxes littering the floor, book after book piled up on stick like furniture as if it was the cell of a mad professor desperately looking for the meaning of life.

'We're going to sort you out, my man,' he said, rifling through a chest of drawers, throwing things onto the floor in his haste to find whatever he was looking for, finally holding up a syringe like it was the answer, mad kind of glee in his eyes.

'That's sorting me out?' said Graham, heading for the door.

'Fucking trust me. You wanna forget, right. Try this shit,' said Vincent, blocking his path, forcibly sitting him on the side of the bed. 'Why you think I wear the long-sleeved shirts. I gotta do some cooking. Back in a tick.'

He listened as the Canadian busied himself, though he realised he wasn't cooking them up a late-night snack. Graham trembled again as he sat but it was as though something was stopping him from just walking away, walking out. On his return he let Vincent expertly tie the rubber tourniquet tight, feeling snug just below the main artery on his right arm, the big blue vein just pulsing as if in anticipation. He felt the prick of the needle, the horribly discoloured liquid going into his vein. As Vincent withdrew, he jerked back but his body was warm, tingly all over, the pain across his shoulders magically gone, a kind of weightlessness and he whipped his head around left to right to make sure he wasn't floating two feet off the floor like he felt. Graham threw himself back onto the bed, buried himself in the pillows, the widest smile stretched taut across his face, Vincent saying something but it was just soothing babble, his mind filled with the most wonderful of thoughts that were passing gently by like big fluffy clouds on a mid-summer's day.

***

'Shit,' he said, putting a hand to his thumping head, slowly opening eyes that felt like they'd been glued together, trying to ignore the insistent throbbing of his phone, light from the window clashing horribly with the pain in his head.

The vibrating of his mobile stopped as Graham propped himself up on one elbow, slowly dawning on him he was back at the River View, the horrible chintzy logo on the lumpy pillow attesting to that, last night coming back to him in odd fragments like a video on fast forward but he was transfixed by the nasty bits, looking down at his arm, rubbing at the crust of blood. He slammed a fist into the bed at the fact it hadn't all been a dream, though had no idea how he'd got back to the hotel.

'Bloody Vincent,' he said, daring to look at the phone, heart racing again as he saw the seventeen missed calls, past midday too, so no chance of that cosy breakfast with Roen, be lucky to make his bus. He still hit dial, needing more than anything to speak to him, willing the boy to pick up.

'Hi, mister,' said Roen, voice sounding distant, flat, not like the sing-song of before.

'Hi, look… I'm really sorry, I…'

'Don't. Graham, just don't. You're going to miss your bus.'

'Roen, I'll make it up to you, I promise,' he said, barely able to get the words out due to the thickness in his throat, digging nails into his palms, drawing blood, having to lie back down again due to the throbbing in his temples.

'White man always say that. Hey, you just call me when you come back to Phnom Penh.'

'I will, I promise,' he said but he thumped the bed again, realising he was talking to dead air, Roen had already hung up, was getting on with the rest of his life, now all Graham had left was Bangkok.

***

Having completed formalities in Cambodia, queuing to get back into the Thai side, waiting to be readmitted to a country that was close to ruining him was always a time of contemplation, never a good feeling. The officer gave him the once-over, the identikit immigration official – middle-aged man gone to fat, disdainful look fixed on his face like every foreigner was vermin and Graham could only avert his gaze, awaiting the stamp.

'What's this?' barked the officer, fat fingers rifling through the passport.

'I'm a tourist,' he said so softly it was like a whisper, the man flicking through his travel document again, slower this time, as if to complete his humiliation, glaring at page after page of visa stamps.

'This is the last time,' said the officer, finally flourishing the stamp, bringing it down with a bang, little trestle table underneath wobbling with the force as he scribbled something in red across the top of the visa he'd just issued.

'Welcome to Thailand,' he said under his breath, shaky legs only just propelling him forward.

Chapter twenty-one

Awakenings

'So sorry about your mum,' said Art.

'There's a saying in Thai – *mai pen rai*, which means 'everything's okay, don't worry'. It's obviously not how I bloody feel but I'm getting there. I'm more worried about Dad,' said Graham, leaning into the embrace of his old schoolmate in the Heathrow arrivals hall, feeling awkward but needing it, having booked a flight straight home as soon as he'd got the awful news staccato from the old man.

'You're not going all hippie dippy on us now, you daft sod. Men can show their feminine side now, you know.'

'It's a shock but Mum had a good innings, Emmy went before her time. Art, I'm still struggling with that.'

'I know, mate, I know,' he said, grabbing Graham's small suitcase, heading for the lifts. 'Come on, let's get you home.'

'Home? No, it's not home no more.'

'Gray, you know what I mean. I reckon you'll be back anyway. How's that new missus of yours?'

'I won't be back. I'm gonna make this work whether it kills me. The missus? I'll tell you about it later,' he said, feeling his body tense, wondering how much Art knew.

'Oh, it's like that, is it? Trouble in paradise?'

'Kind of,' he said reddening, the lift lurching upwards. 'Still on for that drink? We can discuss it then.'

'Yeah, though people been saying things down the pub.'

'What kind of things?'

'Word gets around, you know you splitting up with Sheil, shacking up over there with…'

'With what? What the hell's it got to do with anyone else? I do things my way now,' he said, looking across at Art.

'I know, mate. I know.'

'Sheil's asked to see me, by the way,' he said, as they exited the lift into the car park. 'I'm seeing her this week. We're going down to Seaford, where we scattered the ashes. My Emmy's ashes. She said we're going to have coffee or something. Didn't even know she drank anything other than the old vino. Coffee?'

'People change,' he said, pointing Graham to a car at the end of the row. 'Maybe she's trying to impress. She wants you back, you know. She told Jen she's devastated.'

'Devastated? She spent the last twenty years telling me how crap I am. She blames me for Emmy. I got a new life now. I might not be ecstatic but I'm living, I'm in charge. How are you and Jen?'

'Fine, just fine,' he said, starting the car up, putting on the radio, turning it up – loud.

'I mean really,' said Graham, snapping the radio off, looking at his friend.

'Don't want to talk about it. Now, where are you off to my old son?'

'The Holiday Inn in Sutton please, driver.'

'Wow that's glamorous.'

'Yeah, I know how to live,' he said laughing, feeling in his pocket for the pack of Xanax, popping a pill out of the foil, swallowing it down with the little drop of rancid water he had left over from the plane.

***

He sat on the bench, laying down a bunch of flowers, digging a finger into the letters carved into the wood, like it was the very essence of her, Emmy. The bench along the front at Seaford they'd donated, him and Sheil, in a more civilised moment, the ashes scattered in the sea just a few yards away from where he was perched. Graham pulled his coat a little tighter, the promenade deserted, chill wind whipping around him, gulls screeching on the breeze, lime green sea dragging at the pebbles.

'God, I miss you so much, so bloody much,' he said, nails digging into his palms so tightly were his hands curled around, remembering the happy times they'd spent on the beach as a family, when Emma only came up to his knee, her first swim, the joy on her face when he bought her ice cream, the dad and daughter race to the end of the prom but what did he have left of any of that?

He looked out to sea, the ferry from Newhaven trundling past from just down the coast on its way to Dieppe. Even that evoked memories, how they'd gone on a 'booze cruise', filled the car up with the cheap plonk Sheila loved and it was cheap then, Emmy just a girl, arms crossed on the back seat of the car like Lady Muck, laughing at his comedy French accent, his piss poor attempts at driving on the wrong side of the road. And all Sheil could do was give him grief, even then, an underlying hatred there like he was just one big disappointment. Words like 'limp dick' and 'shit for breath' would always tumble from those twisted lips if he so much as tried to initiate anything, then there was the pinching, the slapping, the biting because she hated him but it was obvious she also hated the world. It was like he'd done his duty by agreeing to marry her, giving her a daughter and now he was bloody useless, like a racehorse that'd gone lame. He should've been put out of his bloody misery, shot. Through those years Em was the only thing that kept him going and when she went that was the end, he thought, wiping away tears, his eyes swollen from crying, heart so heavy in his chest.

An old lady walking by caught his eye, began moving towards him but he waved her away, warned her off, not wanting to engage, couldn't. No, this grief was all bloody his, nobody could make it any easier. But he knew something good had come out of it and that Emma would be proud of her dad.

'You told me to go, didn't ya, love. 'Get away from the bitch,' you said. The best thing you ever said to me. 'Dad, go and get a life. She hates herself but she hates you even more', I remember you saying that to me,' he said, feeling in his pocket for the pack of emergency fags, cupping his hands, lighting up, taking a long drag.

'I'm not sure what you'd make of me now but I reckon you'd approve. You and Nat could share fashion tips. Em, I'm not even sure I'm in love with 'er anymore but I'm in love with the life over there, the freedom. Yeah, it's a struggle but I'm gonna fight with everything I have for it. Want to know something, your old man's becoming a fighter,' he said, throwing down the cigarette, a dog walker eyeing him suspiciously, unkempt bearded man talking to himself on a seafront in the middle of winter but Graham didn't give a toss because he wasn't alone.

'You better know something else, my love,' he continued, patting the bench. 'Your old dad might be gay, a fag, shit stabber, your mum would call it. I reckon she always knew. That's part of the hate. But you're the first person I ever told. I wish I could've said it when you were alive. I don't know what I was afraid of but I lived the first half of my life in sodding fear, on the run. I'm not doing that now.'

''Ave you gone completely bonkers?'

'Sheil, how long you been there?' he said, whipping around to see his ex-wife.

'Having a nice chat were we? You always did prefer her company. Daddy's girl weren't she,' she said, bending down, pecking him on the cheek.

'Don't,' he said, cringing at the familiarity of the dry lips, holding up a hand. 'This is a peaceful place.'

'You should've thought about that before you left me in the shit,' she said, sliding across the bench next to him, considerable, intimidating bulk bearing down on his thin frame.

'Really, love, not today. I thought we met here cos we wanted to…'

'Wanted to what? Kiss and make up? Gray, you fuckin' left me for that… that thing. And you expect everything to be hunky dory. Well, I got news for you,' she said, poking him in the chest.

Graham flinched at her pincer-like touch, one he knew only too well, that he hadn't missed. 'You know why I'm back?'

'You want me to feel sorry for ya, is that it? I know your mum's died and I'm sorry about that, though we never saw eye to eye. I was always too uncouth for them, weren't I. But you don't get a free pass.'

'I'm not asking for your sorrow, your sympathy. We've got to move on from this though. I've got a new life. You need to look forward not back.'

'Is that what you learnt from all the flaming counselling? Pissed all that money up the wall, didn't we, just to come out with that crap. Well, some of us don't find it so easy moving on.'

'I know,' he said quietly, shaking with the cold now, though it was more a nervous tremble than something caused by the weather. 'Can we go for that coffee?'

'I'm hungry, don't know about you. Fish 'n' chips?'

'Yeah, okay then,' he said, getting up, preparing to leave Emmy, food the last thing on his mind, shooting pains in his stomach.

'You're shaking,' she said, pointing at his arms. 'Happy pills not working?'

'I'm cold, stressed.'

'Yeah, don't suppose you have to worry about the cold in Bangkok, do you,' she said, looking him up and down as she waddled on ahead. 'Lucky if I can afford to put the heating on here.'

'I shouldn't 'ave come.'

'Nonsense. We're here now,' she said, as they came to a stop outside the condensation stained window of the chippie.

'Table for two,' he said, feeling vaguely ridiculous as the restaurant was half empty, the vinyl banquettes and Formica tables looking like something post war, as did most of the clientele.

'This way, love,' said the waiter, guiding them limply to their seats, shoving a menu in front of each.

'I'm not hungry,' he said, grabbing at his arms again, trying to still them.

'Eat, for God's sake. Look at you. You're wasting away.'

'What can I do you both for?' said the waiter, grinning like some camp end of pier comedian.

'Two beers, please. Cod 'n' chips twice,' said Sheila.

'You a battered husband then?' said the waiter, looking intently at Graham. 'Get it, battered…'

'Very good,' he said but blushing as the waiter turned on his stacked heel.

'Oh, who's gone all red. New friend is 'e?'

'For God's sake. You can't help yourself. All you do is put me down. It's all you've ever done.'

'Sorry, love,' she said, putting a chubby hand on his knee.

'Don't,' he said, looking down at the table, away from the intensity of her stare, eyes as grey as her greasy, lank shock of hair.

'No, Gray, listen. I didn't want this to 'appen. I know I've been a bitch. Is there any chance we can get back together? Any at all?'

'Your beers, guys,' said the waiter, banging the glasses down.

'It may seem odd that I was talking to Em today,' he said, guzzling back the beer, needing it. 'But I often did. Way back when she told me I needed to get a life, leave you. Know what, I was always too bloody scared. Scared of what was out there in that big wide world, scared of my own feelings.'

'Don't bring Emma into it…'

'No, Sheil, listen. It's important. But I've done it now, I love it. It's not about lust, love or whatever you wanna call it.

248

You bloody hated me during our marriage. The pinching, the poking, the name calling, that cold, hard back when I came in from a night's cabbing. There's no way I can do that again. I'm free,' he said, arms having stopped shaking, warm feeling inside, like for once she couldn't bring him down, get to him.

'It'll all fall apart. You just wait, you arsehole,' she said, launching the remnants of her glass of beer into his face.

'I'm just doing what I should've done years ago, you bloody cow. My daughter was right,' he said, wiping frantically at the beer going sticky in his hair with a napkin, standing up, giving her one last lingering look, hoping he'd never see her again.

'Life's a bitch, then you marry one,' said the waiter approaching.

Graham forced out a laugh as he exited, never looking back.

**

He still felt fuzzy headed in the late afternoon, his body clock more attuned to Bangkok time, like his sensibilities, as he trudged shivering through the slush-covered footpath of Sutton Rec. It was short for recreation ground, though he'd come to think of it as 'wreck', bordered as it was by dilapidated post-war terraced houses, nestling crowdedly against one another like jumbled teeth, scarring the skyline the battleship grey tower of Killick House, the council high-rise with families piled on families. Shouts and hollers came from kids as Graham wandered through the scrubby south London suburb, lads playing in what was left of snow stained an indiscernible shade from the park's dog shit and mud.

Reaching the other side the street lamps were already coming on, the rough part of town appearing even seedier, bathed in a horrible orange glow. He turned right on exiting the Rec on the well-worn path to the pub, left would have meant home, correction, a year or so ago it would've meant home. How things had changed, he thought smiling to himself.

'Hey, mate,' said Art, clapping him on the back as he came through the door of The Sydney.

'All right,' he said, forcing a smile, looking around at the same old faces, the threadbare afternoon shift, expressions as unchanging as the flock wallpaper that had been there since the 1970s.

'Drink?' said his mate, waving a half empty glass, the enticing brown liquid foaming around inside.

'What do you think?'

'I'll have an IPA and whisky chaser for this chap, please. Oh and stick another half in there, would you,' he said to the rotund landlord.

'How's it been going in the 'Kok? Heard you been making friends,' said the governor unsmilingly, pulling his pint

'It's surprisingly easy to make friends. You should try it some time.'

'I bet. Though I'm better off where I am. You never know with some of those ladeeez, I heard. Just run a mile if they've got Adam's apples.'

'They got apples all right,' said some wag standing at the bar to attendant laughter from the rabble.

'Yeah, yeah, heard it all before. Just jealous because you're getting none,' he said, grabbing his drinks, refusing to laugh along, knowing all they ever did in The Sydney was take the piss, jokes as ancient as the worn carpet but it was always spiteful rather than funny, tinged with the bitterness of lives unlived, unloved.

They slid into one of the nearby booths, catcalls from the gallery receding in Graham's ears.

'Bunch of wankers,' said Art. 'You okay?'

'Oh God, that's nothing. This lot are pussy cats compared to where I've come from. They'd eat 'em for breakfast. Art, I was always so worried about what people said about me, that's what held me back. Sheil, she was…'

'I know, I heard. I didn't want to say it when you were together, like, but she was cruel. She was so cruel and cold. I've never met anyone that cold. She could cut you dead with a word or just a look.'

'Yep. This is what it all did to me,' he said, waving the packet pills in the air.

'I never knew.'

'It's fine. You look around this bar. No, look. I reckon thirty per cent of 'em are on the pills. It's modern life, the stress. They've spent their whole lives in this place, this place. And they're gonna die here. How's that not depressing? How can that not make you anxious? I feel like I'm getting better. I might not need these soon,' he said, throwing the packet on the table.

'What about me then?'

'It's different. You've got a solid marriage, your own business, plans. You're not in here every afternoon.'

'If only you knew.'

'Knew what?' said Graham, leaning in, listening harder, tuning out the inane banter coming from the bar.

'The solid marriage is bullshit for starters. She's been having an affair, Jen. With the fucking painter and decorator. It's over now but I'm not like you, Gray, I don't have the balls to just go.'

'I'm sorry but there comes a point, you have to leave,' he said, patting his friend's arm.

'Yeah. What about your missus?'

'She's a he,' said Graham, scanning Art's face, looking for a familiar hint of disapproval, disappointment.

'So it is true.'

'It is and so what? I might not be over the moon happy but I'm not living a lie no more. And I am living, unlike this bloody lot,' he said, raising his near empty glass.

'So you've always felt that way?'

'Probably yes but it was being here, God-fearing parents, expectations, bloody Sheila, it was all buried so deep down inside. It was like being here I had to live a certain way but it just wasn't me. It's not me.'

'You feel guilty?'

'What is this a bloody confessional?' he said laughing, looking into his friend's smiling eyes, downing the remainder of his pint. 'I don't feel guilty. My brother's dying, my poor old mum, bless 'er, has just passed. Emmy's gone. When do you start living?'

'I know, I know,' said Art. 'Cheers to that.'

'Cheers.'

'I'll get another round in. Same again? Seems like you're in need of something strong.'

'You're hanging around? You're not worried your best mate is a poof?'

'I always had me suspicions,' he said laughing. 'Look, whatever turns your 'ead. It doesn't matter to me. It's good to see you with a smile on your face for once, you miserable bastard.'

'Same again then. I had a lot to be miserable about,' said Graham, picking up a discarded copy of *The Mirror*, the same celebrity bullshit, like there wasn't a real world out there, he thought, tossing it aside.

'There you go. On the house apparently,' he said, placing down the drinks.

'Wonders never cease. Trying to kill me with kindness obviously. Just nipping to the loo.'

He unbuckled and pissed into the stinking urinal, tensing as the door creaked open behind him, guilty memories flooding back of snatched moments in public toilets, desperate fumbles. Graham quickly zipping up.

'Is it true then?' said the man standing next to him, face red with booze, contorted into a snarl.

'Is what true?' Graham replied, standing his ground, where in the past he probably would've walked away pretending not to hear.

'Sheila told me you shacked up with one of the those ladyboys,' he said, unleashing a stream of piss, looking Graham straight in the eye as he did so.

'Yeah, her name's Natasha, if you must know.'

'Fucking queer,' he mumbled, zipping himself up, turning for the exit.

'What did you just say?' said Graham, grabbing the man's shoulder.

'You heard me.'

'Say it again,' he spat, nose to nose in the small space, smell of piss in his nostrils, drip, drip of a leaky tap in the silence. 'Go on, I wanna hear it.'

'You're a fucking queer,' said the man finally, finger wagging in Graham's face.

'I learnt something in Bangkok. Don't fuck with me, I fuck

253

back!' he shouted, fist connecting with the man's cheek with a crack, sending him flying backwards, sliding limply down the condensation spotted wall onto the tiled floor wet with sludge.

'I'll get you thrown out for this,' he said, holding a hand to his cheek, staggering to his feet.

'See if I care,' said Graham, watching as the man headed pathetically for the door.

'Where you been? I thought you'd got lost,' said Art as he sat back down.

'I kind of did. Lost in another century. This place is like going down the rabbit hole.'

'There's been a complaint,' said the landlord approaching the table, twenty sets of eyes having followed him.

'A complaint? Your beer's shit and the company's not much better, apart from my friend here of course,' said Graham, leaning back.

'You got all the answers. But I want you out of my pub,' he said with a smirk.

'Out? What the hell's he meant to have done?'

'It's okay, Art,' said Graham, standing up, preparing to address the pub as a whole. 'I was just called a queer in the toilets by one of you lot. And that's obviously why I'm being thrown out. He's right though, a queer, a nonce, shirt lifter, shit stabber, knob jockey, uphill gardener, bender, homosexual. Whatever you want to call it. At least I'm being honest with myself, how many of the rest of you are about anything?'

***

'Hello, Dad,' he said, having been waiting on the doorstep awhile.

'You better come in, Son.'

'I'm sorry,' he said, gently pushing the hand away, hugging his dad to him, skeletal like body so fragile in his arms, as if this is what life had come to.

'She had a good innings,' he said, turning back as they headed down the dank hallway.

'It's not her, Dad, it's you. I'm sorry you've got to handle all this on your own,' said Graham, sitting on the sofa, old man in his normal armchair, a yawning gap beside him that he patted absently.

'Sorry won't bring her back,' he said, lighting one of his cigars, or half of one that had been put out earlier.

'I know,' he said, getting up, opening a window, airing out the stuffy room, atmosphere heavy with the reek of tobacco, fear. 'Cup of tea?'

'Yes, please. You know where it is.'

He clattered around in the kitchen, though everything was just so, all within arm's reach, Mum's sense of place, organisation so evident, tears springing to his eyes as he looked out on the immaculate back garden. The bench where they sat in the summer just outside the window where she'd be reading the *Daily Mail*, listening to her little portable radio he'd bought her one Christmas like she really didn't have any concerns other than what she was going to cook his dad for tea. Would it be a nice piece of fish? Sausages and mash? Liver and onions? Names of those evergreen dishes going through his mind, like they'd been stuck in a time warp, forever 1950, but they'd been happy, hadn't they?

'Oh, Mum,' he said, eyes misting over again, cleaning the cups that had become a little gungy with the Charles and Diana tea towel, her last illness wracked days obviously disrupting her habits.

'There you go,' he said, handing his dad a mug celebrating some distant England Ashes win against the Aussies.

'How's it going over there, you know, over in Thailand? Business good?'

'Dad, it's not easy but we're getting there. I'll make it a success,' he said, putting down his cup, looking him right in the eye.

'We're getting there? You know you could have done worse than staying with Sheila. She came to see me and your mum recently. You know your mum was very ill. But Sheil, she helped out with the shopping, did a bit of cooking and cleaning. A good girl.'

'It's over between me and her. We're divorced. Dad, she hated me. Throughout our marriage she was evil. You know we hadn't had sex for about ten years. Ten bloody years. I'm not a monk... Look what she did,' he said, rolling up his sleeve, sticking an arm in his dad's face, an arm scarred by her bite marks, the wounds having healed but not in his head.

'We don't talk about those things. It's death do us part.'

'Death do us part? Death do us bloody part? Oh spare me. You may have been lucky with Mum, that's probably one in a thousand, one in million. Sheila thinks I'm disgusting. How can I live like that under the same roof? She blamed me for Emmy's death, says I'm a murderer. A murderer,' he said, bringing the mug shakily to his mouth, tense body ravaged by pain again, ache throbbing across his shoulders.

'And what about now? You happy now?'

'It's not just about being happy. I get to choose what I want to do, for the first time in my life. I can choose my own path.'

'Own path, right you are,' he said. 'Sheila told us all about it.'

'All about what for God's sake?' he said, slapping the arm rest.

'You know.'

'I'm not a mind reader, no. But I think you're talking about the fact Natasha's a he? That your son might be gay,' he said, propelling himself forward, in his dad's face.

'I don't want to talk about it,' he said, aggressively stubbing out the cigar.

'That's your bloody problem. It's the whole family's problem. We don't talk. We never do. There's my brother, on his last legs in Canada, there was Emmy and now Mum. You know what, you've never marked Emma's birthday since she's been gone, not even mentioned it, mentioned her. And me being gay will be just the same, won't it?'

'I've got gardening to do,' he said, heaving his frame out of the armchair.

'Gardening? Your wife's just died. It's the middle of winter. Your son's here from Bangkok and you're off gardening,' he said, unable to look at the old man, wanting to shake him.

'Bye, Son,' he said.

Graham listened as the door clicked sadly shut.

***

He felt uncomfortable in his suit on reaching the church, hot and sweaty despite the bone-chilling cold of a December day, the grey of the sky reflecting his mood. Graham had come to say goodbye to his mum but felt he was saying goodbye to everything, at least everything he'd once known.

'Hello,' he said as he passed Sheila, though she could only

257

nod, a twenty-year marriage reduced to the curtest of civilities, surprised she'd even showed, like she was still trying to make him feel bloody guilty.

'Would you like to say a word or two?' said the vicar, taking him by the arm.

'Yes, I'd like to pay tribute in my own way. I won't be reading from the Bible.'

'As you wish,' he said, the same man who'd married him and Sheila all those years ago but barely a hint of recognition, warmth, as he squinted at Graham over half-moon glasses. 'I hear you've moved to Bangkok.'

'Yes, Vicar. A new chapter,' he said, shifting uneasily in his suit, moving from foot to foot, sombre strains of the organ music in the background seeming otherworldly, nothing whatsoever to do with life, his life or Mum's.

'I see. Well good luck with it all. I'm sure I saw Sheila here somewhere,' he said, walking away.

'Yeah, she's here all right, you shit.'

'I'm sorry, Son,' said his dad, shaking him by the hand, cold, clammy skin, face drained of colour, life.

'Me too,' said Graham, patting the old man on the back, waving at a cousin, finding an excuse to disengage.

'Gray, what can I say?' said the cousin as he approached, giving him a bear hug.

'It's okay. She had a good innings,' he replied, repeating the mantra, aping his dad's stoicism but drinking in some familial warmth, finally untangling from the embrace but guiding his cous gently by the arm to a pew.

'She was a lovely lady.'

'God,' he said under his breath, listening as the service

droned, the dirge music, the empty words of his mum's life painted by someone who barely knew her, more a disservice. 'And here to say a few words, her son Graham…'

'I loved Mum. We all say that don't we?' he said, gripping the lectern, like he'd slide down it otherwise, sweat prickling at his underarms, dripping down his back as he looked out at blank faces. 'I still love her. I'm not sure I told her that when she was alive though. I certainly didn't tell her that enough. We didn't talk. And when I say we didn't talk, of course we did but we didn't talk properly, not about anything that mattered.'

He cleared his throat, other people in the congregation coughed, nervous shuffling coming from somewhere but otherwise silence.

'Please talk to one another. If that's one thing I've learnt. Mum never knew anything about me. She didn't know about my life. That's a massive regret. I'll never be able to undo it. See one of the most important things about me… I'm gay. She didn't know that. I'm sorry Mum. So sorry. I love you,' he said, feeling the hot tears rolling down his cheeks, Dad's glare sending those shooting pains through his stomach, shoulders twisted as if by a vice of pressure but then a ripple of applause that gradually built, seemed contagious, roaring in his ears, people coming up to him, grabbing him by the shoulder, shaking his hand.

Chapter twenty-two

An uncivil war

'Shut up,' he said, bolting upright in bed, wondering where he was, heart thumping in time to the shrill ringing of his phone, batting his hand around on the bed in the darkness feeling for the mobile.

Bringing it to his face, it was as though the illuminated screen was screaming at him to pick up, shaky finger hovering over the answer button, eyes locked on to the caller's name.

'Hello,' he said, hearing the tremble in his own voice, barely able to get the words out, tongue thick, mouth painfully dry, though Graham knew this was it, time to stand up for himself.

'Gray, you still in Thailand? I try calling every day but phone out of service.'

'Look, Nat, listen, I been meaning to call… my mum… she died. I had to go back to England. I just got back this morning, then I passed out on the bed for a few hours. So tired. Just so bloody tired,' he said, imagining her snuggled up to the Yank even as he revealed how raw it all was, hate for Von Eil like poison coursing through his veins, aching want for Natasha.

'Oh, I'm so sorry, babe,' she said with a gentle sigh.

'Yeah,' he said, straining his ears, sure he could hear someone in the background, low rumble of a man's voice, pain pricking at him all over again.

'I miss you but I know you angry. I was waiting for you to calm down.'

'Miss you too,' he said, voice quaking, biting what was left of his nails. 'But we need to talk about us, the money, everything. I mean really talk.'

'Baby, we can't talk about this over the phone.'

'I need some answers,' he said, unable to stop wondering about Von Eil, reaching into the fridge, grabbing one of the miniatures, wanting to still the shakes, blot out the terror.

'We don't discuss it over the phone,' she said, voice an octave deeper.

'Okay, when then?'

'Tomorrow, six pm at the club. Someone will meet you at the door,' she said after a muffled pause.

'Okay,' he said but it was to dead air, Natasha already having cut him off, Graham punching the wall, wincing at the hurt arcing along his arm, seeing her head buried in the American's sturdy chest.

It was six in the evening, another day lost, but number one on his 'to do' list after having spoken to Natasha was moving out of the Paradise into a cheaper apartment. He had little ready cash left and he didn't want to raid the piggy bank as Graham had no clue what would happen after tomorrow's meeting. He just had to lay the groundwork to ensure whatever the outcome he'd be able to stick around.

'As long as it takes, old son, as long as it takes,' he said under his breath like a mantra.

One certainty in a world of uncertainties was that there was no way Nat, Von Eil and Daeng would give him a bucketload of cash to just walk away, they didn't need to when they could make him disappear for nothing. Thailand, he'd found out to his substantial cost, didn't operate on money-back guarantees, it was very much 'let the buyer beware'. Graham remembered on his holiday with Sheil, he'd bought one of those fake Rolexes, sweat pouring off him in the buzzing night market as he bartered the seller down to what he thought was a bargain price. It stopped working the next afternoon and taking it back to the same stall that night, the seller looked him directly in the eye and insisted it was a 'different shop' that had sold it to him. He'd been dismissed with a falsehood and a smile because the seller knew he had no comeback, exactly the situation he was in at the moment with the money he'd sunk into the club and he now had to play *their* game.

***

He'd heard bar flies refer to it in sombre tones, like this was where one could end up, but Graham had never been there himself, to Sri Bamphen Apartments, merely walked past while quickening his step. The 'last chance saloon', according to wags who'd frequented the old spit 'n' sawdust Natasha's before the sparkly makeover, and one thing was for certain as the cab pulled up outside the forlorn apartment block, it certainly hadn't had the makeover treatment. Someone had daubed 'Bangkok Hilton' in red paint on the front, the leaky crimson script giving the impression of an open wound, the graffiti referring presumably not to the luxury hotel chain but the other end of the market – the nickname given to the city's notorious

Bang Kwang Prison aka the Monkeyhouse. If Ban Chao Phraya was the place you gravitated to living in Bangkok when you'd made it – as with a certain Von Eil – Sri Bamphen was where you hit bottom. That gloomy thought, the fact he'd reached so low there was nowhere further down, enveloped him as the cab pulled away leaving him and his bag on the kerb, pavement discoloured by putrefying piles of rubbish, cockroaches scuttling around scavenging, whiff of cheap cooking and worse, much worse, filling his nostrils.

'You want room?' said a woman behind the reception, pristine trouser suit and immaculate helmet of hair so at odds with the poverty of the surroundings.

'Yes,' he said but shaking his head, looking out beyond the slum landlord at the dilapidated state of the rest of the building, washing the colour of dishwater hanging limply from each room, concrete walls the hue of tombstones, the obligatory bars on windows.

'How long?'

'One month.'

'Two-thousand baht.'

'Okay.'

'One-month deposit first,' she said, providing the kicker.

He handed over the notes, laughing nervously after the terse exchange, calculating how little he had left, knowing there was no charm in renting a hovel as he grabbed the key and was waved vaguely upwards. Entering the main building, struggling under the weight of his bag, an emaciated white man, translucent skin like it'd never seen the tropical sun, was clinging on to a young girl, possibly illegally so, heralding his awful arrival.

'Yep,' Graham muttered in their wake, those were his new

neighbours and he wondered what he'd done, how he'd ended up in hell – again.

Finally matching the fob number to that on a piss-yellow door, room 101, which figured, he thought, the Orwellian vision of torture. He wrestled with a padlock, which amounted to security, like he was entering some kind of crude lock-up, coughing as he came into the dusty, stifling cell-like space that contained just a bare, stained mattress on a rickety bed. Mercifully there was a bloody window but the sun was blotted out by the fact he was facing into a courtyard with walls on all four sides that seemed to stretch forever up. Resignedly dropping his bag, he switched on the ceiling fan that doubled as air-con, then went into the poky little bathroom, for want of a better word, just a squat toilet, a sink and a showerhead hanging limply from one wall. Graham fished in his pocket and did what he'd been meaning to do for a long time, pulling out the Xanax, throwing the pills into the toilet bowl. He was done, knowing that if he could survive what had happened to him over the last month or two, then he was ready for anything and he didn't need anti-depressants to get through it. Sheil could no longer call him a pill head, she could go screw herself, they all could, it was him versus the rest, the way he now liked it, masochistic smile lighting up the grimy bathroom mirror.

Despite having fallen further than he thought possible, he was still functioning, which meant either he was a bloody idiot or that he did actually possess some resilience. However, it wasn't optimism he was looking for tonight, it was oblivion, the need not to have to think for tomorrow he was returning to the ring. He wasn't about to become another sorry footnote in city folklore, or worse, a three-paragraph story in the *Bangkok*

Post, in local expat parlance what was now known as 'doing a Nigel Monroe'. No, Graham knew he had to be more guarded against that happening to him, being perpetrated on him, for after his experience on Rama IX bridge he saw first hand how Nige had ended up, still feeling sick whenever he relived that chilling night, the blankness of Von Eil's eyes a thing he'd never forget. Or forgive. He still had to avenge Mark's death too, help rid himself of a guilt that had become almost corrosive.

***

His default response to feeling lonelier than he ever had was to go out. While he knew that could make him feel even more alone, for there was no more desolate experience than sitting in a bar full of strangers, he was short of options, friends, he thought sadly as the taxi wound its way through the burgeoning streets, feeling at odds with the city's dynamism, energy which even the warring red and yellow shirts had failed to completely extinguish.

The cab dropped him outside Natasha's but he crossed to the other side of the road, dreading one of the advanced guard still stationed outside spotting him and reporting straight back to the lady herself. He could hear the rapid-fire, neurotic chatter of the ladyboys as he passed, glanced over to see their plumage shooting straight up into the Bangkok night as they twirled gracefully around showing all their finery, though there was nothing graceful about the money-making machine it'd become, the array of coaches parked where Christie's, Mark's place, used to be attested to that – talk about dancing on his bloomin' grave. The Liverpudlian just another obstacle that had been ruthlessly got rid of. He had to hand it to Natasha, she'd got one sniff of the big time and she'd pursued it with two taloned, murdering hands, which is what he was dealing with. Though his mind went back to when she'd said so tenderly she loved him, the way they held hands as if it was forever after he stood up to her old man – their greatest hits stuck in his head on a loop, wondering if they could get back into the groove. But stealing one last glance across the road as another queue of people entered the club, money going into the pockets of Natasha, Von Eil and Daeng, Graham kicked out at a passing stray dog, one with the most grotesquely pregnant of tummies, sending it staggering away with a whimper.

He headed further into the heart of the red-light district, devoid of the glitter and glamour of Natasha's, where there were no such pretensions of seeking the real tourist dollars, just a flash of neon and more than a flash of flesh – the lean-to bars where 'lowlifes', as Chubby Bird termed them, came to fritter away their last baht. Graham sauntered into his regular no-name bar and even though he hadn't been for a while the girls knew better than to approach him for he only spoke in these places when he wanted to be spoken to – part of the unwritten rules of the established Bangkok *bon viveur*. As soon as he sat down, however, a Chang beer was unceremoniously plonked in front of him.

'All right, man, how are you?' said the owner from his usual vantage point behind the counter, a wispy Englishman, thinning strands of white blond hair plastered over his head, grinning lopsidedly with a cigarette clamped between jagged teeth, brimming glass of drink in telltale shaky hand.

'Not bad, mate. You?' he said, looking at his compatriot, thinking how their faces were almost interchangeable, the glum expressions… Nigel, Mark, his?

'Ah, ducking and diving, just avoiding the snipers' bullets,' he said laughing, revealing those tombstone teeth. 'I thought Northern Ireland was tough but this place takes the piss.'

'You were in the army?' said Graham, thinking back to Mark again, another ex-squaddie who'd got lost on the way to paradise, body tensing, that ache across his shoulders.

'Falklands when I started out, Northern Ireland… the lot. Glad they're rounding up these fucking red shirts. It was feeling like Belfast on a bad day. Bad for business,' he said, taking a gulp of his drink, rheumy look in his eye.

'You thinking of getting out?'

'Ah, man, Bangkok's my last tour of duty,' he said, unleashing another laugh. 'But you realise once you've been here a year or two all that glitters, if you see what I mean. It all appears lovely but look, don't touch. I wish I'd have listened to meself.'

'Did you touch then?'

'Man, you know how it is here. In a way, I want to go back to England, I dream of that place, you know, but I don't think I'd fit in there anymore. I don't fit in here. I'm floating, out there somewhere. I just live to pay the fucking bills, the police.'

'Yeah,' he said, turning away, looking out into the sad void of the bar.

'Another drink, fella? This one's on the house.'

'Be rude not to,' he said, laughing hollowly, another drink the usual solution to the city's problems, at least in England it was just a cuppa.

***

'Hello, handsome.'

'Hello,' he grunted at the requisite 'dusky maiden'– reference C Bird – at the entrance to a bar where he really was anonymous, knowing however rude he was, someone would be around to cater for his every whim for the entire evening, or how little left of it there was.

It was just what Graham was looking for, oblivion waiting behind the tacky facade promising 'Big Jugs', the legend picked out in pink neon, self-loathing having brought him to a girlie bar rather than what he was really looking for, what he really liked. Always one step forward, two steps back, knowing he was tempting fate even asking the question of himself. But what was there even left to question? What the hell was wrong with him? He spat on the ground before entering, trying to get the vile taste out of his mouth, taste of defeat.

None of the other girls arrayed slovenly across the plywood bar took any notice as he plonked himself down on a stool. Their disinterest despite the fact there were more staff than customers, with just a couple of old white men wrapped around two lithe, young things that were probably the same age as offspring long abandoned. The woman who'd grabbed him at the entrance had come back inside and was now making a fuss, obviously slim pickings for the night.

'Beer, mister?' she asked, fanning out what looked like freshly painted blood-red nails.

'Call me Graham. Chang, please, and whatever you're having,' he said, looking at the peacock displaying her feathers, or a cat her claws more like.

'Okay,' she said, doing her practised little *wai* – the local greeting where hands are placed together accompanied by a bow of the head.

But instead of the prelude to some holy ancient Thai tradition, it was simply dressing up another sordid transaction this part of town excelled at, thought Graham, reckoning she was twenty-five, which equated to about forty in Bangkok bar girl terms, vaguely remembering someone had told him the formula was double the real age and then take ten off. He was still contemplating this, and whether any of it really mattered, when the girl placed the Chang gracefully in front of him along with her own garishly coloured concoction – presumably the most expensive drink on the menu – resting a hand on his knee, splaying out those nails again that screamed operator rather than tart with a heart, bringing to mind someone closer to home. She smiled as if to break the silence, what silence there could be with the proverbial Thai pop trash blasting out in the background, but he wished she hadn't bothered, the higgledy-piggledy teeth betraying the poverty of another uneducated country girl with no other option but to sell herself. Just another illusion shattered but he knew to expect nothing less, instead taking a long swig of his drink with one hand, squeezing that firm thigh with another, something he'd normally shy away from in public but he was seeking something, anything that would mean he didn't have to think. Tomorrow looming so large in his mind he was trembling.

'You okay, mister?' she said, as he groped her mutely.

'Graham, my name's Graham,' he said, wondering if she'd heard the first time, whether she even cared. 'Yours?'

'Noi.'

'Where you from?' he asked but stifling a yawn.

'Isaan. Northeast of Thailand. You know?'

'Yes, I know,' he replied, as she looked down ashamed, like they all did, felt like saying 'bingo', having witnessed countless of these conversations in the past with the predictable questions and answers – Isaan being the poorest part of a poor country.

'Okay. You have girlfriend? Wife?'

'No,' he said, flinching as he felt her hand go between his legs, just another practised bar girl move.

'Oh, honey, nothing going on downstairs. You not gay are you?' she said laughing.

'What makes you think I'm bloody gay? I'm completely normal,' he said, slamming down his glass, tears stinging his eyes.

'Honey, just joking. Take it easy,' she said, moving her hand to his thigh.

'Can we go,' he said, draining his drink.

'Go? Now?' she replied, hands to her chest as if shocked.

'Now,' he said, not wanting to dance around the topic like they always did, making it look exactly what it was, though her eyes suddenly hardened into what he guessed was her normal countenance, scrutinising him, wondering, calculating – Was he violent? Did he want to fuck without a condom? Would he tell her he loved her? Put her through school? Save her from this? Or be just another disappointment?

They drove in silence in the taxi. For the length of the journey the fingers of her left hand were fanned out across his knee, as if to stop him having second thoughts, running off when the car stopped, those blood-red nails like a warning.

'This your place, honey?' she said softly, as the taxi ground to a halt.

'Yeah… I just stay here a short time,' he said, wondering whether the gentleness of her tone was just for the benefit of the driver, part of the act, for she struck him as hard, unsympathetic like the morning, first grey streaks in the sky a depressing indicator night was over, day fast approaching.

She looked forlorn seemingly with the realisation he was not her prince charming as he led her up a floor to room 101, the intermittent strip lighting in the gloomy hallway giving a pathetic, disorientating strobe effect. He roughly undid the padlock, like a gentleman allowing her to enter first, his only gentlemanly act of the evening.

'Take off your clothes,' he said, falling to the bed, knowing despite everything Thai girls were modest, wanting to humiliate her, make her feel as small as he felt.

'Light off,' she said, emitting a tiny giggle.

'No,' he barked and watched as she did as she was told, a little girl now in a strange room with a strange man far more bitter than she'd ever know but the dark, slender body, the ample boobs bouncing free did nothing to arouse him, knowing for sure the answer to the sick question he'd posed himself.

'What you want?'

'Just come here,' he said, the girl looking timid, vulnerable in her nakedness, not the forty years of age he'd stupidly computed before, not even looking twenty-five but Graham nuzzled into her, finally feeling numb, happy to take the release sleep soon gave.

***

'You!' she said. 'You! Money! Wake up!'

He groggily lifted his head off the pillow, sunlight streaming

271

through the window like it did at its height for one hour a day, Graham finally realising where he was, what had happened but wanting to turn over, go back to sleep and forget. The night he'd wanted to go and find oblivion had become just something else he wanted to erase from his memory.

'You!' she said again, shaking him, even more insistent.

The little girl lost act replaced by something more sinister but he just laughed, laughed or he would've cried, both returning to type as he hurled money at her, 1,000 baht above the obligatory rate, just to be rid of another mistake cluttering up his room. Absently checking his phone as the girl flounced out, he was surprised to see someone had actually texted.

'Hello, Mr Gray. Just wondering how my funny Englishman is doing? Come and see me soon. Roen,' Graham read, unable to stop smiling, the fact he'd been forgiven, thinking there was something about that guy.

'Soon, Roen, soon. I promise x,' he replied, feeling stupidly guilty.

***

He walked past Wong's, felt a tinge of happiness through the pain but also regret, the random neighbourhood bar was a sometime refuge in the early days of Natasha's not only from the club but Thailand in general, a real expat enclave. He hadn't really known any of the clientele by name but there'd been a kind of camaraderie of the hopeless and looking at the sadly shuttered up shophouse he wondered where they all were now as he knew Wong, the genial, chain-smoking host, had died of lung cancer not long ago. He'd become another Bangkok casualty, thought Graham, looking through the dusty window at the emptiness, such a disappointing epitaph to his larger than life reign.

'Where you go?' came the shout from a *tuk-tuk* driver pulling level with him.

He waved him away, knowing to stand still too long in Bangkok meant the vultures swooped and he started walking again headed for the coffee shop of the Paradise, the only restaurant with proper air-conditioning in the rundown vicinity. But walking along the dusty, blanched street sticky with detritus, he questioned what he was still doing in this alien land for he sensed even if he learned the language, having picked up a smattering so far, he'd always be an outsider, would never belong. His attempts at conversation with taxi drivers always laughed off, like how could this *farang* ever be able to master the Thai language without the inedible fish sauce – which stood on every dinner table throughout the land – running through his veins. It was as if Graham had never had his eyes opened more, seeing through the illusion, the fantasy – booming traffic noise in his ears, polluted air clogging his nose, coating his tongue, the filth, the chaos overwhelming. He wanted to scream but instead plodded on, an unbearable ache in his body, mind, that old anxiety always there, though he had no compulsion to reach for the pills, the drugs long gone, flushed out into the Chao Phraya.

'Hi,' he said as he stumbled into one of the numerous small travel agencies that lined the street, the legacy of a neighbourhood that had been the forerunner to hippie ghetto Khao San Road but before Thailand had got metaphorical beads in her hair and become 'gap yah' trendy for the likes of James and Jemima.

The appropriately named Bangrak district he knew was now sex tourist central where the landlords operated a 'don't ask, don't tell' policy and residents formerly included such luminaries as a renowned American musician recently tracked down by the FBI on paedophile charges, more adept at playing children than the piano. But in his present state the down at heel suited Graham, feeling almost at home in the cluttered little box of a shop, gratefully slumping into a rickety chair as directed, cooling his face in front of the rudimentary electric fan. He smiled to himself at a dog-eared poster on the wall of a Beefeater, a bloody Beefeater, hardly contemporary London, but one of the old school accoutrements that told him he was in the right place if he wanted to escape, a cheap one-way ticket as he guessed the hippies who'd congregated here in the past had bought. In some ways he felt some kinship with the 'tune in, drop out' generation with his straggly hair, unkempt beard growth, ever-diminishing wad of cash in his pocket and head full of nothing saved shattered dreams.

'Hello, Sir,' said the woman, finally looking up from a computer.

'What is your cheapest fare to England? London?'.

'One way or return?' she said, chewing on some fruit.

'One way.'

'Girlfriend trouble?' she asked, emitting a little giggle as she greedily swallowed down the last piece of mango, coated in some sauce the colour and consistency of engine oil.

'Something like that.'

'When you want to go?'

'As soon as possible, maybe a week's time,' said Graham, kidding himself he'd have a few days at the beach before he had to go back, like he could pretend the whole thing hadn't happened, that Natasha, Von Eil, Mark, Nigel, Peeklong had all been some bloody bad dream, nightmare, rather than characters in a very real modern-day tragedy.

'Pakistan International Airways leaving next Sunday. Exactly a week. Fifteen thousand baht.'

'Pakistan International Airways... Okay.'

'You want?'

'Yep.'

'Full name.'

'Graham Floyd,' he said, spelling it out to her, listening to the sound of her tapping away, mapping out an escape route as easy as that.

'You pay now?'

'Er, no.'

'Oh. I can hold for 24 hours. You pay tomorrow?'

'Yes, can I get a printout?'

'Sure,' she said, tapping another key, printer whirring into life.

Graham visualised his name appearing on the flight manifest, another step closer but closer to what? He didn't want to lose, thinking of Natasha and Von Eil drinking a toast to his departure, victoriously sipping the vintage champagne the Yank so loved. He took the sheet of paper, glanced at it on exiting the shop, screwing it into a ball and throwing it in the gutter with the rest of the rubbish. He felt an ache, almost a sense of loss about what he'd discarded, though the likes of Mark and Nigel hadn't even had a choice, they'd 'lost touch' with back home, that awful expat bind. It was only people like Smale, the well-off, who seemed to be fully in control of their destinies, able to move on when the East impinged too much on their gilded existence, when the natives figuratively rucked up the Oriental rugs. But he knew he couldn't go back, for what would he be going back to?

'Hello, Sir,' said a woman in a garish uniform as he entered the Paradise coffee shop.

Graham nodded curtly but he was more concerned at finding a free table what with the place so crowded, yet a funereal silence pervading. That figured, he thought, it was the morning, or to be accurate, afternoon after the night before, the evidence of Saturday's misadventures arrayed before him – young, skinny Thais with mostly white companions at least two to three times their age and three to four times bigger. There was male with male, male with female and male with not so sure. The continued silence, the staring out into space, the almost lifeless faces indicated most of these were transactions rapidly heading to a conclusion, the grudgingly polite end to a nasty little charade. Not that what he was surrounded by made Graham feel superior, his particular Saturday night liaison not even making it as far as muted embarrassment over morning coffee, instead the demanding of money with menaces he'd responded to with a fistful of notes.

'What you like, Sir?'

'Give me two minutes,' he said, perusing the two-page menu he was more than familiarly acquainted with, just not wanting to be bothered.

'Sir?'

'Chicken fried rice and Singha.'

'Big or small?'

'Big,' he said, shooting her a sarcastic smile, as if she really needed to bloody ask, loser white man who's just ordered the cheapest meal on the menu for breakfast, of course he wanted a big beer to not only blot out his own sorrows but the whole town's given the cheerless faces surrounding him, the battle still raging on the streets not so far away.

He'd picked up a complimentary copy of the *Post* on the way in, unfolded the paper at the front page though immediately discarded it as there was more political mumbo jumbo, most of the rebel leaders having been stunned and captured like zoo animals but it was a soap opera. This or that commission was due to be appointed but wouldn't be able to heal the wounds, civil war territory with both sides neither able or adult enough to listen to bloody reason.

'Man, is this free?' said a young Westerner having approached his table, looming above him.

'Waiting for my friend,' he said, looking at the telltale dreads, *on a white guy*, guidebook under one arm, the newest adventurer to have found heaven or at least the Paradise, but Graham picked up the paper again, listening gleefully as the interloper slapped-slapped away in flip-flops, disabusing the backpacker of the notion that everyone was his new best friend to bore with travellers' tales.

He tossed the paper aside once he spotted him harassing some other poor victim across the dining room, animated arms and mouth in unison, ten to the dozen, all youthful optimism and not a lot else. Graham sighed as the uniformed one placed his food and drink down with the lack of ceremony it deserved, alternately shovelling rice into his mouth, then gulping beer like a just released convict.

Pushing the plate away to signal he was done, he checked

his watch, not long to go now. And he wondered whose bed she was in, really fearing like the red and yellow shirts that the feeling of mistrust might run too deep for there ever to be real meaningful reconciliation, tic under his right eye pulsating with his overworked heart, beads of sweat popping out on his forehead.

Chapter twenty-three

Friends reunited

'So this is it then, old chap,' said Smale, with one concession to the heat, dispensing with his linen jacket as they were seated in the garden restaurant in Graham's far from salubrious 'hood.

'This is it for you, yep,' he said, looking at the English professor who seemed ruffled for once, out of his usual refined surroundings, though it was common knowledge he didn't mind trawling the gutter when he had to.

'I never thought the day would come. Back to Blighty and all that,' Smale said with a sigh, face wreathed in an uncharacteristic pallor. 'I'd reasoned out leaving in my head, it makes total sense of course, but the problem is this place defies any kind of logic. Bangkok is such an experience, I'll feel part of me is missing without it, like part of me has died.'

'Stay then. Some of us have to. At least the roads are clearer now they've locked up most of the bloody red shirts.'

'They can't lock up an idea though, the army can't blow up an ideology. But listen, I'll be staying in spirit, if nothing else. Or in spirits,' he said, hint of a smile, no longer even able to laugh at his own jokes but still managing to undress one of the boyish waiters with his eyes.

'Can I help you, Sir?' said the waiter.

The lad was looking at Smale in that shy, subservient way Graham suspected he'd exploited too many times, yet the professor was his closest, no, only Bangkok friend, underlying how the place had changed his view of the world, people. And even if that change pricked at his conscience, he was no longer cocooned, restricted by the mindset of marriage, mortgage, death, managing to smile at how far he'd come – no longer afraid of his own desires, of who he actually was.

'Mike, as it's your last day, I'll let you choose,' he said, the boy waiting expectantly, obediently as the professor finally reeled off a number of dishes in Thai, then a few words at the end that seemed expressly for the lad's benefit, the waiter grinning but Graham wondering whether that was just a polite way of batting away the attentions of another dirty old man.

'A feast, dear boy, a feast,' said Smale, clapping his hands as he watched the lad's rear end disappearing off to the kitchen. 'How much longer will you stay?'

'As long as it takes,' Graham replied, gratefully reaching out for the just proffered ice-cold beer with an unnervingly shaky hand.

'That there's fighting talk,' he said as they clinked bottles. 'Surely it depends partly on tonight, no?'

'Yes. What's your advice?'

'Ohhh,' he said, stroking his chin. 'That's a very tough question. They're tough people here, as if the stench of poverty that always hangs in the air focuses minds. Someone with a chance of escaping it, who has escaped it, who had nothing but now owns a successful club, for example, will not relinquish that without a fight to the death...'

'You're talking Nat here?' he said, writhing his hands around under the table.

'Dear boy, the names are interchangeable but, yes, Natasha, Daeng etcetera.'

'But her parents aren't poor,' he said, taking another snatched swig of his rapidly diminishing beer.

'They cut her off though, didn't they. How do you think she survived?'

'You seem to be very well acquainted with her past.'

'Graham... Graham. It was one weekend, a long time ago. We went to Pattaya.'

'Go on,' he said, throwing up his hands, like nothing could surprise him as far as she was concerned but feeling a painful ache in his guts, that throb across his shoulders.

'Look, she was working the red-light district, you knew that already, and we went to the beach for the weekend.'

'She's never really talked much about what happened when her parents cut her off, though I've not wanted to know. Ignorance is bliss sometimes.'

'Believe me it's not. How about another idiom? Forewarned is forearmed. And like when I gave you the knife, be prepared.'

'Yes,' he said, patting his pocket.

'Anyway, on the drive to Pattaya she pointed out these gruesome factory blocks blighting the landscape, discoloured, blackened places to make you shudder. They had big letters stencilled on top of each – A, B and C like they were denoting prison blocks. It was a factory where she worked ten hours a day, they slaughtered and processed chicken. The feathers, the blood, the squeals. She can't eat chicken even today.'

'What else?'

'They lived on site in these big dorms. One of the foremen, an older, chubby Thai man, who reeked of sweat and chickens, she said, kept the young girls, her, in line by raping them in his stifling little office, blinds always drawn at the windows, blotting out the sun.'

'Bloody hell,' said Graham, having stopped eating his food, pushing it away, wishing he'd been interested enough to ask about her past, feeling almost as culpable as the rapist, as the men who bought and used her just like a commodity. What did he expect in return? Respect? Love?

'Her and another couple of ladyboys managed to run away, established a little fund to set up in a Bangkok hovel, get acquainted with the red-light district, make some real money as they'd heard friends had done. She was so shy though, particularly after her experience at the factory, she didn't want to do it at first, sleep with men for money, just any old man, her dreams of meeting a prince charming had already been shattered by the foreman. He showed her what a man was really like, what he was capable of. But seeing her friends' new phones, clothes, fancy shoes, eventually Natasha couldn't not do it. She learned to treat men how they treated, no, abused her. A means to an end.'

'And then?'

'Then came Natasha mark II, what we see today. She saved and saved the money she made on the game and had the various operations, procedures, to make her Queen of Patpong,' Smale said with a chuckle.

'What did you think about all this when she told you?'

'Dear boy, that's the way it is. Too many men come here and deludedly float along the surface, survey the pretty scene, without realising the water is infested with sharks. When they come a cropper, it's a shock but that's only because they never once stopped to ask the reason why. Did you never think to ask Natasha about how she ended up the way she did?'

'No.'

'Why do you think I'm leaving,' Smale said, furiously waving his arms about to indicate the other tables in the restaurant, most of which were filled with Thai and Caucasian couples with huge, if not embarrassing, age differentials. 'Most of that, *this*, is bullshit. Tell me who's the abuser and who's the abused?'

***

Daeng was at the door at six pm, the club eerily quiet before the hordes turned up from about seven-thirty onwards. Graham couldn't help but notice the boy's 'Little Miss Bitch' T-shirt stretched across his muscled chest and on any other day it would've been funny but the laughter caught in his parched throat, the half bottle of whisky he'd chugged before he left having done nothing to still his trembles, the awful thoughts. Instead of engaging, the Thai simply looked at him with those searching, beady eyes, so dark, hard, they appeared black, any pretence of civility dispensed with, hatred openly on the surface. However, he'd always known the boy despised him, knew it from the moment they met, the only thing he hadn't been deluded about in his early Bangkok days.

'Follow me.'

Daeng strode ahead, Graham lagging as though a naughty pupil being taken to see the headmistress. They padded through the innards of the dimly lit club, a long way from the glitter and glamour of showtime. In the bowels where the punters never trod were dark corridors, anterooms that he knew with a shudder could see anything happen, and probably did. Even the sound of pre-show rehearsals was absent, just the humming of the bare strip lights above him and Daeng's disconcerting footfalls ahead, wondering with each of his own laboured steps whether what was behind the next door was the end.

As they entered a small box room his heart thundered in his chest, spasming lips rendering him speechless for sat around a table, blank eyes illuminated by the almost blinding fluorescent lights above, were Natasha and Von Eil side by side. The Yank motioned silently for him to sit opposite like all that had gone before had never happened. Daeng slipped elegantly next to Natasha as if even the seating arrangements had been preordained, like some upscale dinner party for old friends. The functional but claustrophobic, windowless space very much the old Natasha's, behind the gold paint, the illusion, awful silence punctuated only by the labouring of an air-conditioning unit, Graham flinching at their collective gaze, feeling the sweat ooze out of him, the fear.

'So,' Von Eil said at last with a clap of his hands.

Graham jumped, frantically wiping at the slickness of his forehead, face reddening under the scrutiny, stomach muscles painfully contracting as the American's relaxed but intimidating smile indicated just who was in charge. The nod of recognition to his girlfriend unacknowledged, like who the hell did he think he was, no way he was just going to be welcomed back into her life with open arms.

'Why don't you just get rid of me? You were so close to it

on that bloody bridge. You got rid of Nigel, Mark. What next? You got blood all over those hands,' he spat, jumping back up, leaning right into the Yank's face. 'You murdered my friend. I'll never forget that. You're not gonna scare me. And yeah, you could've dropped me off that bridge, but maybe you just didn't have the bollocks.'

'Man,' said Von Eil with a sigh, Natasha patting his hand.

'Well?' he said, halfway out of his seat again but a light shove from Daeng sent him sprawling pathetically back into his chair.

'I already told you before but you better ask your girlfriend the whys. And don't you forget, it was Graham Floyd that got rid of Mark. The last person to see him alive, according to a certain police-general,' said Von Eil, having stood up, removed his jacket and neatly placed it on the back of his chair, pacing up and down now, flexing his obvious muscles constrained by a pristine pink shirt. 'Man, you just don't get it. We're giving you a chance here…'

'A chance? A chance to do what? Work for nothing in a place I own, with no say in anything, while you fuck my girlfriend because you can? You think I'm that pathetic. It's not gonna bloody work like that,' he said, trying to still his trembling body, screwing his hands into balls under the table.

'Gray, baby, you need to listen,' said Natasha, placing a hand on his arm.

He batted it away. 'No, that's not how it is. You can't scare me anymore. None of you. I'm not scared of dying. I wasn't on that bridge and I'm not bloody now. I could've got on a plane back to England but I'm still here. You don't get rid of me that easy. So I want you…' he said, stabbing Von Eil in the chest. 'Yeah, you. Leave Natasha the hell alone. She's my girlfriend.

I also own fifty per cent of this place so back off.'

'Back off? Back the fuck off? That's not what Paul von Eil the Second is all about my man. You don't come here…'

'Paul, shut up. Gray has point. We need to work this out,' said Natasha, holding up an admonishing hand, talon-like nails looking as if ready to strike.

'Jeez,' said the American, leaning back in his chair, lighting a cigar, looking at Daeng as if for support but the Thai just stared stoically ahead as though he hadn't heard any of the conversation.

'Cigarette?' said Natasha, chucking a packet at Graham.

'Yeah,' he said but aggressively pushing away some iced water the Yank had placed in front of him. 'Another thing, I want to hear you admit to killing Nigel or did you get your bloody boyfriend Ronnie to do it for you? The Freak. Bet you didn't have the balls for that either.'

'That limey loser Nigel. If it makes you feel better, yeah it was me,' said Von Eil with a smirk, beating his chest, sheen of sweat on his brow.

'Evil scumbag,' said Graham, eyes boring into the American's, digging nails into the palm of his hand, wincing with the pain.

'I actually don't know what you're talking about. You read the paper. Nigel was a depressed loser. He jumped from that bridge. You and your whacko conspiracy theories. Listen… you got a girlfriend, you got a nice apartment, you own part of a successful club. It's booming, baby. Don't worry, be happy,' said the American, exhaling the remnants of his cigar all over him. 'I'm not gonna touch Natasha but I ain't going anywhere. And you're not gonna get a big pay-off just to go away.'

'What's the alternative?' said Graham, gripping the sides of the table as though to keep himself upright, having smoked the cigarette in about three puffs.

The room filled with sudden laughter and he was back on the bridge, the mocking sound returning him to the cold dread of that night, a night when he thought he wasn't going to see the next morning.

'There isn't an alternative. The door's there if you want to leave but there's no coming back,' said Von Eil, aggressively stubbing out his cigar.

Graham looked from the Yank to Natasha, who simply nodded.

Chapter twenty-four

Last dance

'I'm really sorry about your past. When you had to work in a factory,' Graham said, looking out to sea, the darkness of their table briefly illuminated by one of the fragile Chinese lanterns spiralling up, lit for luck by another of the patrons at the romantic little beachside resort on Samet island.

'You know?' Natasha said.

'Smale told me,' he said gently, for whereas in the past it would have been barked like some accusation he knew he now had to accept her and shoulder some of the weight of her considerable past or it just wouldn't work, they wouldn't work – and it had worked so far, in the month since they'd been seeing each other again but living apart. Though for some of that time Natasha had been visiting her sick grandmother, the constant hushed phone calls home a daily distraction since but an acceptable one.

'Gray…' Natasha said, diamond ring he'd bought for her recent birthday glinting in the soft candlelight as she wrung her hands. 'It's difficult for me to talk about.'

'I know,' he said with a shudder, not wanting to revisit those dark places with her either.

'It was fucking hell. I not going back there.'

'I know,' he repeated.

'Daddy, can we light one of the lanterns?'

'Of course. Next time the seller comes down the beach.'

Silence descended again but a pleasant one, no longer that between strangers or warring partners, though too soon interrupted by the infernal ringing of Natasha's phone, a device she never seemed to be without.

'Grandma?' he mouthed almost silently, for he already knew the answer.

'Yes,' she replied, nodding meekly, as though in reverence. 'I will take it nearer the reception as better signal.'

She hadn't waited for any acknowledgement from Graham as he watched that slender back disappear towards the reception of the resort they were staying in, nearer the telephone mast.

He was enveloped in silence again, though snippets of stilted conversation wafted over from the adjacent table and he couldn't help noting the white man and Thai wife with their children, along with what he guessed were her parents. He'd actually been observing them most of the night, when he hadn't been looking longingly at Nat, but saw that even though the white man could speak the language, the Thai father in law never gave eye contact, not even engaging, as though pretending he didn't exist. He wondered was that the fate of foreigners in a place that was almost mono-racial, where a vague kind of tolerance took the place of any kind of real acceptance, cruelly extinguishing any sense of belonging. It was the way Graham felt most of the time around the indigenous population, studiously ignored in the main, like he was invisible with the odd 'what the fuck are you doing here?' stare thrown in, though he guessed they did have a point given his motivation – and a lot of other men's – for being in Thailand. However, watching this father with his Thai wife, half Thai son, doing the right thing, going to the beach with his in-laws, smiling in all the right places, it was as if in the patriarch's dead eyes he'd never be good enough, never measure up, because he just wasn't and would never be – Thai. He didn't have fish bloody sauce running through his veins.

'Hello,' she said, sidling up to him playfully, pinching his cheek.

'How's Grandma?'

'Hmmm… Did lantern man come?'

'No.'

'Hey,' she said cheerily, frantically waving the vendor over.

After some negotiating in Thai she was soon handing over small change in return for the lantern, which came in flattened, cylindrical form. Natasha was one side, him the other as she'd unfurled it gently and lit the wick beneath, them both edging eagerly across the shore to the inky ocean, sky spectacularly illuminated above by myriad pinprick stars.

'Make a wish,' she said.

But the sinister way her face glowed orange in the flame, dark eyes like black marbles, made him shiver, brought him back to the night Christie Cabaret was an inferno and his mind so full of goodwill before went blank, though he'd let go like she'd indicated and watched as the lantern took flight for a couple of feet then nosedived. There was a faint sigh from the other watching diners as if witnesses to an impending tragedy as it crashed flaming into the sea.

'I get another,' she said, waving her arm in the air, vainly trying to attract the seller's attention again.

'No,' he said, grabbing her arm, the Thai patriarch on the adjoining table glancing over with that disapproving look Graham wanted to beat out of someone one day, unable to 'keep a cool heart' as the locals always exhorted.

Maybe that was his problem, he thought, the lack of their cool calculation, patience, since everything he'd done to get to the point he was at was through being impulsive, though if he hadn't been impulsive he'd still be in a marriage where the only feeling was rejection, in a life where the only emotion was regret.

'What you thinking?'

'Nothing,' he lied, clinking Natasha's glass, her having refilled them both, the bottle of Thai whisky now empty.

'Come on?'

'Nothing,' he repeated.

'Drink up then,' she said, swigging back hers.

'Natasha, it's okay, I'm glad we're here together, doing this. Where else would I bloody be?'

'Why bloody all the time? I'm going to toilet,' she said, scraping her chair back.

As she flounced away it was then he saw it, his heart thumping in his chest, Nat having left in such a huff she'd forgotten her phone, the Nokia lying there on the table black and shiny like a secret diary – the phone she was virtually glued to. He flipped it over and over in his hand, the handset heavy with the weight of its potential secrets but there was just one thing he wanted to know, had to know. Dialling 'Grandma' she answered on the fifth urgent ring, his sweaty hands leaking all over the sleek phone, stupid distracting thought about how he'd wipe it down afterwards like destroying evidence at a crime scene.

'Hello, baby, what is it now…' the voice said into his ear, but it wasn't his ear that reverberated it was his heart, his mind, both ached with a physical intensity that hurt, the few words sapping his will, turning the future black, pitch black, darker than the sky above.

'Baby? You there? Baby?' said the Yank's insistent voice, Graham banging the phone down, unable to listen any longer, finally relieved when there was silence, the awful babbling from the speaker having ceased.

'It's perfect,' she said returning, looking up at the starlit sky, then at the phone discarded in the middle of the table.

'Nothing's bloody perfect,' he spat. 'Nothing can be perfect. Ever.'

'Gray…'

'No,' he said, holding up a hand as she sat down. 'I know who Grandma is. Why? You were away for a week with damn Granny. Now I know.'

'Sorry,' she said, stoic expression melting so easily into tears, but she still managed to scoop up the ringing phone, silencing it as she did so, removing it from view. 'He won't let me go. I try…'

'Try bloody harder… Look, I just don't know what to do anymore. I'm not welcome in England, I'm not welcome here. I gave up everything for this. Everything!'

'I know,' she said, seeking out his hand, grabbing it.

The expression on her face was at least believable for once, thought Graham, not rehearsed in some grubby mirror or requiring the syrupy dialogue she'd rote learnt in the old days

292

when she worked the bars. 'I can love you, really love you…
I'm not going to use you up like some commodity, some bloody
plaything. You know what Von Eil calls his conquests? Well
do you?'

She was shaking her head, looking down like she was totally
ashamed. 'Fuck toys, that's what he calls them… you,' said
Graham, spreading his arms as if to indicate how many of
them there were, though he didn't know what was under the
surface – the kids, the silenced screams, the druggings, the
rapes, the killings.

She shook her head again, then she nodded, like all of
sudden, for the first time, or the first time since he'd known
her, she'd lost her bearings, didn't know where she was, maybe
back in that fat foreman's office.

'I want you to move back in with me,' Natasha said finally,
grasping the hand Graham had put in front her that little bit
tighter.

'This really is our last chance. Mine, yours and that fucking
Yank's. I've had it with him,' he said quietly, looking out at the
dark emptiness of the sea.

Chapter twenty-five

Death trap

'Drink, baby?'

'Gin and tonic, love,' he said with a grin, sinking lazily into one of the comfy wicker chairs they'd just bought for the balcony, looking at the lights of Bangkok blinking back at him, thinking he was wrong to have judged so harshly – the city and Nat.

'Here.'

'Thanks,' he said, taking the G&T, a little habit he'd picked up from Smale, ice and a slice floating on top, the neatly adorned drink almost matching the perfection of their evening. Natasha had taken the night off to not only celebrate him moving back in but also to mark their anniversary, which had earlier seen them eat at Rossini's – the Sheraton's Italian restaurant, which was the place to see and be seen, indicating how far he'd bloody come.

'Here's to a year,' said Natasha, lighting a cigarette.

'Feels like ten,' he said with a laugh, averting his attention from the dazzling skyline, taking her in, as if for the first time, feeling those familiar stirrings of desire, amazed to have them reciprocated for the first time in forever after years of the ice queen. 'You not having one?'

'No, I drink too much,' she replied giggling.

Waving a carefree hand in acknowledgement he took a swig but grimaced at the too much gin not enough tonic, knowing she always mixed 'em strong.

'Good?'

'Sorry,' he said, laughing again, finishing the drink in another couple of gulps.

'You enjoy tonight?'

'A wonderful night, thank you,' he said but she shot him the weakest of smiles, which was No 57 in his subconscious index of Nat's myriad facial expressions, before returning her gaze to the city.

'I want to move from here,' she said, absently tousling her hair, still not looking his way.

'Where to?' he said, biting his nails, unable to compute how they'd gone from loving couple to what felt like strangers in a Bangkok minute.

'Ban Chao Phraya.'

'That's where he lives. The Yank,' said Graham, her laughter riling him further, feeling short of breath, the mugginess of the night closing in, patting his pocket for the Xanax that was no longer there.

'I'm joking, Gray.'

'Natasha, I still want this to work. Remember that,' he said, motioning to pat her knee but missing, his reactions uncoordinated, clumsy, vision blurred as he looked out at the lights of Bangkok, smudged as if through a kaleidoscope, awaiting a response that never came.

***

He woke with a jolt, thick, chemical smell in his nostrils, fumes at the back of his disgustingly dry throat, forcing eyes open, lids so heavy as though they'd been stuck together. Thrashing around in the blackness, frantic with the overwhelming stench of fuel, he felt instinctively for the light switch but it was dead. Dead, dead, dead, that one word screaming in Graham's throbbing head over and over as he grabbed for the door handle. It wouldn't budge. He hurdled across the room, bashing his body against various bits of furniture, not feeling the pain, except the one in his mind, looking stupidly at his only other exit, peering into the void, the twenty-storey drop out of the window, heart thrumming crazily against his ribcage, acid spit of panic pooling in his mouth.

'Natasha… for God's sake, Natasha,' he shouted, the rising hysteria in his trembly voice like it was not his own, Graham pummelling pathetically on the door, the heavy wooden door.

'You bitch!' he screamed, going back through a manic jumble of jagged thoughts – the fact she'd asked him to move back in, how she'd insisted on the night off, the flip-flopping mood from cooing to growling, the odd tasting drink, the odourless, colourless drug Von Eil had talked about with glee that time and he imagined her carrying a filthy, flaming rag in the shadowy hallway, flames reflected in those dead eyes, the Yank looking on with a similarly blank expression, just how it had ended for Mark, Nige.

Hammering on the door again, so hard his knuckles had become a mush of ripped skin and blood, he wished he'd been let go from the bridge, realising how pathetic it all was, he was.

296

But survival instinct kicking in, Graham dived back to the window, just managing to focus from eyes almost blinded by sweat, imagining himself on the other side, though it was then he heard the door lock turning, so wired the sound reverberated around the room. The grogginess in his head was replaced by clarity of thought and racing back to the door, breaths short, shallow, he could see survival, knew what he was going to do. Had to do.

'You fucking bitch!' shouted Graham as he stumbled out of the room, grabbing Natasha and pushing her against the wall, petrol fumes making him retch, eyes watering.

'Go… leave,' she said, eyes looking at the floor, the fuel-sodden carpet.

'You fucking bitch!' he screamed again, pounding her head into the wall with the rhythm of each word but he let go as her watery eyes finally caught his and Graham knew he'd been wrong all along for in front of him was not the cool, calculating killer, instead there was the abused factory girl, discarded by her parents, by society, to become a rich man's plaything, puppet, subject only to his whims.

'Take your chance… Go.'

'Why?' he said, voice reverberating in the hallway, the petrol making him gag again, double up, telling him he must get away, run, but he needed to know why.

'Go!' she shouted, shoving something at him.

'No,' he said but looking at the passport, *his* passport, turning it over and over as if there was anything left to ponder. 'Tell me why.'

'Just leave…'

'No. Why did you do this to me?'

'Von Eil, he won't accept you being with me. Gray, he use me all the time, rape me. It's not sex anymore, we don't do sex, he rape me because he can. He don't want another man with me. He's like that man in the factory and so many after him. So many. But it's worse, he won't let go, he owns me!'

'Owns you? Bloody owns you? That bastard. I'm… I'm so sorry,' he said, brushing her cheek but she pushed him away and it was then he pictured the grinning Von Eil, the brash American waltzing around town, dragging Natasha after him like a dog, as if he owned her, owned the whole damn city.

'Go.'

'What about Daeng?' Graham said, grabbing her again.

'Go!'

'Fucking tell me,' he said, shaking her, fixated at the red marks he'd left on those skinny arms, ones he'd kissed up and down, over and over, like they were his, no better than the bloody Yank.

'We together. We've always been together. Even Von Eil don't know. Daeng my one and only love,' she said with a sigh, sliding down the wall.

Graham had difficulty breathing, like he was suffocating, the walls like his thoughts, closing in, and he ran, ran past Natasha now a crumpled heap on the drenched floor, didn't stop running until he reached the street outside.

***

He entered the foyer, chest heaving up and down, drenched in sweat, scummy clothes, haggard look out of place with the perfumed cool of the lobby, huge chandelier, along with the garish statuettes and water features of Ban Chao Phraya like something out of renaissance Italy gone wrong.

'I'm here to visit Mr Paul. Von Eil,' said Graham, throwing two 1,000-baht notes at the guard behind the marble desk.

'Top floor,' the security replied.

But he was already back across the lobby stabbing a finger repeatedly at the button with the up arrow, no time for pleasantries. The lift a hall of mirrors, his craggy face reflected back at him infinite times, Graham fixated by the determined look, but the lurching halt shook him out of it. Faced by a corridor snaking both left and right briefly threw him but there was only one door, nearing it he saw it was yawning ajar, as though Von Eil thought nothing could touch him in his ivory bloody tower. He kicked it wide open.

There was a chemical smell in the air that he knew to be amyl nitrate, something Natasha had introduced him to, along with the reek of sex. His head throbbed with the overload of it all as he pushed on down a grand hallway but it was defaced by snatched glimpses of porn, just boys and girls, naked, wasted, lovingly rendered in expensive frames, softly lamp lit, whiff of sleaze thick in his nostrils as he shook. Coming to a gilded set of double doors, rumble of music from within, Graham unsteadily wrenched them open.

'Von Eil!'

The American who'd been hovering over a low-slung sofa, towering half naked above what looked like a girl no older than about fourteen, petit and trembling, spun around.

'Freaking A,' he said above the nightclub music that was pounding from the speakers, eyes burning but not a hair out of place on his perfectly coiffed head, holding a cut crystal glass of what looked like something expensive in his hand.

'Bet you didn't expect to see me,' said Graham, approaching the Yank, taking in the ornate furniture, coffee tables strewn with glossy magazines, as though it was the apartment of a sophisticate, the thing he aspired to, but the young girl dwarfed by the expansiveness of the place, half-dressed and shivering in the air-conditioned chill indicated otherwise.

'What the fuck are you doing here, loser?' he said, though thrusting his arms up defensively.

'I might not have Natasha but you never will either, you fucking scumbag. You think you can buy her like you flash your gold card at everything else but you can't. Her and Daeng are together. An item. You hear me. Her and that little runt. She's playing all of us. You don't own anyone.'

'Stop... just stop,' he said, covering his jug ears.

'No, you're going to hear this,' said Graham, wrenching the American's muscled arms away, feeling a sudden strength pulsating through his body. 'You raped her repeatedly. My woman. When you could've had anyone? Anyone? Do you hate me that much. Her? Then you wanna burn me alive?'

'It was her idea...'

'You can't help yourself. You won't stop,' he said, nodding at the girl.

'Mind your own business, loser. You'll never have what I do.'

'That's because I hate what you have and how it corrupts in this place, this fucking place!' he shouted, spittle covering that perfectly waxed chest they were so close, a glinting flash of silver as he withdrew the knife and thrust it deep into Von Eil's side, the American falling back onto the floor clutching his stomach with a howl, luxuriously piled cream carpet turning a deep shade of red, crimson spreading outwards like ink on blotting paper.

'You go,' he said gesturing to the girl, her face scrunched up and pale, looking from Graham, back to the prone, silent Von Eil splayed over the floor. 'Now!'

She soundlessly grabbed items of her clothing that looked like they'd been disrobed in a hurry and ran for the door in a blur. Graham took a look back at the Yank, unmoving, his face putrid white, as he strode across the living room to what appeared to be the master bedroom. He wrinkled his nose at the unmade bed, silken sheets in an untidy ball, grabbing at his windmilling arms to steady them, locating the floor to ceiling wardrobe at the back of the massive space. Looking down at his own shirt defaced by fountain-like spatters of blood, he ripped it off as he rifled through row after immaculate row of finest Italian silk, picking one that felt cool and light against his red-hot skin. Entering a ridiculously marbled en suite bathroom, mirrored walls accusingly picking out his blood-spotted, gurning face he threw cold water over himself, water running red down the plughole. He didn't look back at what seemed now just a bundle on the floor, doing up his shirt as he crossed the living room. A dead man's shirt? And all was quiet apart from the boom, boom still reverberating from the Bose speakers, the raging thump of Graham's heart in his ears.

He was buoyed to see the dark sky flecked in the distance with the first hopeful light of morning as he dived out of the building. A cab slowed on seeing him and jumping in the back Graham imagined the phone ringing on Peeklong's jumbled desk in the broom-cupboard office. He didn't have long.

'Airport,' he croaked, body wracked by the shakes, burning pain across his shoulders, in his head, no options left other than one.

'No bag?' the cabbie said, eyeing him quizzically in the mirror.

'No bag… I have nothing,' Graham replied, managing to offer up a smile, about all he had left to give, smiling for the fact he'd finally stood up for himself, Natasha, feeling different, alive, not the 'white ghost' who'd arrived in Bangkok what seemed a lifetime ago. He had plans.

'You go home?' said the driver.

'I'm going to Cambodia. Phnom Penh,' he said, picturing Roen's little riverside bar.

As the taxi lurched onto the motorway and they picked up speed, absently flicking through his passport a photograph fell out, the picture taken in Samet of him and Nat, holding hands, the happiest they'd ever looked, smiles radiating outwards. Turning the photo over, as though looking for a clue, anything, in her curly, girlish script was scrawled one word: '*Sorry.*'